NOW STREAMING

AYLA CHANDLER

AYLA CHANDLER

NOW
STREAMING

PROLOGUE

MIN

The zombie's head exploded with a satisfying squish of impressive blood and brain splatter. Min took a moment to admire the death of the creature in front of her as it collapsed onto the ground in a heap. The work behind that simple moment of art was astonishing, and the end result was vibrant and beautiful in the grossest way possible.

Finally snapping out of it, Min glanced over at her stats.

"Shit. That was the last of the 9mm ammo. I gotta find some healing around here."

Clicking several buttons on her light-up keyboard, Min navigated around the game map, making sure to keep her character ducked and her zombie vision on. Spotting an icon in the distance that said it was an item, Min had her avatar make its way toward it, being cautious, making sure her rifle was equipped and loaded. Her chat screamed at her.

"Guys, I know it could be a trap. But I'm in the red. I got to take this chance."

The music was quiet, putting her nerves on edge in spite of her confident words. She knew the zombies were out there, waiting. Min also knew the other players were somewhere doing exactly what she was doing—loading up on items and weapons to prepare for battle while trying to stay as hidden and quiet as possible.

She'd managed so far to avoid most of the traps laid in this particular area, but the game was good at throwing curveballs and she didn't want to be overconfident. She couldn't just keep an eye out for her competitors—she had to be careful an NPC zombie wouldn't jump out of nowhere and chomp on her. That would lose her the game.

Min fucking hated to lose.

She pushed on her headset, sparing a quick glance over to her second screen, showing her chat. Her fans loved it when she played Bleeding Sword, loved the tournaments even more, and she knew they were cheering her on. And while her pink wig was making her head itch, her contacts were making her eyes dry, and her makeup felt caked on after several hours of gameplay, Min never felt happier than she did when she was streaming.

Bleeding Sword was the latest competitive first-person shooter video game, blended perfectly with the horror aspect of a zombie survival. While it had only been out for a few months, it was on track to win Game of the Year thanks to an overwhelming amount of stellar reviews. Min and her other professional streamer friends had already logged hundreds of hours of gameplay, both against each other and as teams, and they often organized competitions to boost their viewership and sponsorships. Min had made it to the final four of this particular competition for Bleeding Sword, to no one's surprise, and now the mission was serious. She was determined to beat DeathsHead.

As if summoned, his deep, dark voice came through her headset.

"You know you can't hide from me, FlameThrower."

She pressed the button to talk in-game so he could hear her. "C'mon, Death, you gotta be used to girls hiding from you by now."

His deep chuckle was his only response, rumbling through her headset and bringing a grim smile to her face.

Min didn't have to look at her chat to know they were losing their minds. She and DeathsHead were engaged in their usual game, a survival free-for-all, with the last player standing declared the winner and earning bragging rights. They were playing one of the larger and trickier maps, one that could handle several players at once, so she and her streamer friends could boost their viewing numbers, cross-promote, and mostly just play the game with their friends. It took strategy and skill and a certain amount of luck to win, and therefore the game often brought out the best and worst in all the players.

Especially her and her arch-nemesis, DeathsHead.

He had appeared on the scene a few years ago, his sinful voice, biting comments, and game skill launching him into one of the most popular streams every time he signed on. Unlike other streamers, he refused to show his face on camera, relying instead on his distinctive deep voice and in-game antics to keep his audience entertained. Even with that limitation, his viewership had exploded, with clips from his streams being replayed over all social media. When their group of friends had started getting into Bleeding Sword, it took very little time for the main draw of those lobbies to be DeathsHead versus FlameThrower. They were both excellent players and would taunt each other relentlessly whenever they played against each other, both doing their damnedest to outmaneuver the other. Sometimes she won, sometimes he did, but it was always a good time, even if he constantly pissed her off.

And boy, did he piss her off.

He was good, she would give him that. But he also played dirty, or at least as dirty as a video game would allow. He would set traps and lure her into them with items. He would make deals with other players to take her out. No matter who was playing in the lobby, DeathsHead made FlameThrower his number one target, constantly baiting and pushing her, pissing her off until they would end up yelling at each other through the course of the game. At first, she had been self-conscious about how easily he got her temper up. But her fans loved it, so she let it go, let herself banter back with him, taunt him, needle him, in the hopes that she would trip him up.

In this current tournament, they were playing a rural map, with long stretches of farmland dotted by various houses, barns, and stables. Min kept her avatar—pink, FlameThrower's signature color—crouching in a field of wheat, scanning the terrain. They had been playing for a while now, and they were down to the last legs of the game, item drops few and far between. Spotting a house on the other side of a field, Min made her way slowly toward it, constantly scanning the terrain with an eye out for the other players. If they saw her in this vulnerable position, they'd shoot in a heartbeat, and she wouldn't blame them. It's exactly what she would do.

Once she crept near the house, she slid her character into it as soundlessly as she could, closing the door behind her and peering out the window to see if any of the other players were out there waiting for her. A glance to her second monitor showed her chat yelling encouragement, and she grinned, loving it all—the support, the love of the games, everything.

Min played a lot of different kinds of games on her stream,

some social and relaxing, some puzzle oriented, some stressful as hell. She was grateful for the day she had been able to quit her day job at the coffee shop in order to be a full-time streamer, and would happily sign on for any type of game to try it out. But her true love was the competition, the games where she got to sneak through an environment and take out the other challengers. And though she'd never admit it, she lived for the times she got to play against DeathsHead.

They had never met in person. DeathsHead was strict about his anonymity and privacy. He never met up with other streamers in person, even though at this point, they had all known each other for years. As far as she knew, no one even had his phone number, since they all just messaged through an online server. He was just a voice. A dark, gravelly, admittedly sexy voice that played video games.

As if he could hear her thoughts, his deep voice filtered through her headset.

"I can hear your heart beating."

She quickly ducked under the window she had been looking out of and did a quick scan of the area. Was he lying? Or was he really that close? Bleeding Sword was a horror-themed game, meaning the atmosphere was created to scare the shit out of the players while they hunted each other down. So the creak she was hearing could be DeathsHead coming through a door, or it could just be idle noise from the game. Details like that kept players on the edge of their seats, hearts racing with fear and excitement. Exactly the type of game DeathsHead loved.

"I think you're lying, Death." She was all bravado as she scanned the house for weapons—any weapon, really, since her 9mm had run out of ammo taking out another player, and then the zombie who had attacked her on the way here. All she had was her rifle, and that ammo was dangerously low. Her blinking red health icon warned her that she was one lucky shot away from being out of the game. She'd have to work fast if she wanted to win.

She crept her way upstairs as his deep chuckle filtered through her headphones, giving her goose bumps. A glance at her chat showed that they were loving the interaction. The rivalry between them always spawned Min's best streaming numbers, and she couldn't blame her fans. Who wouldn't want to hear that voice calling for them?

Min couldn't help but physically jump at the sound of the front door slamming in the area she had just left. Shit, he was telling the truth. She had to find a weapon.

"Keep hiding. I'll find you wherever you go. You're my favorite prey, Flame."

Min rolled her eyes at his dramatics. "I'll remember you said that when I'm shoving a grenade launcher up your ass."

She crept into room after room, staying as silent as she could, but there were no signs of any sort of weapon drop, nothing she could use against him. She briefly contemplated the lamp on the nightstand, but even in a video game, his head was probably too hard to feel that.

Min made her way into the last room, thinking, if anything, she could jump out the window. If she hit the button to roll at the right time before impact...

Shaking her head, she knew she was kidding herself. Even the minimal amount of damage from the fall would take her out of the game. Which meant she had to figure something out, and she had to figure it out fast. She sent the camera around the room, searching for anything that could help her out of her current predicament... but the place was empty of anything, a bare room with a closet and a wire frame twin bed. Min was screwed.

The game filtered his heavy footsteps as he walked up the stairs, not even trying to be stealthy or sneaky. He was stalking her, wanting her to hear him and know he was coming, knowing that she didn't have a lot of health left. He would know she was trapped and considering her limited options. And he knew as well as she did that the fall out the window would kill her.

"Tell you what, Flame. I'll make you a deal." Somehow his voice went even deeper, quieter, as if it really were just the two of them in this video game house. Min felt the sound of it slide down her spine, and she fought a shiver as she tried to think of a plan—any plan. Desperate, she angled her camera just right... and saw a marker on the floor. *Jackpot.* She pressed the buttons for her avatar to pull out her combat knife.

"What kind of deal?" she asked, playing along. She didn't want him guessing what she was doing, so she very much needed him to drag out this villain monologue as she went to work carving a hole into the floor.

"You come out. We work together and take out the other two players. Then we worry about each other. I know you're low on health. I have a med kit. It's yours, as a symbol of good faith."

A glance at chat showed that they would love this, love any interaction between her and DeathsHead, but especially the novel idea of them working together. She and DeathsHead were rarely on the same team, but when they were, they were unstoppable. Chat was yelling in all caps for her to take the deal, but she still shook her head, the pink hair from her wig hitting her cheeks with the movement. She wasn't falling for this again.

"You've said that before, Death. Remember how that turned out for me?"

His laugh was her answer. The last time he had offered that deal, he had immediately shot her when she showed herself. She wouldn't make that mistake twice.

"Okay, that's fair. But I'm serious this time. You and me against the world, Flame. What do you say?"

His footsteps were right outside the door of the room she was currently hiding in. She knew he knew she was in there. But he was assuming she was hiding, that she was low on health and ammo and therefore out of options. *Big mistake.* The hole in the floor was slowly growing, and she started to hope she would actually make it out of this room alive.

"I think you know the answer." She let the sarcasm bleed into her tone, wanting to keep him distracted. She felt the tension in her bones as she sawed away at the marker on the floor, so close to escape, the anticipation of him opening that door running through her veins. *Almost...*

He gave a deep sigh as if disappointed. *"Well. Remember that I offered."*

The door opened just as Min's avatar ripped the floor up. She laughed in victory as she immediately sent her avatar jumping down through the hole, away from DeathsHead.

Except... when she spun the camera to laugh at his avatar, it wasn't Death. The guy with the gun pointed at her was another player, KevinKillsU. Min's mind raced as dread pooled in her stomach. If Kevin was who was coming up the stairs...

Min's avatar dropped to the floor below, landing with a thud. And she found herself staring down the barrel of a machine gun, held by none other than the masked DeathsHead.

"No!" Min yelled, but it was already too late. The machine gun fired, hitting her right in the chest several times, destroying what was left of her armor and leaving her avatar a bloody and broken mess on the floor. She could hear his dark chuckle as she cursed into the microphone.

"You made a deal with Kevin, you lying son of a—"

"Kevin knows a deal when he's offered one. Maybe next time you'll listen to me."

Min practically growled into her microphone. "The next time we play, I'm going to paint the walls with your blood."

"You can certainly try."

Shaking her head, Min glanced at her chat, wanting to commiserate on her loss. But they weren't talking about her incredible defeat. They were talking about something else, something about a photo drop. Min quickly muted herself in-game, speaking only on her stream.

"Chat, what's this about a photo?"

As she scrolled through the chat, trying to figure it out, her heart dropped into her stomach, her room spinning. She didn't even hear the other players on stream as they continued the game.

Someone had posted photos of her online.

Photos of her still in her wig and heavy makeup—the usual costume of her online FlameThrower persona, the one she used to hide what she really looked like while still showing her face on stream. But in the photos, she wasn't dressed in one of her signature over-the-top outfits, the dresses with a corset and fishnets and some sort of skirt. Nope.

She was naked.

Straddling what appeared to be a naked man, his face conveniently hidden in the shot, leaving only her with her distinctive wig and her very, very naked body to be easily recognized. They were clearly engaged in a sex act, or at least were about to, and when the next shot showed her on her knees in front of the man, the man whose face was still somehow unidentifiable, Min could see a familiar couch, a familiar room, familiar surroundings that she knew belonged to her asshat of an ex-boyfriend.

Alex.

Alex had asked her several times if he could take intimate pictures of her, just for himself, and had even asked to make a video a few times, promising it was for his eyes only. Min had honestly been intrigued by the idea but had ultimately said no every time, too worried about what might happen if his phone was hacked, or if someone had somehow found the recordings.

Which meant these pictures of her, naked and on top of him, or naked on her knees in front of him, weren't anything she had consented to. Hell, she hadn't even been aware he had set up a camera, but he obviously had. Now either someone had hacked him, or he was taking the breakup harder than she thought he would. And though she still had to get the whole story from him, her gut was screaming at her that he had done this on purpose.

They hadn't ended on the best of terms. They were both streamers and had met in a gaming lobby where they had hit it off immediately. Alex had been charming at first, a seemingly nice guy who wanted nothing more than to play video games and hang out with friends. But after only a few months of dating, Min had started to feel like they weren't really connecting, that he saw her more as a status symbol than a girlfriend. So she had ended it after six months together. He hadn't been happy, had kept texting her and calling, trying to convince her to give him a second chance, but she'd ignored him. After only a few days apart, Min quickly realized she didn't miss him in her life. They were better off apart, especially when she learned that he had been hooking up with some fans while they were together. After she heard that, Min blocked his number on her phone and never looked back.

But now there were naked photos of them together on the internet. Photos she hadn't even known existed.

A quick glance at the chat showed the comments were streaming in, some warning her, some sympathetic. But there were others, the trolls that always lived somewhere on the internet, that had found her public stream and were calling her names.

Whore. Slut. Cheap. Trash.

Min couldn't breathe, could feel the walls closing in around her. Pictures like this were literally her worst nightmare. She worked hard to keep her private life private, to make sure she could have her normal life outside of her streaming world. It was why she always made sure to dress up in her Flame-Thrower persona before she streamed. She didn't want any photos of her real self out there connected with her job. Min was protective of her family, her retired mother and younger sister, who were her biggest fans. She had always made it a goal to never drag them into the craziness that was the internet. She wanted to keep them separate from that.

And while she was technically still wearing her Flame-Thrower wig in the photos, she still felt sick, violated. Her naked body was now out for any scum on the internet to ogle, to judge. A rise of emotions rose into her throat, leaving her choking with outrage and vulnerability. And anger.

So much anger.

"Fuck."

CHAPTER 1

HAYDEN

"Obviously, this is an incredible opportunity. Both for you, and for our company."

Hayden sat back, trying to look cool and detached but not able to stop his fingers from drumming the armrest of the chair he was sitting on. He hated meetings, hated conference rooms, hated meeting with new people. If it were up to Hayden, every business dealing would happen over the phone or email, with him staying in the safety of his home. But this offer had seemed like a good one in the email, and the money they were offering would go a long way to help him with his long-term goals. So, even though he felt out of place wearing his zip-up hoodie and old jeans in this conference room that screamed money and privilege, he sucked it up and took the meeting.

After making the two men in the room sign several NDAs.

Hayden took a deep breath, trying to keep his anxiety under wraps as the businessmen across from him gave their sales pitch. One of the suits, the less sleazy one, Brad, leaned forward, giving what looked to be a sincere sales pitch.

"Bleeding Sword is still rising in popularity, and we'd like to keep it that way. Which is why the company is planning a huge tournament at Kickoff this spring. Massive publicity and marketing campaign, several prizes and swag, panels every day of the convention. We're reaching out to several popular streamers to have them participate, using the tournament as a way to roll out our most expansive map yet. Having Deaths-Head participate would be a huge get for us. Your number of subscribers alone is in the millions. If even half of your followers watch, Bleeding Sword and this tournament will be a huge success."

Hayden let his eyes fall to Brad's tie, which probably cost more than Hayden's entire outfit, as he took a moment to think about it. Every year, Kimball, California, held the Kimball International Convention of Fans, aka Kickoff, a huge event and one of the most attended conventions in the world. Every year the otherwise sleepy city would be flooded with people, all wanting to immerse themselves in the media they love, attend panels, meet up with friends, and purchase exclusive merchandise. Kickoff was a highly anticipated event, with the revenue from the convention funding the town for the whole year. Hayden knew streamers everywhere would be flying in to participate, to speak on panels, to sell their own merchandise and set up their own streams. If people only had the chance to go to one convention each year, they went to Kickoff. It was the biggest and the best.

Hayden had been several years, but never as his streaming persona. At heart, Hayden was a fan, and so he loved going to panels, walking the exhibition floor, and losing himself in the crowd of people who loved content as much as he did. But since he had started his streaming channel, conventions had become harder and harder for him to attend. For one, his voice was too recognizable, so he had to be careful when and where he spoke aloud. His anxiety would spike in crowds, worried he'd let a stray comment slip and suddenly have heads turning toward him. And for another, being around that many people started to wear on him, causing an exhaustion that often took him a week to recover from. The convention was fun, but slowly it was becoming something to endure rather than something to enjoy. And he hated that.

But this was a new situation, one that seemed too good to be true. Bleeding Sword was offering to pay for his travel and hotel, as well as a stipend, in return for him participating in a tournament filled with other well-known streamers. The tournament would be a mixture of pros and rookies coming to try the game for the first time live. The game itself was one that Hayden enjoyed, and many of the participants they had already recruited were online friends of his. For anyone else, this was a no-brainer.

The problem, as always, was him.

Hayden didn't like attention. In the current digital age where influencers were everywhere trying to climb the ladder of success, trying to become a household name by competing to get famous, Hayden valued his privacy above everything else. His online persona, DeathsHead, was created with the mantra that he could be himself and play games online, but still keep himself real. The only part of himself he shared on his streams, besides his love of games, was his voice. And while in hindsight he probably should've set up a system to disguise his distinct voice, he couldn't deny that it was part of what his fans loved about him. So he let that part of him out onto the internet, while he constantly wondered if even that much was a mistake.

Hayden's very real anxiety was mostly under control, but it could spike with the right trigger. He was always worried someone would hear him order coffee and immediately know who he is. One picture on the internet and he would become fodder for all kinds of garbage, from people criticizing his looks to stalkers, and probably worse. Hayden had known that starting out, and now that he had a fan following, he knew it would be even worse if he revealed his face. People had now had time to build up in their minds what he could look like, which meant no matter what, a face reveal would disappoint and anger everyone who followed him. Hayden couldn't handle that, so he did everything he could to keep his identity secret. He wore a mask and concealing clothes if he ever appeared in public. He never showed himself while streaming. And he never, ever, met his fellow streamers in person. He knew from bitter experience how quickly those friendships can turn on you for likes and follows. And he was determined not to be clickbait for someone else.

He surveyed the two men in front of him. Hayden was definitely interested in the tournament, in the possibility of winning the prize money and the sponsorship that would move his secret dream further into reality. But he needed assurances first. A lot of them. "How do you plan on handling my need for privacy?"

Brad leaned forward, clearly having anticipated this question. "We're willing to work with your comfort level. Obviously the tournament has to be fair, but we can provide a separate entrance to the convention center for tournament times, a private room set up to stream with your own specifications. We can throw in whatever security you feel is needed, and we're willing to work with you on anything else you need. To be completely upfront, we're offering this to all of our high-profile streamers, but we're invested in including you on our tournament roster."

Hayden drummed his fingers more as he turned to look out the window. The building was one of the pretentious ones on Wilshire that towered high enough to have a view of the Hollywood Hills over the never-ending brake lights that was Los Angeles traffic. If he wanted to have less than an hour's drive home, he'd have to make up his mind soon. But there was something keeping him undecided. His instincts were yelling at him, but he wasn't sure why. In the past he would turn something like this down fast, the chances of getting recognized too great. But the money was good, even better if Hayden won the tournament. It was hard to turn that down.

The other man with Brad cleared his throat, and Hayden turned to him. He didn't like this one. Something about the look in his eyes reminded Hayden of sharks. Always swimming forward, never looking back at the destruction they caused.

"While obviously you would be a huge get for Bleeding Sword and the tournament, we would also be willing to work with you if at any point you felt like revealing your identity to your fans. The number of streams alone, added with the online interactions from the other social networks, would—"

"See, this is what pisses me off." Shark Eyes stopped talking as Hayden cut him off. Hayden felt his anger burn deep in his gut, his anxiety spiking when the douche began talking and a familiar feeling of rage coursing through him. Hayden was certain the look in his eyes was fucking fire. He hated guys like this.

"You bring me here, and you talk up how well you're going to treat me and respect my privacy wishes, and then you try to push me to expose myself for your bottom line. It's not going to happen. If you knew anything about me, if you had done even the most basic research about me, you'd know that."

Brad stepped in, trying to bring it back to before his idiot coworker had spoken. "Mr. Phillips, I assure you, there is absolutely no pressure. Our main goal in setting up this meeting was to earn your trust to hopefully build a future partnership. We're prepared to offer everything we can to make you feel comfortable. Dylan was just making an offer, in case it was something you had already been entertaining."

Hayden snorted. "Again, if you've watched me, you know very well I have zero plans to reveal my face, and I don't take kindly to the pressure. Especially when you use the tournament offer to try and persuade me. It's shit like this that reminds me why I don't work with businesses like yours."

Still, Brad tried. "Mr. Phillips, please, if we could just forget what Dylan said and go back to just the offer for the tournament—"

"It's a no for me. I don't work with people I don't trust." Hayden stood, raking his fingers through his dark hair. He should've gotten a haircut instead of coming here. What a waste of time.

Shark Eyes jumped up, something like panic on his face as he probably realized how much he just fucked up this deal. "Mr. Phillips, please, let me apologize. I led this meeting off track."

"Save it."

Hayden was out the door before they could say anything else.

CHAPTER 2

MIN

Min glanced around the lobby, noting the lack of water rings on the glass coffee table, the lack of receptionist, and the absolutely stellar view of Los Angeles through the floor-to-ceiling windows all along the far wall. She had never been in a waiting room this empty. Usually when she took meetings, the place was bustling, with other people waiting for their own meetings, assistants passing out water, and workers chatting about their day. But the offices of Bleeding Sword were completely empty.

Which made her nervous.

It had been three months since the pictures had leaked. In that time, her streaming numbers had dwindled, and her usual sponsor had dumped her. Her social media profiles were flooded with hate from strangers who were determined to run her off the internet. It was only through her sheer stubbornness that she kept the accounts open. Let them scream at her. She used their anger to fuel her own rage and drive. Min was determined to come back from this. At twenty-six, she knew her happy place was streaming, gaming with her friends, and introducing others to her love of video games. She was going to fix this. And she was hopeful it started here, with this meeting.

She checked her phone, confirming the date and time of her meeting for the tenth time. She was nervous, could feel her leg bouncing, and did her best to concentrate on staying still. She had been contacted about participating in a Bleeding Sword tournament at Kickoff, the biggest fan convention in the world. The stipend was generous, and the email had mentioned prize money for the winner, as well as a year-long sponsorship. After the last three months, Min needed this offer like a sip of water after days in the desert.

Min tugged at her auburn curls, attempting to make them behave. It felt weird to be going to a meeting as FlameThrower and to not be in her usual persona disguise. She didn't mind being on camera, but that didn't mean she wanted people to know exactly what she looked like. While she always sighed in relief when she removed the pink wig after a stream, right now she felt naked without it, without the heavy winged eyeliner and her normal pink contacts in.

She always wondered if people were disappointed when they actually met the real her. Real Min was short, didn't wear a lot of makeup, and was more likely to wear a torn band T-shirt than the corsets and fishnets FlameThrower loved. Real Min was the picture of normalcy, of blending into the crowd, whereas FlameThrower made sure she stood out. Usually Min enjoyed the contrast, but something about today had her feeling nervous.

One of the blessings of the leaked photos was that she was still in her wig and makeup for them. So while people online could call FlameThrower a slut and a whore, someone on the street would have to stare at Min a little longer to recognize her. And usually no one stared at Min for too long.

The time since the photos leaked had been hell. Alex denied posting them, but Min assumed he was lying. But she had no real proof he did anything other than take pictures without her consent, so she had no legal recourse against him. At least, that's what the cops had told her when she tried to press charges.

She had been an idiot to stay with him so long. And now she was paying the price.

Min's follower numbers had dropped significantly. She was known to be a good streamer for adults and kids alike, so these pictures changed her persona and her audience. And while she had released a statement saying she had never posed for the photos and that they were taken without her consent, the internet didn't care. Always on the lookout for the next great scandal, Min's naked body had been memed and ridiculed across the globe. She was now the face of "gamer girls" according to cis het white men who didn't like women in games, didn't like female streamers, didn't like anything about women who refused to suck their cock, and they made that clear in their campaign against Min. She had lost a sponsor stream, her merchandise deal, and thousands of followers.

And then last month Devery, her little sister, had her car t-boned by a drunk driver. The accident had been brutal, with Devery needing emergency surgery. That had truly been the worst moment of Min's life, hours bleeding into each other until the doctor finally came out to tell them Dev was going to pull through. She still remembered the relief engulfing her body at his words.

Among other injuries, her sister had badly broken her right leg, leaving her with months of rest and physical therapy in her future. And though her family's flower shop made a modest income, the medical bills were already piling up. Their mom, who had recently retired, was ready to step back into her role to run the shop while Devery was recovering, but it wasn't enough. And while in better times, Min could help support her family with her streaming, the well had run dry in the three months since the photos dropped.

She needed this tournament.

Min knew she could win. She had played most of the announced streamers in the past and had beaten them. Before the scandal, FlameThrower had been recognized as one of the best players of the game. She had a real shot at getting the money and, more importantly, the sponsorship. She was surprised they had approached her after the fallout from her scandal, but she wasn't one to question an opportunity.

Min needed the money. Bleeding Sword had the money. That was all that mattered.

Just then, her phone dinged with a message. Min checked it to find a picture from her sister—her sitting with their mother in her hospital room. Devery had a big smile on her face, almost as big as the hip-to-ankle cast she was sporting. The doctors were finally releasing her to go home today, and Min couldn't wait to have her there. She knew Dev was dying to be home, and Min already had planned to cook every last one of her favorite foods to celebrate.

Min smiled at Dev's obvious excitement, texting back a quick *"Looking good"* before enlarging the photo to study it. And it's while she was smiling that she heard a voice coming from down the hall.

"It was a mistake to come here."

Deep. Like, abyss deep. She knew that voice. She had heard it several times in her headphones, mocking her right before shooting her avatar in the face. Forgetting about her phone that she was holding, Min looked up just in time to see a man storm out from the hallway. He was taller than she had expected, well over six feet. And he was broad, not even his black hoodie hiding the expanse of his shoulders, his well-worn jeans hugging him in a way that Min felt was borderline indecent. He strode into the waiting room like he was going to war, clearly pissed, his dark eyes snapping, his dark hair chaotic, waves and curls rioting with every movement he made, looking like a buff, angry Tom Hiddleston. The executives chasing after him really had to hurry to catch up, his long legs eating up the distance to the elevators.

One of them tried. "Mr. Phillips, please, if you would just give us a moment."

"No. This was a waste of time," he said in a hard voice that Min was very happy wasn't directed at her.

Struggling with her shock of seeing DeathsHead in person, Min forgot that she was still holding her phone. And that she had been holding it upright, coincidentally pointing directly toward where DeathsHead and the execs had entered. She suddenly snapped into herself, quickly clicking the phone off and lowering it. But not before his eyes snapped to her, locking on.

Furious.

His anger radiated off of him as he changed directions and stormed toward her. With his long legs, it was only a moment before he was right there, towering over where she still sat on the bench.

"Delete the picture you just took." His voice was somehow deeper with anger. Min had played with him several times and had never heard him this enraged before, this serious.

She shook her head, trying to look innocent. Because she was innocent, damn it.

"I didn't take a picture," she insisted.

He hovered even closer to her, and she could smell the clean scent of his aftershave.

"You did. I know it. You know it. Don't be an asshole and just delete it already."

Min felt her own temper flare. She respected his need for privacy. Hell, she shared it. But she hadn't done what he was accusing her of, and now she was getting pissed. And like it did when she was angry, her mouth was about to take over and probably make things worse.

"I didn't take your fucking picture. Back off."

Instead of listening, he came even closer, leaning over her, an arm on the back of the wall behind her. Min couldn't help but feel completely surrounded. So she straightened her spine, not letting herself back away from him in any way.

"Don't lie to me. If you know who I am, you know how serious I take this."

Min glanced to the guys behind him, the two extremely nervous executives hovering nearby, clearly not sure what to do. One of them spoke up, his voice uncertain.

"I'm sure she didn't—"

"I wasn't talking to you." Death cut him off.

Min vaguely realized that they must have been recruiting him for the tournament. Even as pissed as she was, she knew it made sense. DeathsHead was a big draw. He would easily skyrocket their streaming numbers.

Min locked eyes with the dark tower of a man leaning over her, doing his best to intimidate her, and she thought about her shithead ex, Alex. How her life and business had been ruined when that asshole decided to post pictures of her naked body, and she felt her anger burn with the deep fire of women everywhere fucking tired of men pushing them around.

And she snapped.

"I do know who you are, fucknut. Which is why I didn't take a photo, because I know you'd hate it. And I really don't appreciate being spoken to like this. I was invited here for a meeting. I'm not here for you. So get. The fuck. Out of my face."

She stood while she spoke, forcing him to lean back and let her. Their toes practically touched as she glared up at him, her high heels only doing so much to add to her modest height, bringing her head up to his chin. In her peripheral, she saw the two executives exchange glances, but she ignored them. Ignored everything except his dark eyes hot on hers.

She barely registered a flicker of heat in her stomach, a fluttering of... something... but she ignored that, too, assuming it was her temper.

His eyes narrowed, clearly not impressed.

"<u>You</u> were invited here for a meeting?" His voice was skeptical, and while Min couldn't tell if it was because he didn't recognize her or because he didn't think she'd merit a meeting, it no longer mattered. DeathsHead was a bigger draw than FlameThrower even before her photo scandal. The two executives staring at them had to be the ones in charge of the tournament, and they clearly wanted DeathsHead. They were watching this all go down and were saying nothing to defend her or verify her story. If Death was pissed at her, there was no way he'd let them keep her in the tournament. This meeting was fucked no matter what she did now.

She exhaled sharply, very suddenly done with this entire situation.

"Fuck this." She should have known this meeting was too

good to be true. She was an idiot for thinking something was finally going right, that she would actually be able to salvage her streaming career and dig her family out of the oncoming medical debt. Disappointment was threatening to engulf her, and she had to get out of here before she let any of these assholes see.

Grabbing her purse, she bumped his shoulder hard enough to move him out of her way and made a beeline toward the elevator. She smashed the call button before the executives had a chance to remember how to talk, if they were even inclined to try to stop her. She was done with this meeting, done with the farce of pretending she can simply win her old career back. Alex wanted her destroyed, and so far, it had worked. But she was far from done fighting for herself. Maybe she couldn't do this tournament, but she would figure something out, something to get herself back on track and to help support her family. Min didn't need this, didn't need these people.

And she certainly didn't need DeathsHead.

Min was gratified when the elevator doors opened after only a moment. For once, the universe was on her side. She hit the button for the lobby and stepped back, leaning against the back wall of the elevator, waiting for the doors to fully close before she allowed herself to breathe.

But just as they were about to close and free her from this nightmare situation, a hand slammed between them. The doors were pushed open and there he was again, tall and over-whelming, the energy around him crackling, his eyes wild. That heat fluttered inside her again, and once again she ignored it, her eyes narrowing, her spine straightening with outrage.

"What the hell are you doing?"

He didn't answer, stepping into the elevator with her and

just… standing. Staring at her. Their eyes locked on each other, heated and powerful and something else Min couldn't define, some sort of combustible chemistry that was unique only to them. She glimpsed the two executives behind him, not coming near the elevator, letting whatever was going to happen, happen, and she felt her fury rise at that, at once again being left to fend for herself in a shitstorm that she didn't create. But she wouldn't let that show. Not to him.

Their eyes clashed as the elevator began to move. And then, without breaking eye contact, he reached toward the control panel and pulled the emergency stop. The elevator lurched a little as the brakes complied.

"You're not going anywhere until you delete that picture, babe." His voice was soft, softer than it had been before in the lobby, but still menacing, and she could almost feel it caress her skin. Despite herself, despite how pissed she was at him, she couldn't help but notice that they were alone in the confined space, with only the soft elevator music cutting the silence. She kept still, clenching her phone in her hand, sensing that he was tensed for her to try to escape even though there was clearly nowhere to go. She was trapped.

But she sure wasn't going to show any vulnerability in front of him, so she raised her chin up and stood her ground. "For the last fucking time, I didn't take your picture. Get over yourself."

He exhaled sharply, raking his hands through his hair, his curls even more unruly, his dark eyes snapping.

"People like you are the problem, you know?" he growled.

"You mean innocent people who get stalked and yelled at for just trying to attend meetings they were scheduled for?"

He snorted at that, clearly not believing her. "People who claim to be fans, who say they love you and want everything for you, support you through it all. When in reality they don't give a shit about you. They never did. They're just waiting for their chance to steal a piece of you for themself. Something to mount on their Instagram like a fucking trophy."

Despite her anger, she could feel the truth in his words, the cynicism that must have been proven to him time and again. A flicker of sympathy fluttered through her, but she refused to let it show. However true his statement was, whatever his experience, it had nothing to do with her.

"I'm not that person," she said, her voice softer than before, trying to appeal to him. "I swear."

He wavered, and she thought he wanted to believe her. But then his expression hardened.

"Then prove it."

His hand reached out for her phone, and on instinct she drew it back, away from him, which only pissed him off more. He reached for her again, and this time his hand was too fast to dodge, grabbing her wrist tight and unyielding as he pushed it against the wall behind her, holding it there slightly above her head. He stepped closer into her space. Min found herself surrounded by his clean scent, inhaling it deeply before she could stop herself. He gazed down at her, nostrils flaring, and she wondered vaguely how the fuck she was going to get out of this.

She attempted to push him away with her free hand, but all she found was hard muscle underneath his black hoodie as if she was pushing on a wall. Unphased, he put his free hand on the other side of her head and pushed his body into hers, anchoring her into the wall with his hips so she couldn't move. Their faces were so close she could feel the rustle of his hair as he leaned down toward her ear.

"Give me your phone." His voice rumbled from his chest,

and this close, she could feel the vibration shiver through her body.

"Eat shit and die." Her reply came out as a whisper, but she refused to back down. She tried pushing her body against his to move him away, but he wasn't budging.

"This would be over if you'd just let me look."

"I have just as much right to privacy as you do." A muscle in his jaw flexed at that, like he agreed but didn't want to show it. He was silent a moment, studying her, probably trying to figure out his next move, and she tried pushing him away again, but he was too strong. Too solid. Too much.

With a deep sigh, he reached over and plucked the phone out of her trapped hand, not letting her go as he tapped the screen. She tried to struggle again, to dislodge him, but he slid one of his legs between hers, holding her more securely pressed against the wall. He held the phone up to her face, waiting for facial recognition to kick in, but nothing happened. She almost smiled at his frustration but settled for glaring.

"I don't do the facial recognition lock. Always too worried someone would use it against me. Ironically." She smirked as his lips pinched into a frown. "Now let me go."

He didn't move. "Code."

"Get bent."

Only because she was so focused on his mouth did she see his lips twitch, a different expression fighting to overtake him before he controlled it. Instead, he leaned closer, his breath whispering into her ear, his heat surrounding her

"You want to know the worst part? If you had just played it cool, just smiled at me with that fucking candy pink mouth and introduced yourself with that smooth as silk voice, I would've done whatever you asked. Anything."

He whispered the last word, and she couldn't stop a shudder from running through her. His eyes flared as he felt it.

"But you ruined it." His voice was suddenly cold, and she couldn't stand it, not when she had heard how hot it could be only a moment before. Before she could think about it, she turned her head toward him, their mouths now only a breath apart.

"I didn't. And when you realize that, you better have the best fucking apology for me. Because if you had just not been an asshole, I would've smiled and introduced myself. And my fantasies about you would've been very, very different from the homicidal ones they currently are."

She couldn't believe she had just said that, but it was too late to take it back. Especially since she only realized as she was saying it that it was true.

"So you admit you've fantasized about me?"

Not one to back down, Min gave him a savage grin. "Of course. The current one involves slow dismemberment."

They both held their breath, eyes locked. She saw the moment he decided to try a different tactic, feeling him pull away even as he kept her against the wall.

"I don't really have time for this, babe. Those suits up there already wasted enough of my day, and now you're making me late."

She felt her panic rise at that. "Wait, you're not doing the tournament?"

He studied her, seeing the change in her, curious. His thumb almost caressing her trapped wrist as he stared at her, considering.

"No. The douche made it clear that they wanted to cut a deal for me to reveal my identity during their stream. I don't like being pressured, and my privacy is too important to lose it to one lame tournament."

She ignored the 'lame' comment. Min quickly put the pieces together in her head. This was why Bleeding Sword was willing to give her a spot in the tournament, even though her recent viewership had tanked. She was being offered this chance because of her rivalry with DeathsHead. Their streams together always resulted in both of their highest ratings, and the tournament wanted those kinds of numbers for themselves, even if Min's star had fallen.

And if Death wasn't going to be in the tournament… it's possible the company would decide they didn't need her, didn't need to risk having to sponsor such a controversial streamer if she won. While she had walked out in a temper, a clearer head was currently prevailing. Min couldn't let him walk away from the tournament. If she was going to go back up there and grovel for a spot, which she was currently gearing up to do, she would need DeathsHead signed on to boost her chances of success.

Fuck, she needed him.

"I'll give you my code if you do the tournament." The offer rushed out of her in a long breath before she could stop it.

He was surprised. "What's in it for you?"

"My sister just got out of the hospital." She hated telling him the truth, but she couldn't let him walk away. She glanced away from him, not able to meet his eyes. "Car accident. Her surgeries were expensive, and the bills are piling up. I haven't been able to work for a few months now. Winning the tournament would help. The sponsorship… it would help a lot."

It would change her miserable life, and she knew it. He was silent, his gaze dropping to her mouth before traveling back up to her eyes. She could see him weighing his options, torn between whether to believe her.

"You really think you could beat me?" He smirked at her, and Min suddenly remembered that he didn't know who she was. He clearly believing her to be a rookie streamer, and a rookie would have almost no chance against a pro like DeathsHead.

Min met his smirk with a cold smile. "I have before."

He froze at that, his eyes searching her face, still not recognizing her without the heavy makeup, without the wig, without the outfit, and she found herself both grateful and disappointed that he didn't know her without it. Or maybe that he had never really cared to know her.

"Who are you?" he asked.

"Do we have a deal?" She held her breath, not sure what she would do if he said no. His thumb absently caressed her wrist again as he gazed at her, and she wondered if he even realized he was doing it. Finally, his mouth compressed into a flat line.

"Deal."

Her breath whooshed out of her as she sagged against the wall.

Min recited her code, and he kept hold of her while he typed it in. The phone immediately unlocked, showing him her texts with her sister, seeing the picture of her with her mom in the hospital, Devery's leg encased in the large cast. He scrolled through some of the texts, then went to her photos. She straightened her spine, her mouth flattening as he invaded her privacy even further.

"I told you I didn't take your picture."

He ignored her, scrolling through her pictures, seeing her with her sister, her mom, cooking and laughing and being together. He checked her trash file, finding nothing. If anything, she could feel his body grow more tense as he violated her phone, searching everything he could before finally clicking it off. When he finally met her eyes, she could see the regret flash through them before he hid it. He handed her back the phone.

"I'm sorry."

His voice was sincere, and cold air rushed over her as he stepped back, letting go of her wrist. The sensation was so sudden that she almost stumbled, rocking toward him a little before she caught herself. His hand reached over to the control panel and released the elevator. He leaned against the wall furthest away from her, staring at her, his eyes hooded but still on her as they rode the rest of the way to the parking garage in silence.

The doors dinged open, revealing the two executives from before standing there, waiting for them. Min could only guess what she and DeathsHead looked like. She could feel her face was flushed and her breath was short. DeathsHead, however, was calm, showing nothing of their conversation or of how close they had been only moments ago. He gave the execs a cold look before turning his eyes back to her. She didn't say anything, worried the slightest thing would cause him to renege on their deal.

Finally, he turned back to the executives. "I'll do the tournament."

The suits practically sagged in relief, and one came forward, hand up to clap Death on the back before thinking better of it and running his hand through his own hair.

"So glad to hear it. Really, really glad. How about we go back upstairs and hash out the details?"

DeathsHead nodded and the executive turned to Min.

"I'm assuming you're Minerva Hayes?"

Min tried a smile, but wasn't sure how genuine it came out. "That's me."

He held out his hand. "I'm Brad, Vice President of Bleeding Sword. We're so happy you could make it. And I apologize for… the misunderstanding."

Minerva nodded, not sure what else to say. The whole situation was beyond anything she had dealt with before, and clearly Brad was feeling the awkwardness as well.

His coworker, however, seemed to have recovered. He chuckled as his hand waved between her and DeathsHead.

"As odd as this is, I have to say it's an honor to be here with both of you. We're big fans of you two."

DeathsHead turned to Min, a question in his eyes, and Min found herself filled with cold anticipation for how he was going to respond. Her lips curved into a sardonic smile.

"Who are you?" he finally asked, suspicion filling his voice.

Her lips curved into a sardonic smile. "Minerva. But you know me as FlameThrower."

The shock on his face was worth it.

CHAPTER 3

HAYDEN

She was fucking FlameThrower.

Hayden couldn't stop himself from searching her face, looking for the signs he had previously missed. Her eyes seemed bigger without the lashes, the winged liner, and everything else she layered on for her streaming channel. Her hair—her real hair—was a deep auburn, probably the fire of her namesake, and it curled around her like flames. Without the pink contacts, her eyes were dark brown, with flecks of gold when the light hit them right. But dark enough to pierce straight through Hayden when she focused.

She said her name was Minerva. Hayden had trouble reconciling her real name with her online persona. FlameThrower loved attention. She was bold and funny and had a laugh that could infect others. The disguise she wore while she was streaming was cute, a little sexy, something that seemed completely the opposite of the fierce, argumentative woman he had played against... and yet it all wrapped up into one intriguing package.

The woman in front of him was different than what he had

come to know for FlameThrower. Cold, quiet. More likely to listen than to talk. But when he thought about it, Hayden had to admit, the temper was the same.

He couldn't get over the fact that the woman next to him had been playing games with him for years. Sometimes Hayden won. Sometimes she won. Their rivalry was legendary, and the fans ate it up. Hayden would often find himself watching her solo streams, trying to learn her latest strategies to use against her the next time they played. He had spent hours talking with her, playing with her, watching her. And now that she was near him, sitting next to him, he couldn't believe he hadn't recognized her right away.

He was an idiot.

Hayden had never before felt like such a piece of shit. His brother liked to joke that Hayden was the calmest person he had ever met, that nothing short of a house fire could get his temper up. As a tall, large man, Hayden made sure to control himself, knowing how easy it would be to intimidate and scare someone. He never wanted to do that. But when he had entered the lobby, his blood already up, and had seen this gorgeous woman, something had screamed inside him. He had seen her big brown eyes flash with recognition, and he had seen her lush, pink lips drop with a gasp. And on any other day, he would've relished it, relished approaching her and finding out exactly what her story was.

And then he'd seen her fucking phone in her hand. Held up as if she had just been taking a picture of him before she caught his eye and tried to hide it.

He should be used to it by now. The last girl to approach him had made her interest seem genuine and had never indicated that she followed the streaming world. It wasn't until he caught her about to sell her photos to some online rag that she confessed she was more interested in revealing his identity to the world than she was in dating him. His anxiety had spiked then, causing him to spiral and abandon streaming for a while, until his brother helped drag him out of it. After that, Hayden swore to himself he was done with trusting strangers. He stuck to his brother and the people he already knew, keeping to himself as much as he could, and stayed away from even the online friends he had played for years, knowing that in the end they would probably betray him.

Except this woman hadn't. She had just been texting what looked to be her sister, a young, tired-looking woman with a huge cast on her leg. An innocent text between family members that had absolutely nothing to do with him.

And Hayden found himself feeling like the villain.

He hated it, hated that he had pried into someone else's privacy the way he had always despised. The memory of her face when she had told him about her sister, clearly not wanting to share but feeling she had no choice, was going to haunt him. And he would deserve it.

Now here he was, once again seated in this conference room he despised, the executives across from him looking like they had won a battle.

But this time, FlameThrower sat next to him.

She hadn't met his eye since the elevator, had clearly been tensed for him to back out of their deal. But there was no way that was going to happen. Not when he had fucked up so royally.

The suits had been talking for a while, something about bottom lines and red tape that he didn't find himself caring about. It was getting late and traffic was going to be a nightmare, so it was definitely time to wrap this up. He leaned forward on the table, interrupting whatever Brad had been about to say about procedures and paperwork.

"I will not be revealing my face. I want to make that clear."

Dylan, formerly Shark Eyes, leaned back in his chair, a little disgruntled and not meeting Hayden's eyes. But Brad was already nodding.

"Of course. Your identity is your own. Bleeding Sword is simply happy to have DeathsHead in the tournament."

"I'll send you my specs for the setup. I'll need a private entrance and a private room. I shouldn't see anyone else on my way to and from."

Brad nodded, jotting down a note on his iPad, then glanced at the woman next to Hayden.

"Ms. Hayes? While we're talking about setups, is there anything in particular you'll need?"

She cleared her throat and Hayden couldn't help how aware of her he was. She sat next to him, but there was a gulf of space between them, something she had made sure of before she sat down. But Hayden could still smell her perfume, the light floral teasing his senses as she did everything she could to ignore him.

"I'll need a private dressing room, a place I can change into my persona before the tournament so that I can enter and exit unnoticed."

"But you're fine to be on camera?"

"Of course." Her voice was almost cold, a little detached, and Hayden remembered vaguely someone talking about some photos of her that had circulated a few months ago.

He didn't keep up with streamer gossip, preferring to simply play games and then work on his own projects, but now he was annoyed he hadn't looked into it more. There was something behind her answer that he didn't understand, and he suddenly wanted to. Very, very badly.

"What about accommodations?" Her voice was all business, and Hayden felt it itch at something in him. That mouth that had told him to fuck off, that had whispered in his ear, was now grilling these suits like she'd eat them for breakfast, and Hayden couldn't deny it was making him hot.

"You'll both have rooms at the hotel near the convention center."

"We'll want rooms away from where the other streamers are staying. For privacy."

Min raised her brow at Hayden's use of "we," but she didn't contradict him. He got the feeling she wanted to avoid the other streamers, too.

"Done," Brad said. "We'll book the rooms under whatever pseudonym you would like. We can also assist you with your travel."

Hayden looked to Min for confirmation. After a short hesitation, she nodded. "That would be great."

"Excellent. Is there anything else?"

She turned to Hayden, her eyes on his, waiting for something to happen. And Hayden realized she was waiting for him to back out, to say no, to reject the deal they had made and to leave her high and dry. Now that he knew she was FlameThrower, he knew why she wanted him at the tournament—their rivalry was popular among their fan base, and their streams together were always the most successful and the highest rated. She tensed, and Hayden could tell she was holding her breath. She needed this.

And hell, if he was being honest, Hayden wanted her there. Of any of the other streamers Hayden had played with, Flame-

Thrower was the one who actually had a chance to beat him. She made the game more fun just by challenging him.

But Hayden wasn't going to make it easy for her. If he was going to do this, stream for a big tournament at the biggest fan convention in the world, he was going to go hard. The money from the win and the sponsorship would speed up his plans and goals considerably.

Which meant he wasn't going to let her win without a fight.

Hayden quirked an eyebrow at her, which she glared at. He didn't know if that was because she sensed what he was thinking, or if she was just glaring, but he was finding he didn't care as long as she was looking at him.

"Well?" she finally asked. No, demanded.

"Ready if you are, babe."

CHAPTER 4

MIN

Min hated being late.

She raced through Union Station toward her train, dragging her small carry-on behind her, trying to read the signs for directions while she raced by them. In an effort to miss traffic to Kimball, she had booked herself a seat on the train heading south, hoping to get some reading and emails done during the four-hour trip. She had taken the train to Kickoff many times in the past, and had always loved how relaxing a journey it was, loved watching the glimpse of the ocean outside the windows as they rolled past. After the last month of settling Devery into their mom's house and driving her back and forth to her doctor's appointments and physical therapy, Min had actually been looking forward to unwinding for a few hours by herself, lost in the crowd of the train.

But that relaxation was looking harder and harder to grasp. She had missed the subway she had meant to take downtown, which meant she had to wait for the next train, throwing off her schedule. She could feel the slow passage of time leeching out of her, eating at her anxiety that she was attempting to breathe through. By the time she reached Union Station, she only had minutes to spare, so when she finally spotted the sign pointing her to the platform she needed, she sprinted.

A little out of breath, she finally stepped out onto the platform and the night chill sank into her bones. Los Angeles was beautiful at all times, but the sun had set, leaving a bite in the air that made soft Angelenos like herself shiver. She kept up her pace, heading to the back of the line for business class. The tickets were more expensive, but worth the splurge as they were the only seats guaranteed on the train. After her first year going to Kickoff when she had purchased an unreserved seat and had found herself stuck for hours under the sun in a line waiting to make it onto a train, she swore to herself she'd always pay the extra money for the peace of mind of a guaranteed seat. Even if it meant she was eating ramen for a few weeks.

She was one of the last to board, and still felt the stress of her tardiness as she climbed the narrow stairs to the second-floor seating. People were everywhere, negotiating seats, stowing bags, and Min slowly made her way through the crowd, finally spotting ahead of her an empty aisle seat. She slowly shuffled forward to claim it... only to stop short at the guy in front of her, clearly about to sit in the seat she already thought of as hers. He was tall, his wide shoulders blocking her from finagling her way around him, so she cleared her throat, hoping to get his attention. He turned toward her and their eyes locked, and Min silently berated herself for not seeing this coming.

It was DeathsHead.

No. *Hayden.*

She hadn't spoken to him since the meeting last month. They weren't really friends online. They streamed in different circles for the most part, only coming together for larger group games. And since Min's scandal, she hadn't been invited to those lobbies, her presence replaced by newer, greener streamers whose scandal wouldn't overshadow the other players. She had to admit, she couldn't blame them. Every time Min had tried to stream since the photos had leaked, her chat and feed had been filled with hate, name-calling, judgment, and threats. Everything under the sun a bored internet troll could think of was thrown at her, until she had finally just stopped. She told herself it was only a short break, to give her followers time to process and herself time to grieve what had happened. Her other streamer friends had been sympathetic, but since views and likes were the life and death of a professional streamer, they had made it clear that she was on her own. Min understood their position, but she'd be lying if it didn't make her burn.

Hayden's mouth quirked, and Min realized too late that they had been staring at each other for far too long in the busy aisle. A glance around told her that most passengers had settled into their seats already. He quirked his head into the empty seats for her to go first. But the amusement in his eyes was too much, his accusing words from the day they met too fresh in her mind, so she glared at him and sat in the seat across the aisle, next to a businessman who she silently hoped would be quiet and sleep. For his part, Hayden helped an older woman into the window seat and then sat, only the aisle separating them.

But even across the aisle, she was too aware of him pulling out his laptop, settling in for the trip, his deep sigh of being able to finally relax. Min started to worry the aisle wasn't wide enough.

Taking a deep breath, Min focused on shuffling her carry-on, pulling out the items she had planned to use during the train trip. She grabbed her phone, and even though she was intent on ignoring him, she couldn't help throwing a sarcastic remark his way.

"I'm waiting for a text from my sister, so don't freak if I have my phone out."

She heard him snort, and a glance through her lashes showed he was not looking at her, settling into his seat and focusing on his laptop, clearly as determined to ignore her as she was him. Not able to decide if she was annoyed or relieved, Min took out her own laptop to do some work, letting the quiet of the evening train settle around her and loosen the tension in her shoulders.

Before her photos had hit the internet, Min had been invited to speak on a panel for Women in Gaming. Well, she had been invited to speak on many panels, but the Women in Gaming panel was the only one that hadn't dropped her after the photos made the rounds. Min was grateful for the small act of kindness and settled in to study the list of panel questions that had been emailed to her. She wanted to be as prepared as possible.

But it soon became clear that wasn't going to happen. The guy next to her was disruptive, pushing her elbow off the shared armrest, taking up more space than his skinny frame needed, talking loudly on his phone even though other passengers were clearly trying to sleep. Judging from his conversation, he was a lower-level executive at a film production company, and he very much felt he was more important than he probably was. He glanced at Min every now and then as if reassuring himself that she was paying attention to him, and Min was annoyed that she was, that she couldn't help it. He kept knocking her off the armrest, his legs kept shifting, spreading, taking up space in what she considered her "zone," and it was pissing her off.

"Could you stay in your area, please?" she tried to ask him quietly, her tone polite, all while hating that she actually had to engage with this guy.

He only flashed her a grin that made her skin crawl. "The boys need to breathe, honey."

Ick. Min couldn't stop herself from glancing at his crotch skeptically, not really seeing a bulge worth the spread he was claiming, but he somehow took her skepticism as interest. He threw her a wink as he dialed someone on his phone and proceeded to talk even louder. Min saw a woman a few rows ahead jerk upright, probably awoken from a good sleep by this scum ball and his need to prove he could have a loud phone conversation. She could see people glancing at them and wanted to shrink. While FlameThrower dressed outrageously and loved attention on the stream, Min hated being the center of attention, especially for something like this.

Not able to stop herself, Min glanced across the aisle, wondering what Hayden's response was to her loud neighbor. But Hayden had some large headphones over his ears and looked as if his entire focus was on whatever was on his laptop, not paying her the slightest attention. His wild hair had fallen into his eyes, and his hoodie was pulled around his body like armor. The older woman next to him had fallen asleep almost immediately after the train had departed, and Min gazed at her longingly, thinking of all the work she would've gotten done with a quiet seatmate who just slept and didn't keep spreading his legs to knock into hers.

The jerk next to her interrupted her jealous thoughts by tapping her shoulder too hard.

"Snack time, honey. Let me out."

With a roll of her eyes, Min grabbed her laptop and stood in her seat, pressing back so he had room to pass. Of course, even with all the space she had made for him, he still somehow managed to brush up against her body as he moved past her, sending her a smirk before heading down the aisle toward the cafe car. She breathed a little relief when he was gone, reveling in the silence now that his constant clamor for attention had left with him. She quickly dove into her work, knowing her quiet time was limited and wanting to make the most of it. Because she was so intent on it, Min only vaguely sensed Hayden stand up and head out of the car, probably needing to stretch his long legs.

She wasn't sure how much time had passed before both Hayden and her seatmate returned. She jumped back as the jerk reached over her and grabbed his small bag from under his seat, pulling it to him over the aisle. A glance up at him had her curious, since he was pointedly not meeting her eyes, his face carefully blank, his smirk gone. She kept staring at him, confused, as he took his bag and spun around, settling into what she belatedly realized was Hayden's now empty seat.

And then her vision was blocked by what she knew to be a hard chest tucked into a black hoodie. Her eyes reluctantly made the slow trek up to meet Hayden's dark eyes.

"Scoot over."

Confused, she picked up her stuff and slipped into the window seat. Hayden quickly dropped into her vacated one. He didn't say anything else, just stored his bag, set up his laptop, and slipped his headphones back on. Her confusion growing, Min glanced around him to peer across the aisle and caught her former seatmate shooting Hayden a nervous look. She was even more surprised when the jerk put away his phone and turned his eyes to gaze out the dark window, actually staying quiet for the first time since he boarded.

Min turned her attention back to Hayden, her eyes narrowing.

"What did you do?"

He ignored her, but she knew they were close enough for him to hear her, even through the noise-canceling headphones. Annoyed, she poked her finger into his side. Hard.

He jumped, eyes turning to her, rubbing his side, frowning. "Ow?"

"What did you do?" She was practically hissing through her teeth, low enough for her voice not to carry in the quiet train car. But Hayden was clearly intent on dismissing her.

"I ran into Mr. Wonderful in the cafe car. He asked to switch seats. Said you were complaining too much. Practically begged me." Hayden's tone was dry and flippant and Min absolutely did not trust it.

"Liar. He was rubbing up against me before he ran into you, and now he won't even look this way."

"Did you want him to look this way?" Hayden's voice went dark, a flicker of something in his eyes that Min couldn't identify.

"Of course not."

Hayden's shoulders relaxed, almost imperceptibly. But Min was staring at him, tracking every movement no matter how small, so she saw. And wondered.

Hayden went back to trying to ignore her. "Then what do you care that he wanted to switch seats?"

"I don't care about that. I care that you're lying to me."

Finally, Hayden turned to her, his eyes burning as they met

hers, and Min was suddenly overwhelmed with how much space he took up, how he encompassed everything.

"What do you want to hear, Minerva?" he asked, his voice soft. "That I followed him to the cafe car? That I told him if he didn't keep his fucking hands off you for the rest of the ride that I'd make sure he would never be able to use them again? That if he didn't find another seat, and quickly, that I would not hesitate to completely destroy his entire life piece by piece?"

She was breathless, staring at him, their eyes clashing with an electric pulse that hadn't been present before. She wasn't sure what surprised her more, the thought of him threatening some guy for being a jerk to her, or hearing him say her real name for the first time.

It had to be her name. Had to be. She licked her lips, realizing that her breath had become erratic. When did that happen?

"It's Min. I go by Min." There was a tense moment between them, something that was hard to define but that she knew meant something. She just didn't know what. And Min, coward that she was, turned away first.

"There's no way you threatened him. You don't even like me." Her voice wavered, and she hoped he couldn't hear it. He had to be fucking with her. There's no way this man who had done nothing but accuse her and antagonize her since she had finally met him had done anything as bold and, well, nice, as confront some asshole on a train just because he touched her.

Hayden's mouth twitched, almost smiling, before he turned back to his laptop.

"You just can't believe you're so annoying, someone would switch seats to get away from you."

She couldn't think of a reply, and she hated that, so after a moment of gaping at him, she reached out and pinched his forearm. He yanked his arm away from her, rubbing the spot.

"Would you stop doing that? You're too small to be so violent."

It was something he had often said to her when they were competing online against each other, and she fought the sudden urge to laugh.

She turned to her own laptop before he could see.

"Shut up, I'm trying to work."

She ignored his deep chuckle, flipping back to her panel questions as he settled deeper into his seat, going back to the document he was working on. She told herself it didn't matter that he had clearly made the guy switch seats, that he must have seen how annoyed and bothered she was even with his headphones on and his face buried in his computer. And it certainly didn't matter that he was now right next to her, their elbows touching on the armrest, the heat from his body radiating into her side as he completely ignored her.

It didn't matter. She had a tournament to win.

She closed out the document for the panel questions and pulled up an internet video from a previous tournament. She had been slowly studying streams from all her competitors, learning their favorite tactics and moves. One of the participants was Fannibal, a fellow streamer who Min knew was also participating in the Bleeding Sword tournament. She watched Fannibal for a while, studying his gameplay, lost in her research, when Hayden leaned over, staring at her screen.

"He likes the shotgun."

Min frowned, throwing eye daggers at Hayden before focusing back on the screen. It was true, Fannibal always traded for the shotgun, loving the wide spread it gave him for damage.

"Easy enough to counteract," she said. The shotgun did solid damage when your target was in range, but it wasn't good for much else. Min preferred to keep her distance, sniping from afar, so the shotgun with its shorter range was less of a worry for her.

"Maybe you'll be safe from Fannibal, but you won't be able to hide in the buildings forever. It's too easy to sneak up on you while you're sniping." He said it idly, more conversational, but she felt her spine straighten in defense anyway.

"As opposed to just scooping up the baseball bat and running headfirst into a firefight?" She let her irritation show, and she hated how amused he clearly was by her annoyance.

"Baby, the point of games is to have fun. If you're not having fun, then why are you playing?"

She glowered at him. "Lose the 'baby.' And maybe I have more fun when I'm winning."

"Maybe I run headfirst into firefights because that's where flame throwers tend to be."

Good god, his fucking voice. Coming from anyone else, the line would sound cheesy, like a bad online dating prompt. But his deep voice rumbled through her, his dark eyes twinkling and his unruly hair curling everywhere, and Min realized she forgot to breathe. She slowly exhaled, and his eyes went to her lips.

"Just remember you said that when I'm roasting you alive in front of millions of people."

He smiled at that, a real smile that changed his whole face, and it suddenly occurred to Min that DeathsHead was handsome. Was actually kind of a hottie. And once the realization hit her, it was hard to unsee it. She couldn't help but feel a slight panic. She didn't want to think her biggest rival in the tournament was attractive. Honestly, didn't really want to think of him at all, other than as another person to beat. This sudden noticing of him had to stop.

Luckily, Hayden didn't seem to register her sudden change of mood, instead focusing on her challenge. His gaze was sinister as he looked down at her, too close.

"Baby, I can't wait to watch you try."

CHAPTER 5

HAYDEN

The train screeched to a stop, and still the woman slept, her head light on his shoulder. The video she had been watching had long ago played itself out and switched over to random, recommended viewing, somehow now playing ASMR content involving a snake. Hayden stayed where he was, telling himself he was avoiding the rush of the crowd who lurched out of their seats to grab their bags, eager to leave the train far behind them. Hayden didn't know how Min managed to sleep through all the commotion. Her head was resting on his shoulder in a way that he knew she would absolutely hate if she was conscious. He was looking forward to her waking up and realizing, if only because the sight of her eyes flashing with anger was quickly becoming one of his favorite things.

People around him were politely jostling each other as they gathered their bags and filed out. Hayden let his eyes follow the guy across the aisle, the one who had very quickly backed off when Hayden made it clear he didn't appreciate his interactions with Min. He especially didn't like watching that dickwad take up space around her, sliding his elbow and legs and everything he could get away with against her, even when she very clearly told him to stop.

Hayden couldn't stand guys who took more than was offered. So he had been itching to put Min's seatmate in his place, even if it meant an impromptu visit to the cafe car.

Not that he would tell her that. They hadn't started off on the best foot, and even on a good day, they were still competitors in a tournament they were both determined to win. Hayden had plans, ideas he had been working on for years, and the money from winning the tournament would go a long way to get his plans realized. He wasn't about to do anything to jeopardize that.

Even if FlameThrower had turned out to be more interesting than he had expected.

Min's head suddenly jerked and she sat up, blinking, finally noticing the people moving around her. When she focused on him, her eyes still dreamy from sleep, he very distinctly felt his cock twitch.

Which he promptly ignored. "We're here, baby. Wake up."

She looked around herself, still a little disoriented, but automatically went to pack her things, not even giving him shit for calling her 'baby.' Which was good, since he had no plans to stop.

Hayden stepped out into the aisle, shouldering his duffel. When she stepped out ahead of him, he took her bag from her and threw it over his other shoulder. She blinked, gaping at him.

"What are you doing?"

He ignored her. "Get moving. I'd like to get to the hotel before two am."

Clearly too tired to argue, she followed the line toward the exit. But when they finally stepped out onto the platform she turned back to him, her hand out.

"Thanks, I can take it from here."

He kept walking, and he knew she had to hurry to keep up with his long strides. He pulled out his phone and pulled up the rideshare app.

"They put you up at the Wayward?"

"Yeah."

He nodded, ordering a car to pick them up, and didn't stop walking until they were at the side of the street. The road was empty except for the others leaving the train. The night was dark, darker than LA ever managed to be, and the streetlamp was their only illumination. Out of his peripheral, he saw Min scrub her face with her hand, trying to wake herself up even more. And then she held out her hand again.

"Give me my bag."

"No."

That surprised her, and he almost ruined it by smiling. She must be used to ordering men around, and he bet with that mouth of hers they jumped to do what she said. Too bad for her. Hayden had too many fond memories of FlameThrower's voice screaming in outrage at him whenever he outsmarted her. And he was aiming to hear it again.

He could see the moment she relented.

"Fine. You can hold it until I get a cab here." She pulled out her phone, and Hayden was quick to put his hand over the screen. She froze, tense, and he could kick himself for reminding her of the last time he went for her phone. He quickly pulled his hand back, shoving it into his pocket.

"I already called a rideshare," he said as gently as he could. "We're going to the same place, so it doesn't hurt to split one." He could see her hesitation, but she nodded, sliding her phone back into her pocket. She looked uncomfortable and he couldn't think why, her eyes going anywhere but to him, obviously working up the nerve to say something. He found he couldn't wait to hear what it was.

"I'm sorry if I, um, slept. On you. That was rude of me."

Hayden wanted to laugh. She clearly hated the idea of leaning on him, of subconsciously trusting him while she slept, and Hayden enjoyed every moment of her awkwardness even as he kept his face neutral, knowing it would drive her nuts.

"Don't worry about it."

They were interrupted when the rideshare pulled up, and after Hayden confirmed the plate and driver with the app, he loaded their bags into the trunk and helped open the door for Min. There was still surprise in her eyes, but she slid in, and he followed, closing the door. They fell into silence, both staring out their windows to watch the city pass by.

"You two in town for the convention?" the driver asked, glancing at them in his rearview mirror.

Hayden ignored him, hating small talk, but he sensed Min turn to catch the driver's eye in his mirror, a polite smile on her face.

"Is it that obvious?"

"Well, you're in less of a costume than my last ride, but it seemed to be an easy guess."

Min laughed at that, and Hayden felt the sound washing over him even as the driver sat up straighter. He clearly enjoyed it as well. This car ride couldn't end fast enough.

"You two traveling… together?"

He was being so obvious Hayden almost snorted, but held it back, keeping his gaze out the window, pretending to ignore them, not wanting to engage, and leaving it to Min to figure out what to say. He felt the heat of her eyes on him briefly.

"Nope, just carpooling."

The guy perked up, clearly ready to lay some groundwork and Hayden found himself interested to hear what he's going to try, ignoring the burning in his gut. Probably just a reaction to the turkey sandwich he'd had on the train.

"So what are you most looking forward to at the convention?"

They talked idly for the next ten minutes, Min polite and engaged in the conversation, but Hayden relaxed when he heard nothing more than that in her voice.

Finally, they were dropped off in front of the Wayward Hotel, Hayden once again holding open the door and grabbing their bags from the trunk. They walked into the lobby together, and Hayden immediately scanned the room, checking for fans or anyone who might recognize him. Conventions like this were always dangerous and stressful, his voice too recognizable, too many people around him that could blow his cover at any moment. Thankfully, the lobby was mostly empty this late. He glanced at Min, who was holding something in her hand. A card. Hayden raised an eyebrow at her blush.

"He gave me his card. In case I needed a ride during the convention."

Hayden just shook his head. "You gotta be more careful with that smile of yours."

"I'm sure he's just trying to hustle. Make extra cash."

"That's not all he's trying to make."

She was a vivid pink now, clearly uncomfortable talking about this, and she turned away from him to head to the check-in desk just as a guy walked by, not paying attention to anything but his phone. The guy bumped into her, knocking her off balance, and Hayden's hands instinctively caught her at her waist before she stumbled too far. He glared after the guy, but he was already gone and out the door.

Min threw a startled look at him over her shoulder and quickly stepped away. His hands flexed on her waist a moment before he let go, and with a skeptical glance his way, she moved up to the front desk to check in.

Their registration went smoothly, and soon they were both alone in the elevator. Hayden pressed twenty-two for himself, then looked at Min.

"Floor?"

Her mouth was flat. "Twenty-two."

He shook his head—*of course*—then stepped back, giving her space as the elevator started moving. Hayden glanced at Min, taking in the hard set of her jaw and how firmly she was not looking at him. And being him, he couldn't help but poke the bear.

"Boy, does this bring me back."

She glared at him, and he did his best not to grin at her, watching anger flush through her skin. Hayden still hated how their first meeting went down, how it all went so wrong so fast because of him and his anxiety and paranoia. But he couldn't help but admit he loved knowing she was thinking about him.

"You're such an asshole."

At that, Hayden sobered. She was right, he was an asshole, and he was finding that he didn't like that she had seen that side of him.

"I'm sorry." Her eyes flew to his, wide, deep brown staring into him as she tried to figure out if he was being genuine. He let her see the truth of it, of him. "I've had bad experiences before with people. But that's no excuse for how I treated you. I'm sorry."

They stared at each other, and he wondered what she

would say when the elevator dinged and the doors opened. She distracted herself by stepping off, tracking down the rooms, only to find that their doors were across the hall from each other. He waited while she slipped her keycard into the reader, getting it on the second try and stepping in, holding the door for him, and he saw the hesitation in her eyes.

He slid her bag from his shoulder, depositing it at her feet just inside the door, his shoulders filling the doorframe as his glance took in her room before landing on her.

"Lock your door."

Stepping away, Hayden was already turning across the hall to his own door when her soft voice hit him.

"I forgive you."

Hayden glanced toward her to see she was standing in the doorway, her chin lifted, her eyes stubborn. "But don't fucking do it again."

She shut the door then, and he found himself chuckling as he slid his keycard into the slot, idly wondering what the fuck was going on in his head when he was near this woman. Hayden wasn't a fan of traveling, wasn't big on hotels or crowds or anything like what the weekend had in store for him. But he found himself looking forward to the convention in a way he hadn't in years.

This should be fun.

CHAPTER 6

MIN

Min finished throwing the dead bolt and other locks on the door, then inserted her own personal door blocker into the lock, making sure the door was firmly shut and as impenetrable as she could make it. She scanned the room, checking the pictures and mirrors, checking the window, checking the bathroom, making sure there were no small lights or anything that could be hiding a hidden camera. The hotel had rave reviews and seemed to be safe, but a woman traveling alone could never be too careful. And thanks to Alex's brand of douche-baggery, Min was now extra paranoid in new places.

Finally satisfied she was as safe as she could get, Min started to unpack, needing to do something with all the restless energy left in her after traveling with Hayden and sleeping the last leg of the trip. She couldn't say she was angry about him switching seats to sit next to her since her original seating buddy had been such a distracting pill. And for all of Hayden's abrasiveness, he had actually ended up being... fine. Quiet, for the most part, but not necessarily in an awkward way. Focused more on whatever he was working on his laptop than he was on what Min was doing. Sure, he made it a habit to look at her screen and comment on the gameplay videos she was watching. But he hadn't been intrusive, and they had eventually fallen into a companionable silence, lulled by the rhythmic rocking of the train. Overall, it was a pretty nice train ride.

But then Min had woken up with her head on his fucking shoulder. She was embarrassed, worried she had drooled on him or done something else that she would never live down. And then when the driver made his interest clear, she had felt Hayden's amusement next to her that had her flushing even redder.

Min tried not to care about what he was thinking about her for the last few hours they had been together. She tried telling herself he was just some recluse streamer who hated her and she wasn't going to let him take up space in her brain. When that didn't work, she turned to the hotel pamphlets neatly stacked on the nightstand. She smiled at the advertisements for the morning buffet. There was French toast in her future, which meant the day was already looking bright.

Pulling out her phone, Min texted her sister that she had arrived safely, and was rewarded with a thumbs-up emoji. She then checked her Twitter account, quickly scanning the new hate tweets that had come her way since the last time she had looked. When it had been announced she was competing in the Bleeding Sword tournament, it had awoken all the internet trolls who had finally lost steam in their vitriol. From the looks of her mentions, she was again being told she was a good-for-nothing whore, slut, thot, and several other names she'd have to look up later because she didn't know the reference. But what was easy to understand was that the vast majority of social media agreed Min definitely didn't deserve any of her success since she must have gotten it by sucking cocks.

Great.

Not liking it, but used to the hate by now, she went to her secret Instagram for a serotonin boost. She had spent months carefully curating it with kittens and horoscopes and the few select friends she allowed to know about it. But of course, the first thing at the top of her feed was a post from her ex. ShakespeareWithGuns aka Alex.

Fucking Alex. If anyone made her want to breathe actual fire, it was him.

Min had come to the realization in the last few weeks that Alex must have set this all up on purpose, that he must have already had the camera installed that night when he had asked her to keep the FlameThrower outfit on during sex. She remembered being excited, thinking a night of spicy roleplaying was exactly what they needed to jumpstart their pretty lackluster sex life.

But instead it had been yet another disappointing evening of Alex bitching at her for not coming when he did the bare minimum and her making a to-do list for her week while waiting for him to finish. She had ended up leaving that night and not looking back, breaking it off with him later in the week. Life was too short and, at twenty-six, she was too young to settle for sex with no orgasms.

And then she found out he had been cheating the whole time.

Looking back, she wasn't surprised. The cheating, along with his jealousy of her rising stardom and his bad attitude toward the time she needed to spend with her recovering sister, made her feel like an idiot for staying as long as she did.

When things had finally ended, she had felt nothing but relief that Alex was officially out of her life.

A few weeks later, the naked photos of her had appeared online. The IP address was traced to a computer at a public library. Untraceable, according to the detective assigned to her case. But Min knew it was Alex. She just couldn't prove it.

The internet had demanded she reveal the identity of the man in the photos with her, but she couldn't bring herself to name him. She wasn't ashamed of having sex. She was a healthy adult woman with a sex drive and she didn't give a damn if people knew that. But if she revealed him online, her name would be connected to his in perpetuity. Whenever someone looked her up, they would always see him in connection to her. She didn't want to give him that power. So she kept his identity a secret and let the internet hate her. Min was a big believer in karma, so she put her trust in the universe that Alex would get his.

But now here was his Instagram picture, fucking up her day. Alex was here. At the convention, which shouldn't have been a surprise but still was. They had talked about going together this year, so she should have remembered he already had a ticket, the one she had spent hours online refreshing her browser to purchase for him. His picture showed a carefully crafted selfie he had taken with one of the large signs advertising the tournament. Which meant he was probably participating, even though Min hadn't seen him on any of the lists.

Good. He was a good player, but she was better. Min was going to use the game to shut him down. Soundly. Taking the win and the money and the sponsorship and leaving him in the dirt where he belonged. That would feel good.

Nodding at her own thoughts, Min put on her PJs, set the alarm on her phone, rechecked the door, and then finally collapsed into her bed. Her mind swirled with everything she had to do the next day, the mental preparation she needed for the first bracket of the Bleeding Sword tournament. But instead of focusing, Min found her thoughts drifting back to Hayden. How different he had seemed in real life, but still familiar to her. Confusing.

She drifted to sleep with the memory of how he had pushed her against the wall of the elevator, his hand holding her wrist away from her, his leg sliding between hers and anchoring her to him, his heat and his hard body and his overwhelming presence turning the moment into something that coiled in Min's stomach.

When her alarm went off the next morning, Min sat up with a gasp, the last dregs of Hayden slipping away from her, leaving her aching and frustrated. With a quick breath, Min rolled out of bed, determined to put her dreams and Hayden behind her. There was too much to do, and Min knew how much of her time would quickly get sucked up and disappear once she arrived at the convention center.

Min loved conventions, loved being surrounded by the people who followed all the same things she did. The first time she had attended Kickoff five years ago, she felt like she had finally come home. That feeling returned every time she walked into the Kimball Convention Center. She looked forward to this every year, and even knowing Alex was there wasn't going to ruin it for her.

After a quick shower, Min threw on her oldest and most comfortable jeans, a plain white V-neck shirt, and her walking shoes. After some light makeup, she drew her auburn curls up into a ponytail to keep it out of the way, grabbed her small backpack with sunscreen and hand sanitizer, and headed out for the day, eager to walk the floor of the exhibition hall.

She was practically bouncing on her heels when the elevator stopped at the lobby, and she took a left to follow the signs for the breakfast buffet. It was early enough that she was hoping to beat the crowd, her inner dream of French toast making her mouth water and her stomach growl. If there was anything Min loved, it was a solid breakfast.

There weren't many people up yet, and she strode immediately to the end of the buffet, grabbing a plate, filling it up with eggs and bacon until she got to the French toast. A man was already there, apparently trying to decide between French toast and waffles. As she approached his eyes lifted to hers, and she could've kicked herself.

Of course, DeathsHead would hit the breakfast buffet. Of course he'd be up just as early as her for the convention. She should've anticipated this inevitability.

They stared at each other for a moment in surprise. Not sure what to say, she glanced down at his plate, the tongs still in his hand, and realized he had taken the last French toast. Her heart dropped right to the floor. When she looked back up at him, her glare was cold.

"How. Could. You?"

He was clearly confused, both by her words and her cutting tone, until he finally followed her eyes to where the French toast lay on his plate, looking delicious and ready to be eaten. Min saw the moment it dawned on him why she was mad, and the amusement that invaded his eyes.

"You mean, how could I get up earlier than you, get ready faster than you, and get to the buffet long before you did only to take the sad dregs of the mediocre hotel French toast?"

She huffed at that. Min knew she was being ridiculous, but she took breakfast very, very seriously. It set the tone for the entire day, a day that she desperately needed to go extremely well.

And he was ruining it.

"However mediocre the French toast may be, if you aren't going to appreciate it then you should've left it for someone who would."

He smiled at that, a real smile, not just the quirk of his lips that she had grown used to, and somehow it made her more tense. It was unfair that he could have real human feelings and look so good while doing it.

"What'll you give me for it?" His voice was deeper now as he leaned toward her, the tongs still held in one hand. She rolled her eyes.

"The satisfaction of knowing you didn't ruin my day."

"French toast does not have the power to ruin your day."

"It does if you continue on this destructive path you're on."

"If that were actually true and not just a manifestation of your insanity, then you should really be a lot more motivated to make a trade."

She eyed him warily, knowing he was enjoying this far too much.

"What do you want?"

He thought about it for a moment, his eyes perusing her face.

"A favor. To be named at a later date."

She narrowed her gaze, glaring. "I'm not throwing the tournament for French toast."

Now it was his turn to roll his eyes. "Good, because I wasn't asking, babe. I think we both know I can beat you fair and square."

It took a moment for Min to realize they were in some sort of staring contest, that the seconds were ticking by as they just stared at each other over the breakfast buffet. How did her life come to this?

"What kind of favor?" The question erupted from her abruptly, and she did her best not to wince at how inadvertently loud it had come out.

Min was wary. In the past, DeathsHead had offered her deals in-game, but half the time he had been lying to her, killing her character with a swift betrayal that she could only respect. She had learned he was unpredictable that way, so she made it a rule to never trust him, especially when he offered a trade.

But a real-life favor… that felt different. More serious. More intimate.

As if he was reading her mind, he lowered his voice, glancing around the rest of the room to be sure they weren't overheard.

"Nothing dirty. Get your mind out of the gutter."

"Then what?" She pinkened at that. Her mind had definitely started spiraling south, and she stood up a little straighter, hoping a straighter spine led to a clearer mind. Worried about how distracted she was.

"I haven't decided yet."

She stared at him. This whole conversation was inane, and she knew it. She could easily grab a waffle or something else from the table and be just as full and excited for the day as she had been five minutes ago. But there was something about sparring with him like this that made her never want to step away.

The swift throat clearing of a server interrupted them, and Min jumped a little, stepping back. She hadn't realized they had come to stand so close together, and would've been embarrassed if she hadn't noticed what the server had brought with him. He moved quickly, and before Min could blink, the server switched out the empty French toast serving platter for a new one, full of fresh, hot, steaming French toast that smelled so good Min's mouth watered.

She shot Hayden a victorious grin and piled a mountain of it on her plate before drenching it in syrup. Hayden shook his head, disappointed.

"Should've put a clock on the deal," he said ruefully.

"Didn't help you the last time you tried it." The last time, he had offered her some spare med packs in exchange for ammo, but with the caveat that she only had ten seconds to decide.

She had shot his avatar in the face.

He just shook his head, remembering the same moment of the game, and walked out toward the tables to sit down. Before she knew it, they were heading to an empty table together, him filling two cups of coffee on his way and handing her one. They were silent while they ate but not awkward, which Min tried not to think about too much. After all, they both talked for a living. It was the life of a streamer. But it was nice to have the moments of quiet, too.

When her stomach was finally full and her coffee drained, she leaned back against her chair in satisfaction.

"That was way better than mediocre."

"You eat like a lumberjack."

"Don't watch me if it bothers you."

"It's like watching one of those nature shows where the snake unhinges its jaw. I couldn't look away. The horror was hypnotizing."

Min couldn't even be mad at his teasing, just rubbed her stomach a little, happy with her morning so far. He shook his head, smiling again as he sipped his coffee, and Min was shocked to realize she was enjoying herself. Who knew DeathsHead could be fun?

Hayden broke the silence first. "What's on the agenda today? You have a panel, right?"

Min tried to hide her surprise that he knew about her panel. Maybe it was announced online somewhere. In fact, it certainly was, but she still didn't expect him to care about something like her con schedule.

"Yeah, but not until the afternoon. I want to walk the floor first, see the sights. Soak in the nerdy atmosphere."

"Dressed like that?"

She glanced down at her jeans and tee. "What's wrong with this?"

"I don't know. I guess it's not very FlameThrower-y."

Min shrugged. "I would prefer not to be recognized, especially now." She took in his ripped jeans and the plain black T-shirt he must've washed a thousand times. It looked soft. And very, very good on him. Not that she would ever tell him that.

"What do you mean, especially now?"

Her eyes flew to his in disbelief, but she didn't see anything to indicate that he was teasing her or lying, just curiosity. Did he really not know? How was that possible?

"After the photos leaked. I always preferred to blend before, but now it's more of a necessity. Flame is a little too high profile to the wrong people lately. I don't want to get yelled at on the exhibition floor."

Hayden frowned at that, gears still turning in his head, and Min had to admit he didn't seem like he knew what she was talking about. It was hard to believe, since when it had happened, it felt like those pictures were on every site she looked, that she was tagged on page after page of either the photos or some article talking about the photos.

But here he was, looking confused. Someone in the streaming community had really managed to miss her scandal. Amazing.

"Do you not follow the news?" she asked.

"If you mean streamer gossip, then no. I have other things to do."

"Like what?"

"Should we head out? The floor is opening soon, and I'd like to get there before it gets too crowded."

He stood up, gathering his tray and looking around for where to put their trash. Min knew what he was doing, knew he was changing the subject, but still her jaw dropped in surprise at his question.

"Wait, you want to go together?"

He shrugged. "Why not? We're both doing the same thing. And it's more fun with company."

Hayden was right, but she still couldn't believe he wanted to hang out with her. On purpose. Without someone forcing him.

"Okay, but I move slow," she warned him. "I like to look at everything. Closely. And I hate being rushed."

"Babe, rushing you is the last thing I plan on doing."

And Min couldn't help it, she blushed, both at his words and his deep voice and her dirty thoughts that went exactly to the places on her body that he could take his time with. She drew in a deep breath, avoiding his gaze, and firmly turned her mind back to the convention, where it desperately needed to stay.

"Then hurry the fuck up. We got places to be."

The brisk walk to the trolley did nothing but fill Min with anticipation. The few other pedestrians they ran into heading in the same direction were a mixture of nerdy T-shirts and full-on cosplay. Min was always delighted to see what characters people loved so much they'd dress up, and she could spend hours admiring all the craftsmanship that went into the costume. She jabbed Hayden in his side to get his attention and pointed to a couple dressed like the zombies from Bleeding Sword.

"My god, their makeup looks professional." She was so enraptured that she almost walked right into the person in front of her, a Winter Soldier that had suddenly decided to stop and take a picture of an advertisement for a new movie. Hayden's hand shot out, grabbing her upper arm and pulling her to a stop in time before she crashed. He then maneuvered her to the other side of the sidewalk, guiding her to the inside of the sidewalk so he could walk near the street.

Min was in such a good mood she flashed him a grin.

"Such a gentleman," she teased.

"If you'd watch where you're going, I wouldn't need to be."

Min rolled her eyes at that, refusing to let him wreck her good mood.

"Part of the deal of us hanging out today is that you can't be grumpy. I wait for Kickoff all year. You're not allowed to ruin it for me."

"You'll ruin it for yourself if you don't keep your eyes up." He grabbed her arm again, pulling her toward him to miss the Mario that she almost walked into. She couldn't help but laugh, which got her a hat tip from Mario.

It was only a short walk before Min and Hayden reached the station. They waited with the crowd for the trolley, loading into a standing-room-only car when it finally came. Min gripped the stability pole in the middle while Hayden stood next to her, his grip above her on the high rail. As more people shoved in, he moved closer to her, blocking her from the crowd and pressing her until the pole as the whole space became cramped with people. Finally, the doors closed and the trolley pulled away from the station.

The movement of the car rocked Min's body against Hayden's. She kept her eyes on the pole in front of her and did her best to ignore it. But his heat was everywhere, and this close she could smell the clean scent of his shampoo, trying not to inhale it. She stole a look up at him to see he was scanning the car, probably looking for other people on their phones he could assault. But at least he was ignoring her, for all that his body was almost completely wrapped around her.

Finally, the trolley landed at the station across from the convention center, and she breathed easier when they exited the packed car, her smile growing bigger the closer they got to the center. They both pushed their way through the crowd and stepped into the entry line.

Able to relax for a moment while they slowly made their way through the line, Min turned to Hayden, noticing how still he was, how his eyes were sweeping over as much of the crowd as he could.

"Are you nervous?"

He didn't answer right away, and Min was starting to wonder if he'd even heard her question when he finally spoke in a soft voice.

"I tend to not be very talkative at the cons. Too easy to be recognized."

Understanding filled her, and she felt a twist in her chest at the thought of how careful he had to be at all times in places like this. While she felt at home surrounded by people like her, he saw it as a threat. It had to be hard, wanting to just love what you love as loudly as the other fans, only to have to hide it for safety and privacy. It was the same reason she wore a wig, contacts, and a whole wardrobe when she was streaming. She wanted to be able to walk around and be herself, especially at Kickoff.

But with his distinctive voice, he couldn't have that.

Impulsively she reached out and squeezed his hand. His eyes flew to hers, and she blushed, feeling the sudden need to undercut the tension between them.

"You talk too much, anyway." She let her hand slip from his, stepping forward with the line, and she heard him chuckle softly behind her.

Min and Hayden slowly made their way through the line, flashing their badges to be scanned and grabbing their souvenir tote bag. Min was practically itching with anticipation, and she headed immediately to the closest entrance for the exhibition hall. Hayden was right behind her, and after once again flashing their badges at the volunteers stationed there, they stepped into the exhibit hall.

Min stopped for a moment, taking a deep breath as her eyes attempted to devour everything at once. It was still early, so the large space wasn't yet filled to the brim with people forced to rub shoulders or bump into each other as they simply tried to walk down an aisle. She gazed around her, the layout familiar yet promising lots of new items and people and displays to look at and purchase.

And she couldn't fucking wait.

She turned to Hayden to find him watching her, taking in her love of the con that was surely radiating through her with a strange look on his face. After a moment, he shook his head, like shaking off cobwebs, and glanced around.

"Well?" he asked. "Where to first?"

Min grinned at the question, figuring it was obvious. "You know where."

She slipped into the crowd, her eyes following the various superheroes, the dinosaurs, all the clever ways that people thought of to dress themselves, and she loved it. She could feel Hayden following behind her, and she was unable to stop herself from throwing him a grin. He stayed as quiet and unruffled as ever, but he was also taking in the sights, in his own way.

They made their way to the video gaming section, the one with various demos set up to try new games or to try your hand at one recently released. Min scanned the choices, torn between what to tackle first, when Hayden firmly grabbed her hand and pulled her with him into a line. She glanced at the display with a laugh.

"This one?"

It was a two-dimensional platform game, about to be released the following month and therefore a hot ticket item at Kickoff. From the design of the characters and the cute graphics, it was aimed more for relaxed players than the usual high-intensity shooters Min and Hayden would stream. Min was a fan of all kinds of games, but she had never known Deaths-Head to play something so… adorable.

His eyes twinkled at her. "Speed run."

She felt the zing of excitement race through her. When she had first started her streaming career, it had been with speed runs, playing the various well-known games she had grown up with at a speed that some would say was too fast to enjoy. But the challenge of the clock made her blood pump, and she was already wiggling her fingers in anticipation.

"*You do speed runs?*" She had never seen him post content like that, and she had watched a number of his videos. Deaths-

Head had always stuck to the more violent games, the survival horror or first-person shooters.

"You don't know everything about me, babe."

"I don't know anything about you."

His eyes flared at that, and he looked away from her.

"You know more than most."

The line moved slowly. The booth limited play to twenty minutes, so it meant any movement was few and far between. Min did her best to watch the people currently playing to get a lay of the levels, knowing Hayden was doing the same. Of course, with his height well over six foot, he had an easier time seeing over people, and shook his head at her more than once when Min would hop a little to see a screen.

When it was their turn, they took the stations next to each other, and she could feel the familiar thrill of the challenge thrumming through her. DeathsHead was her rival, and Min knew he would be able to push her to the edge of her temper within minutes of the game starting. He had a gift.

But he was also her favorite person to play against.

She gripped the remote, the timer for the demo counting down for the start. When it hit she didn't hesitate, powering through the tutorial explanation to the beginning of the first level before turning to look at Hayden… who was already looking at her, waiting. He quirked an eyebrow, and she nodded, counting in her head. *One… two… three…*

They started simultaneously, fingers flying over buttons, jumping over platforms and enemies in a race to get what she knew from watching the other players to be a cupcake at the end of the level. She raced through, easily jumping and dodging and solving puzzles on her way, until she mistimed and her character fell backward, stuck between an enemy and a moving flame platform. Fuck.

She raced ahead, timing it right, hearing Hayden's soft curse as he probably fell into the same trap she did. She continued racing forward, pushing her little avatar until finally she was able to grab the damn cupcake. She held up her controller, showing she had finished, and she turned to Hayden. His character was just then grabbing his cupcake.

She had won.

"Yesssss!" She jumped up from the seat, clapping her hands, elated. Beating DeathsHead at a game was like a drug, and boy, was she addicted. One of the guys running the booth approached her, handing her a T-shirt with a wide smile as he glanced at her screen.

"Great time, there. Probably one of our quickest."

She beamed, high-fiving him with enthusiasm before turning to Hayden, who was already shaking his head.

"You're ridiculous," he told her, his tone dry.

"Don't be a sore loser."

The booth attendant handed Hayden his T-shirt before turning to pass out shirts to the other players as they finished the level.

Min hugged her T-shirt to her like it was the greatest trophy she had ever won. As much as she was basking, Hayden was already scanning for their next game.

"Best two out of three?"

"You're on."

Min studied the other demos around them, trying to figure out the best choice, already feeling the fire of competition rising again when something flashing out of the corner of her eye had her freezing.

A glimpse of blonde hair. A medium build. A band T-shirt she knew too well.

Alex was here.

He was gone before she could really register his face, but the damage was done, ice freezing her veins as her mind raced with questions. *How long had he been there? Had he seen her?*

"What is it?" Hayden was talking to her, and it took a moment to release herself from the panic that had risen at the brief sight of Alex.

With an effort, she shook it off before turning to Hayden, careful to keep her face neutral.

"Nothing, sorry. Thought I saw someone. Let's check out the shooters."

She was already moving, in the opposite direction of where Alex had been, not really seeing where she was going, just knowing she had to move. Hayden fell in beside her, not asking any more questions, and she was grateful.

Needing something to take her mind off the panic of seeing Alex, Min asked the question she had been wanting an answer for.

"So what happened that makes you attack people you think are taking your picture?"

The crowd was thinner here, as if they had found a magical pocket that other attendees hadn't rushed into yet. But even then Hayden glanced around, wanting to make sure people weren't too close.

"I didn't attack you," was his reply.

"You pinned me against an elevator and ransacked my phone."

She turned to him just in time to see his jaw flex. He really didn't want to talk about this. But Min felt like she deserved an answer after everything, so she waited.

With an exhale, he started talking. "I was seeing someone last year. Only for a few months, but we were starting to get serious. She wasn't in the streaming world, but at some point, figured out who I was. We spent a weekend together at Big Bear, and she took a bunch of photos of us together. Cute, couple stuff."

Min could feel in her stomach what was coming, knew in her bones it was going to be bad. But still, she wasn't prepared.

"She came over the next week and live-streamed from my house while I was at dinner with my brother. Announced to the world she was going to reveal who the real DeathsHead was, but only to the highest bidder."

"Holy shit." The words were out before Min could stop them. Hayden nodded.

"I was tagged pretty early in her stream and raced home. Cut off her feed before she could show too much."

"I don't remember seeing anything like that." Min was a little shocked. DeathsHead was considered a big streaming star, and one of the biggest secrets in the industry was his identity. Even a hint of a reveal would've trended on social media for a week.

"I have friends who are pretty good at making things like that disappear, at least when they're caught fast enough. That, coupled with my lawyers serving her cease and desists, as well as restraining orders, kept the information in check. She didn't have any following, so even those who saw the broadcast didn't believe her. She's not the first one to claim they could ID me."

Min cleared her throat. "Is that how it ended with her?"

Hayden shrugged. "Mostly. The following week, I got an email from my lawyer saying that he caught someone trying to sell pictures of me to online gaming news sites. They were all from Big Bear, with her. Lawyers shut that down fast."

Min's eyes were wide. She couldn't hide her horror.

"Hayden, that's awful. I'm so sorry you went through that."

He just nodded. "The situation triggered my anxiety. That's why I'm sensitive about it."

Min shook her head. She knew first-hand how people could be seduced by internet fame, but still. Hearing his story broke her heart a little.

"All that said," he continued, his eyes piercing hers. "There's still no excuse for how I handled our first meeting. You didn't deserve to be treated that way. I should have listened to you. I'm sorry."

Not wanting to admit she felt a little breathless from his apology, Min nodded. "Thank you. I appreciate that."

Min found herself staring at Hayden, him staring back, both of them just standing in the middle of the exhibition hall, not saying anything. But there was something about the energy of the moment that Min didn't want to be the one to break.

And then she found herself shoved hard, losing her balance. Strong hands grabbed her waist, steadying her, as a group of teenagers dressed like comic heroes barreled through.

The spell broken, Min laughed. "C'mon. We got too much to see to stand here all day."

They found two more games to play, a shooting game and a racing game, both of which Hayden won. Min was pouting, but her heart wasn't really in it as the morning passed and she lost herself to the convention. She stopped at every booth that drew her eye, took pictures of several people in costumes, and bought some pieces of artwork from her favorite artists. She had tensed when she had glimpsed Alex, but the exhibition hall was large and packed. The longer they wandered, the safer she felt, and she was grateful for it.

It wasn't until Hayden pointed to the concessions area that she realized how hungry she was. After waiting in yet another line and choosing a hot dog and a much-needed Diet Coke, they found a spot at a large, shared round table already inhabited by a few other attendees, each admiring the convention exclusives they had already managed to purchase. To the side of the tables, several TVs showed various news interviews and broadcasts about the convention, as well as replayed some trailers that had been released during the panels that morning.

Min ate her hot dog with the focus of a starving woman, taking deep gulps of her soda and letting the calories and caffeine flood through her. When she came up for air, she spent a few well-fed minutes watching the crowd swirl around her.

"Why do you wear a disguise for your stream?" Hayden's question almost made her jump, they had been sitting in comfortable silence for so long. She wiped her mouth, crumpling her napkin in her hand before reaching for one of his chips and snagging it before he could stop her.

"To be able to blend. When I'm streaming, my outfit, my makeup, everything screams to be noticed and grabs your attention. After a while, most of my viewers tend to only notice the loud and colorful outfits. It means that I can come here as my plain old self, blend in with everyone, and go completely unnoticed. I love it."

"You're not going unnoticed." She glanced up at that, frowning, wondering if he had seen Alex, or sensed what happened earlier, but he just rolled his eyes at her. "The guy at the demo booth was practically throwing himself at you."

That startled a laugh from her. "He was passing out T shirts. He sees a million women a day, much better looking than I. He didn't give me a second look."

Hayden just shook his head at her supposed naïveté. "The rideshare driver noticed you."

"I was the only one talking."

A muscle flexed in his jaw, and she watched it, fascinated, wondering what was going on in that head of his. Finally, he met her eyes, his own glinting with some emotion Min couldn't identify.

"I noticed you. Right away." His voice was soft, almost velvet, and she felt it run through her, heating her blood in a way that had her adjusting herself in her chair.

"That was completely different," she said. "I was the only one in the waiting room. You thought I was taking your picture. The circumstances alone were memorable enough that anyone would notice me. But trust me, I'm not one to get noticed in a crowd of people."

She wasn't sure why she was arguing this point. It wasn't like it did her ego any favors. She had accepted a long time ago that she was cute *enough*, pretty *enough*, funny *enough*. It's why FlameThrower was such a thrill. When Min streamed dressed as her persona, she felt like she was letting free the part of herself no one would accept in her regular body. The outfit somehow gave her permission to be more herself, while still allowing her to retreat into anonymity when she needed to.

Yet another reason she needed to get her streaming career back on track. She missed being FlameThrower.

Meanwhile, Hayden was looking down at her, something in his eyes deep and dark and… dangerous. Min felt caught, like he was weaving a spell and she couldn't look away.

"Min, if I had seen you at a coffee shop, if you had just been sitting there, reading or on your laptop or who knows what, I wouldn't have been able to stop myself from approaching you. I would've done my best to be charming and nice and the whole time I'd be nervous as hell that you would see right through me. If I got your number, I wouldn't even make it home before I texted you. And if I had managed to convince you to go on a date with me, maybe dinner, maybe a movie, literally anything you wanted, I would've been crawling out of my skin hoping I didn't fuck it up."

Her eyes were huge on him, her thoughts both racing and also somehow blank. She had no idea what to do with the words he just said. A guy had never told her something like that, so she couldn't help her knee-jerk response.

"You're lying."

He leaned closer, his mouth almost to her ear and his voice softer so it didn't carry to the other attendees milling around them.

"FlameThrower is beautiful because everything she puts on doesn't cover up who she is. The wig, the contacts, the outfits, can't hide how fucking gorgeous you are, no matter how much you try to distract from it. You're beautiful, Min. Flame is just an accessory you wear." His voice somehow dropped even lower, his breath stirring her hair. "I'm happy I get to see the real you."

With a shiver, Min pulled back, her eyes wide, flying from his eyes to his lips and back. Her brain had completely stopped functioning.

"Who *says* things like that?"

His mouth quirked at the bewilderment in her voice, but before he could reply, the TV behind them blared, suddenly loud and piercing.

"Online streamer FlameThrower is supposed to be competing in today's Bleeding Sword tournament, and boy do people on the street

have something to say about it. We asked Kickoff attendees their thoughts."

Min spun to face the TV just in time to see a microphone was shoved at a SpongeBob.

"It's honestly disgusting that she would be allowed to compete when everyone knows exactly what she did to get where she is. Or rather, the people she did."

The screen changed, flashing censored versions of the pictures that would haunt Min for the rest of her life. She forgot to breathe as the reporter came on the screen.

"FlameThrower has been mostly absent from her channel since graphic pictures of her were leaked onto social media. The pictures quickly had people questioning how the streamer had become so popular so quickly in an industry that is relatively difficult to break in to. The backlash from the photos led to FlameThrower losing her sponsorships, as well as many well-known online gamers coming out against her alleged methods of promotion."

Min stood, suddenly not able to watch any more, even though it was nothing she hadn't seen before. Her eyes burned. Surprising, since she thought she had cried herself out on this.

"Min—" Hayden started, but she cut him off, not able to look at him. He was the one person she had known who hadn't seen the pictures. Hadn't known what a disgrace she had become. She couldn't stand to see the judgment in his eyes.

Or worse. Pity.

"I have to go. My panel starts soon and I have to change."

She was gone before he could say anything. She slipped into the crowd, leaving him at the table, feeling more alone than she ever had in her life.

CHAPTER 7

HAYDEN

Hayden's eyes followed Min as she strode away from him, heading for the far end of the exhibition hall where he knew the exit was. He wanted to follow her, not liking how dark her expression had fallen when she had noticed the news broadcast. But his instinct told him she needed some time to herself. And that was something Hayden could understand.

He glanced back at the TV, but it had already moved on to another story, something about a movie trailer that was just released, and he felt the tension inside him ease. Hayden hadn't known the reason behind Min's disappearance from her streaming channel. A lot of times streamers took breaks for simple reasons like vacation, an illness, or just needing a mental health break, so it wasn't unusual for someone with her audience to go quiet. But there had been more to it, so much more, and being confronted with the truth and what she must have been going through during her hiatus left Hayden with a sour feeling in his gut.

Not to mention that the image of Min in her FlameThrower

wig and nothing else, in another man's arms, made Hayden burn in a way he had no desire to analyze.

Hayden searched his memory for any mention of who FlameThrower had been seeing recently. Her stream rarely went personal, with Min choosing to focus instead on the games, on the other players, and on her own enjoyment. It was one of the things he liked about her channel, but now his mind raced with the knowledge he was missing. He wasn't really one to keep up with gossip, something he had prided himself on until this very moment.

Another glance at the TV told him no more information was coming, so he walked his trash to the receptacle and slipped back into the crowd. He had been surprised when Min described loving the feeling of getting lost in the crowd. It was one of his favorite things, knowing there were so many people and voices around him that no one would pay him any mind. He wandered from booth to booth, looking at the displays, trying to lose himself in the chaotic energy and the excitement of the crowd around him.

When he grew tired of the exhibit hall, Hayden wandered the main lobby, admiring the ingenious cosplayers posing for pictures, smiling at the small children dressed as their favorite characters. He didn't pay attention to where he was going until he found himself in front of a door, a whiteboard in front proclaiming the schedule. A quick glance at his phone showed that Min's panel was about to start, and he had somehow found himself at the room where it was going to happen. With a feeling of inevitability, he walked inside.

The room was one of the smaller ones, only holding a few hundred people, and he slipped into a chair toward the back. His eyes quickly found FlameThrower's name plate on the panel table, and he heard her name buzzing around him.

Many in the audience had apparently come specifically to see Min.

More people kept filtering in, and soon the room was packed. Finally, the moderator approached his spot, introducing himself before turning to announce the panel participants. Several female game executives, a programmer, and a designer, all well known in their own field. But FlameThrower, as a streamer, was the real star of the panel, for better or worse. When she was announced, Hayden could feel the crowd's collective intake of breath, the applause scattered and timid as she strode into the room.

Min was smiling, big and bright, but he could tell she was bracing herself. She was in full FlameThrower persona, the pink hair from her wig fluttering around her as if she was being followed by a fan. Her large eyes were made even bigger by her pink contacts, her fake lashes, her winged eyeliner. But her mouth was what caught his attention, full and soft, now a glossy cotton candy pink. He could feel his cock twitch as images of her mouth wrapped around him flooded his mind.

Her outfit didn't help, the loose anime T-shirt so large it fell down one smooth shoulder. She had tied it in a knot at her waist so glimpses of her navel peeked out over her tight pink miniskirt. Wide fishnet stockings covered her legs, and Hayden had visions of those legs wrapped around him, holding him tight against her, and he started to sweat. This was a bad idea. FlameThrower on her streaming channel was cute and spunky and outrageous.

FlameThrower in person was fucking lethal.

She slid into her panel seat, her long legs covered by the tablecloth, and Hayden could finally breathe again. She tossed her pink hair over her shoulder and settled in, a challenge in her eyes. This crowd had come to witness her drama, and Min had come ready for a fight.

More people joined her on the panel, and then it began. The moderator did a good job of making sure each participant was engaged and able to speak on a topic, keeping the conversation on the experience of female gamers in the workplace. Hayden found himself enjoying the talk when the moderator turned to Min.

"So, FlameThrower, you're going to be participating in the Bleeding Sword tournament this weekend. You're obviously skilled at the game, but you'll be up against one of your biggest rivals, DeathsHead. Any nerves there?"

Min laughed, and somehow her eyes found Hayden, in the back, in the crowd, and he could feel himself smiling back at her. A secret between them.

"Death likes to talk a good game, and lord knows he's got a great voice to do so, but I've beaten him in the past. I am pretty confident I'll be able to spank him again."

The crowd laughed, and the moderator made some comment, but Hayden missed it, staring at Min and her smirk and imagining her tight skirt lifted up over her hips, his own hand slapping her sweet ass, leaving it red and sore for his eyes only. Something of his thoughts must have shown from his eyes even from across the room because he swore Min's face reddened as if blushing. She returned her attention to the moderator and the other panelists, but Hayden couldn't hear them anymore, he was so focused on her every expression, wondering if her thoughts had wandered to the same filthy place his had.

The panel ended and people lined up for the Q&A portion. It didn't take long before a guy walked up to the microphone, swaggering with an intent that had Hayden on edge.

"Hey Flame. I'm a loyal fan, but I gotta know… who's the guy in the photos?"

The room went silent. The moderator tried to step in, clearly prepped for this, but Min held up her hand and leaned into her mic.

"I won't say much, but I will tell you this. The photos were taken without my knowledge or consent. I was in a relationship with the other individual, and we had parted ways long before those photos were leaked online. I'm pursuing legal action at this time. But that's all I can say on the subject."

Her voice was a little harder than it had been before, laced with the steel from her spine that Hayden couldn't help but admire. The Q&A continued, the rest of the questions thankfully staying in safe territory. Finally, the moderator wrapped it up and thanked all the panelists for coming.

"And FlameThrower, good luck in the tournament."

Her cotton candy mouth smirked and she threw Hayden a wink.

"Thanks, but I won't need it."

The panel ended as Hayden threw her a dark smile. Game on.

CHAPTER 8

MIN

"*F**lame, I have to admit. I have a fantasy of killing you.*"

"That's weird, Kevin, because I have zero fantasies about you whatsoever."

Min smiled at the trash talk. She was deeply embedded in the first round of the Bleeding Sword tournament. She had been randomly assigned in to a group of ten other players, and they had been dropped into a random map for a free-for-all fight. Last player standing in each group would move forward to the second round of the tournament the following day.

There was no way in hell Min was going to be taken out in the first round.

Min had already killed three of the other players herself, the last player's corpse still at her feet. A quick glance at the vitals board told her there were just two others left. She knew KevinKillsU, had played with him many times before, and therefore wasn't surprised by his threat. Similar sentiments were often thrown her way during games like this. It was part of the fun.

FlameThrower's avatar rounded the corner, her sensors out

and casting, checking for other players and any NPC zombies that could be nearby. Min knew Kevin was somewhere close, and she wanted to be ready for him. She quickly reloaded her rifle and scanned her surroundings. He was here somewhere, probably lying in wait to snipe her, just like she was doing. Which meant she had two options: wait for the ever-spawning NPC zombies to flush him out of his spot or get creative.

Min loved to get creative.

She turned to the body of BaxterBro, the player she had just taken out, and grabbed it, her avatar throwing it over her shoulders. A voice crackled through her headset.

"What the hell are you doing?"

"Heard you had a thing for dead bodies," she said over her headset.

"Yeah, but it's not exactly appropriate for a streaming audience, you know?"

She smiled. The players in each group were allowed to chat with each other since part of the game was psyching out your opponents. Plus, the streaming audience loved it. She knew KevinKillsU was gonna be pissed at what she was about to do, but she also knew he'd be impressed, so fuck it. She was winning this tournament.

She walked the body over to the nearby window, scanning. There were a lot of places Kevin could be hiding, but her infrared goggles she had found gave her an edge, so she was able to cross out a lot of those possibilities before settling on the dumpster directly below. The metal would block his heat signature, but with the right equipment, he could still be watching her from there. It's where she would choose in his position. So she took aim... and threw BaxterBro's body out the window.

It landed with a faint smash right on top of the dumpster,

like she had planned, and she immediately took out her rifle, aiming it at the dumpster. Soon, zombies were flooding the area, drawn by the sound of the body hitting the dumpster, and Min knew it wouldn't take long for the NPCs to knock it over. At this rate, Kevin would be lucky if she kills him before the zombies.

"You crazy son of a—"

"Temper, Kevin," she told him. "It's just a game, right?"

His indignant huff was his only answer, making her smile. Min waited, hearing the telltale sound of some of the zombies making their way up the stairs to her. She wasn't surprised, but it meant that now she was in a weird race with Kevin below, seeing who would be killed by the zombies first. She could only hope that she had given herself enough distance, but she wasn't going anywhere. There were no other exits in the room other than the window and the door. She was trapped in a game of chicken. And she refused to lose.

Zombies were everywhere, swarming, but she held still. Gun trained on the dumpster below her. Waiting.

"Come out, come out wherever you are."

"You first, Flame."

She huffed a laugh at Kevin's sass. He was stubborn, probably shitting his pants trying to figure a way out of this instead of accepting his fate. But the AI zombies were already rocking the dumpster. If only they would hurry because she figured she didn't have a lot of time.

Almost on cue, the sounds of dragging footsteps and moans were sounding closer and closer to her, the zombies making their way up the stairs toward her. Her time was running out.

Finally, the zombies below managed to tip the dumpster

over. Kevin's avatar was already running and dodging the undead attack, scrambling for cover. With an exhale, Flame-Thrower fired.

Perfect head shot. Kevin went down.

A siren sounded in the room, lights flashing as the *"You Win"* filled Min's screen, even as the animation showed the zombies breaking into her room. She had won with a literal second to spare.

Min stood up, stretching, and turned immediately to where she knew Kevin's streaming bay was. She pointed right at him, a huge grin on her face, waiting. For his part, he stood and threw down his headset before turning to scowl at her. She knew he was pissed at losing, but even from this distance, she could see a smile forming.

"You got lucky," he yelled over to her.

"Lucky you suck at the game," she sassed back. He flipped her off, and she laughed. He appreciated a smart kill, even if he was on the losing end of it. The room filled with applause from their live audience as the announcers proclaimed Flame-Thrower the winner.

It felt *delicious*.

Min hadn't competed since the photos leaked, and she had missed it with a literal ache in her body. That was another thing Alex had robbed from her—just the simple joy of playing a game she loved with her friends while streaming with fans.

For now, the crowd apparently either forgot or didn't care about her scandal because the ones there in person were cheering loud and screaming her name. Min waved, waved at the announcers, then made her way to the private exit.

In the sudden quiet of the green room, Min snagged one of the complimentary bottles of water and drank while she checked the board for the results from the other groups. She smiled when she saw DeathsHead posted as winning his group, not surprised. He was as serious about this competition as she was.

"Hey, Flame."

She turned to find Kevin there, in front of her. Before she could react, she was immediately lifted off her feet into a tight hug.

"I hate you so much."

She laughed at that, returning his hug. "You love me."

"Same thing."

Kevin was one of the few players who actually knew her real identity. But he was always careful and respectful of her privacy.

She tapped his shoulder. "Can't breathe. You're squeezing too tight."

"I've missed you. You've been gone too long. I've had to play with noobs lately who have no idea what they're doing. Not even a challenge. I'm practically sleeping during streams."

"Okay, but I need to breathe."

He finally dropped her onto her feet with a laugh. "I'm gonna get you for that move with the corpse."

Min's pink mouth split into a grin. "You mean you can't wait to try it yourself."

He laughed and tried to ruffle her wig, but she pushed him away.

"A group of us are gonna get some drinks at the Waterfront tonight. Join us? You can be you or Flame. We'll roll with it."

It was tempting, but she ultimately shook her head. "It's been a long day. I need to decompress and get some rest for tomorrow's bracket."

"You're too serious."

"You're not serious enough. That's why the zombies ate you first."

He flipped her off as he walked away, grabbing his boyfriend around the waist with a big kiss to his neck. Min smiled at how happy he was, even though he'd just lost a high-payout tournament. She would've been crushed.

She headed to her private dressing room and slowly stripped every sign of FlameThrower off and carefully packing the items in her backpack. She then washed all her makeup off, throwing her now sweaty hair into a ponytail. Sometimes the subterfuge of switching her persona gave her a thrill, but sometimes, like today, it just made her tired. She wondered vaguely what Hayden was doing with his first night at the con, then immediately banished the thought from her head. Just because they had had a nice day walking the floor together didn't mean they would spend the whole convention together. He was her competition. She didn't need to think friendly thoughts about him. Ever.

With a mental shake, she pulled on her tennis shoes and stepped out into the world, just another nerdy girl excited to be at a convention. No one around paid her any attention.

The walk to the trolley and then to her hotel took the last of Min's energy, and she found herself having some pretty hedonistic fantasies about showering, ordering room service, and falling asleep while watching a scary movie. When she stepped into the elevator with a small group of other attendees, Min pressed herself to the side and out of the way, trying not to think about that fateful elevator ride with Hayden. The way he had pressed into her space. Held her wrist against the wall. Breathed into her ear. That deep voice resonated down her spine.

Fuck. He had ruined elevators for her.

Finally, the elevator dinged on her level, and she dragged her tired feet over to her door, managing to get it to open on the first try, and stepped in, only to freeze in shock.

Someone had trashed her room.

Hotel bedding was ripped and tossed every which way. Holes were sliced into the one armchair in the room. Her laptop was on the desk, smashed, the screen showing several large cracks, some of the keys popped off and thrown on the floor. Her toiletries were spilled everywhere, and from the smell of it, her shampoo and conditioner had been poured onto her clothes, which were cut up and tossed every which way. Min's gaze took in everything, landing on the bathroom. The door was open, and even from here she could see herself in the mirror... and the word someone had written there in what looked to be black Sharpie.

Whore.

She stepped farther in, finally registering that she could hear the TV on, that there were noises coming from the speakers that were blasting at full volume. When she could finally see the screen, her stomach dropped.

The TV was showing a video. *The* video. The recording Alex had made of them having sex, that he had then made screenshots of and posted on the internet. He had been pissed when they broke up, feeling like it was a blow to his pride and ego that she would dump him, and though he denied it, Min knew this was him getting his revenge. Even in the video, his face had been blurred out, keeping his identity secret while hers was clear to anyone who watched.

Moans from the TV filled the room, and she couldn't tear her eyes away from the screen. She burned with rage and grief and betrayal. She had never said yes to making a tape, even though he had constantly asked her to make one with him "just for them." While Min wasn't opposed to sexy videos or pictures kept between partners, she also wasn't dumb. She knew how easily those recordings made their way onto the internet, and even back then, she suspected enough about Alex to not want him to have access to something like that, instinctively knowing it would probably end badly.

And here it was, her very own scandal, a naked Flame-Thrower on her knees sucking what Min knew to be Alex's mediocre dick. The violation of it sent a wave of nausea through her, and she found herself sitting on the bed, no longer able to stand up as the panic hit.

Someone had found her at the convention, at this hotel, when she was supposed to be safe. Someone had broken in, destroyed everything, and then taunted her with this fucking recording and the words written in the bathroom. She had never known the capacity to hate anyone this much, yet someone clearly hated her. And she knew from the many, many messages she had received since the pictures leaked that they weren't alone. Everyone blamed her for the photos, for having sex, for liking it. Min hated this feeling of losing control, hated that she didn't feel safe. That she probably wouldn't feel safe anytime in the near future.

There was nothing to do, so Min took a few deep breaths and then grabbed her phone. The hotel phone had been torn out of the wall and tossed somewhere, so she called the front desk through the mainline and calmly asked them to send up security, doing her best to fight back the tears

Just because she was alone didn't mean she couldn't handle herself. If whoever did this thought it would scare her away from the tournament, then they had sorely underestimated her. She'd take tonight to take care of everything and have whatever breakdown was on the horizon.

But tomorrow, she was going to win the next round of the tournament.

CHAPTER 9

HAYDEN

Hayden stepped into the hotel elevator. It had been an extremely long day, and he was tired, more tired than he had felt in a long time. First the morning with Min, then the panel, followed by the intense first round of the tournament. Then he had rushed to meet with his brother to go over their upcoming business contracts and to evaluate their budget for the thousandth time. He had left with a feeling of anticipation and cautious excitement. They were so close to their goal. Winning the tournament would give them a huge leg up, allowing them to finish development ahead of schedule and launch early.

Then he could leave the streaming life behind him for good.

It was everything he wanted. Hayden had been working with his brother on their own game, funded by Hayden's streaming money. If he won the tournament, the game could be finished that much quicker, and he couldn't wait. Hayden was tired of living behind a mask and was ready to start a new chapter in his life. One where he was the one creating the games streamers loved to play. Where he was out of the spot-light and didn't have to worry so much about someone recog-nizing his voice.

He would, however, miss playing FlameThrower.

The thought occurred to him just as the elevator arrived on his floor. He shook it off, striding to his room, only to stop dead in his tracks.

Sitting in the middle of the hall with her back to her door was Min. Back in her plain T-shirt and old jeans, all makeup cleaned from her face. Her knees were drawn up to her chest and her head was laying in her arms on top of them. Her back-pack was next to her. Worry, and a sense of foreboding hit Hayden hard.

"Lock yourself out?"

She looked up at his voice, and he froze, his heart forget-ting to beat. Her face was streaked with tears, her eyes red, and the look on her face was complete misery.

"Min, what the fuck? What happened?"

She shook her head, her eyes filling, and she put her head back down in her arms. He crouched next to her, his hand going to brush her hair away from her face.

"Tell me what's wrong. Are you hurt? Are you drunk? Is this about the tournament?"

She takes a big sniff, not able to look him in the eyes even as his hand settles on her cheek, his thumb tilting her chin up toward him.

"The door's propped open," she told him in a shaky voice. "You can see for yourself."

He shot her a questioning look, then stood. The door to her room was ajar, held open by the security lock she had left there, so he entered, bracing himself. Hayden was immediately assaulted by the graffiti. He was speechless as he moved farther in, freezing in front of the TV where a video was playing. A moan filled the room, a low and sultry noise that he felt straight to his cock, and then felt it die when he saw the video.

Hayden was going to kill him.

Whoever had done this. Whoever had made the recording. Min didn't deserve this, and Hayden had to fight the red that had filled his vision, knowing Min wouldn't appreciate him losing his cool right now.

He took a deep breath to pull himself back together, then headed back out to the hallway.

"Who did this?" He was proud of how calm he sounded, considering all he could think about was how much he needed to destroy the bastard, slam his fist into a face again and again.

Min shook her head, her forehead on her knees. "The police are coming to process the scene. The hotel is going over their security footage, but they won't have anything tonight. But the police said on the phone that they won't be able to release my room until they've gone over it thoroughly, and the hotel is at capacity. Everywhere is booked for the convention, and I can't get a hold of a friend I know is here. I don't know what to do." She took a shuddering breath, watery eyes meeting his. "They destroyed everything. I only have what was in my backpack."

Hayden looked down the empty hall, wondering where the police were, but then focused on Min. He held out his hand.

"Come on."

"I'm not really in the mood for company right now, Hayden."

"Well, too bad." He reached down, grabbed her by her upper arms, and easily pulled her up to stand. She stumbled at the sudden movement, not expecting it, and Hayden wrapped his arms around her to steady her, one hand buried in her hair and the other locked around her waist in the tightest hug he could manage. He didn't want to examine why, but suddenly everything in him needed to hold her.

He felt her tense, felt how surprised she was at the physical contact, and then she melted against him, letting him take her weight. With a sob, the tears came. He held her while she cried against him, her tears wetting his shirt. Stroking her hair, Hayden murmured in her ear that he had her, that she was okay, that they were going to deal with this together. He didn't really know what he was saying, but he knew he meant it.

Her sobs turned to hiccups, and he pulled her even closer to him as she quieted. He turned his face into her hair, feeling her breath on his skin, feeling her pulse calm from the hand he had on the nape of her neck. After several long moments, the sound of a throat clearing interrupted them. Hayden looked up to see two officers had joined them in the hall.

"Hi, sorry to interrupt. We're here to process the room."

Hayden nodded as Min's head came up and she pulled away from him, wiping her eyes. Or at least she tried. Hayden kept his arm around her, his hand on her waist, not letting her back up too far. She shot him a bewildered look before turning to the cops.

"Do you need me for anything?"

"No ma'am, we have your statement. We'll call you and let you know when we're done processing."

She nodded, then looked around, clearly at a loss for what to do.

"Come on." Hayden bent and scooped up her backpack. With a nod to the officers, he pulled Min across the hall to his room, keeping his hand at her back as he unlocked the door and ushered her inside.

Hayden led her to the bed and gently pushed her to sit on it. She was overwhelmed, and a little numb, he thought. After the huge shock she had found in her room, he couldn't blame her. She had had just as long of a day as he had, and he felt dead on his feet. He couldn't imagine how she felt coming back to that scene in her room.

To that fucking video.

"What do you need?" He was already grabbing a bottle of water for her, twisting it open before handing it to her. Once he saw her take a sip, he kneeled down at her feet and started to unlace her shoes. She didn't even react, which showed how completely out of it she was.

"Nothing. Everything. The only clothes I have are the ones that I've been wearing all day and FlameThrower's outfit. Christ, I don't even have anything to sleep in."

Her breathing was coming faster, probably on the verge of a panic attack. Hayden took her now bare foot into his hand and squeezed it gently.

"Hey. Look at me."

Her big brown eyes locked on his, stealing his breath away.

"The cops are going to find who did this. The person is going to go to jail, hopefully sometime shortly after I break all of his bones. You are going to continue with the tournament and the convention because you love it. And you are not going to let this asshole ruin it for you. Now breathe."

She took a deep breath, her eyes never leaving his.

"Again."

She took another one, and he could see her shoulders start to relax a little.

"Good girl." He put her foot down, and then went to the dresser, pulling out a shirt and some sweatpants. He handed them to her, then walked into the bathroom, turning on the shower to hot. Satisfied with the temperature, he walked back into the bedroom to find her still sitting on his bed, staring at the clothes he had handed her.

"Min. Take a shower, wash off this day, and I'll order us some food. Sound good?"

She lifted her eyes to his, and he was hit once again with how vulnerable she looked. Without thinking about it, he reached out, brushing some of her hair that had fallen out of her ponytail back behind her ear.

"You're going to be okay, Min." He willed his strength to flow into her, through the barely there touch of his fingers in her hair.

Finally, she nodded, taking his clothes, hugging them a little while she stood and slowly made her way to the bathroom.

"Anything in particular you want from the menu?"

"Something greasy." Her voice was so soft he almost missed it.

"You got it, baby. Go shower."

His eyes followed her until Min shut the bathroom door behind her. He then went to call the hotel restaurant and order some food. Hayden hoped Min was hungry because he was pretty sure he was gonna order half the menu.

By the time she emerged, dinner was there, a large burger and fries waiting for her, as well as a chocolate milkshake. Hayden was in front of the TV, flipping the channel to a mindless comedy before turning to her. And then he froze.

He hadn't been prepared to see her in his clothes. It seemed so innocent when he had offered them to her, just one of his old DeathsHead shirts and sweatpants he figured she'd probably swim in since he was about six inches taller than her. But now she was in them, her hair wet, his name scrawled across her chest, her face bare of makeup, her pink toes curling into the carpet, her uncertain eyes too big and staring at him. He tried to breathe, mentally yelling at himself to act like a normal person and to ignore the throb in his cock that was currently screaming for him to do *something* about this woman. He cleared his throat.

"Hope a burger's okay."

She nodded and sat at the small table, and he sat across from her. They didn't say anything, letting the canned laughter from the TV fill the silence. When she had finally slurped the last of her milkshake, there was color back in her cheeks, and her eyes were clearer as they caught his.

"Thank you. I didn't realize how much I needed that." Her voice was soft, as if she was uncertain how to act around him now that they were… whatever they were.

"I guessed you hadn't eaten since lunch."

When they had eaten together. When she had seen her photos on the TV and then walked away from him. He had hated that but tried not to let it show. Hayden didn't know what was happening with this woman. Why he felt this need to take care of her. But he knew deep in his core he was happy she was here. In his room.

To distract himself, he gathered up their plates, piling them on the tray they had come on, and placed the tray outside, glancing at her door across the hall. It was open, and he could hear people moving around inside, still working on her room. He quickly shut his door, not wanting her to see the activity outside this room, but when he turned, he realized he shouldn't have worried because her focus was completely on the king-size bed in the room.

The only bed.

Hayden desperately wanted to know what thoughts were racing through her head.

She licked her lips, not looking at him as she cleared her throat. "If you give me a blanket and a pillow, I can sleep on the floor."

He snorted at that, even though he knew he should've seen it coming.

"No way. You'll take the bed. I'll sleep on the floor."

She looked at him then, her eyes large.

"Hayden."

"No. I won't argue about this. You've had a terrible day and you're not ending it by sleeping on the fucking floor."

She was shaking her head, and he could tell she was trembling, but he didn't know why. He approached, his hand on her back, not able to keep himself from touching her.

"You're safe here, you know," he assured her. She nodded, her breath catching.

"I know, I just…"

"Just what?"

She paused for so long he wasn't sure she heard him, wasn't sure she'd answer. But then her head finally turned, her eyes catching his, wide and soft and very, very dangerous.

"I just don't think I'll be able to sleep in that bed by myself."

He held his breath. Min's hair was still wet, dampening the back of his shirt. Her hands twitched at her sides as if trying to decide what to do. But he didn't know what she was thinking, so he couldn't tell how to help her. Not with this. She was clearly fighting whatever question she wanted to ask him. Which only made him more and more curious.

And then she exhaled, not able to keep it inside anymore.

"Could you hold me?"

A light went off in Hayden's head, so bright it chased all thoughts out. He reached for her, his hand grabbing the nape of her neck and pulling her into him. On their own, his arms wound around her, one hand buried in her hair while the other spread across the small of her back. His head dipped, his face falling into her neck, and he inhaled, deeply, smelling the hotel shampoo, himself on her shirt, and something light and intriguing that simply had to be her. Her hands were on his chest for a moment before they slid up to his neck, a caress, and he felt overwhelmed with the rightness of it, of how well they fit together, how his gut twisted with the need to take care of her, to chase away her sadness.

And then her hands were in his hair, tugging, pulling him down toward her, their mouths inches away until suddenly they weren't and she was there. Her lips on his, soft and gentle and hesitant and creating an entire solar system within him with her as the sun. The room spun around him and there was nothing but her and her scent and her warmth and her softness. A single word echoed through his entire being.

Mine.

CHAPTER 10

MIN

Min didn't know what the fuck she was doing. But she knew she didn't want to stop.

She could feel Hayden's surprise when she kissed him. His entire body froze for half of a moment, so fast she would've missed it if he wasn't completely wrapped around her. And then he was kissing her back. His mouth gentle, like she was something fragile and precious that he wanted to protect. She wasn't sure how she knew Hayden would hold her if she asked. But she had, suddenly needing his strength and heat surrounding her, and she desperately wasn't in a place to think about why that was so. She just wanted to lose herself to this, his gentle kiss, his steadiness, how solid he felt.

And then the kiss changed.

Hayden adjusted the angle of the kiss, his tongue caressing her lips for a moment before she parted them and let him inside to stroke her, slow and deliberate and purposeful. Min felt her nerve endings curl inside her, coming alive at his touch. With her hand on his neck, she could feel his pulse pounding a rhythm that matched her own. His hand flexed against her hip, and she was pulled even closer, their bodies pressed together and his hips ground into hers with a friction that Min knew she had to chase or she would lose her mind. Her free hand slipped around his waist, sliding under his shirt to feel his skin there. Her grip tightened, her nails scraping his skin, and she felt more than heard him groan into her mouth.

"Hayden…" His name slipped out of her with a low, husky whisper, and she felt him shudder against her, as if she was testing the last of his control. And she loved it. She wanted more.

He pulled away, almost ripping his mouth away from hers. Min tried to pull him back, but he caught her wrists, holding her hands away from him and creating distance between them. Hayden's dark eyes glittered with such heat and desire she could feel herself getting wet in response. He was breathing hard, and she didn't know what he saw as his eyes raked over her, but she felt wild. Her hair had air-dried with waves that would be impossible to tame in the morning. Her mouth was open as her harsh breathing matched his. She wanted to burn. And she knew, from the lightning that struck her when their lips touched, that Hayden was a fire so hot he would consume her.

And boy, did she need to be consumed.

After a moment, Hayden's mouth flattened and he shook his head, almost as if reprimanding himself. He took a deep breath.

"Min, you've had a shock." His voice was gravelly, deep with lust, and Min's body practically swayed toward him. But his hands stayed firm on her wrists, holding her back.

"Make me feel better." She should be shocked at her own words, low and husky with desire. But she saw his eyes flare with need that mirrored her own.

"You'll feel better when you get some rest. Alone. In the bed." His voice was firm, but he was still holding on to her wrists, had probably forgotten he was holding them. Min was suddenly terrified that if she let him push her away here, let him put her to bed with nothing more than that brief kiss, they would never get to this point again.

"Fuck that. Hayden, touch me. Please."

"I can't, baby."

Min took a deep breath, her eyes lowering, doubt suddenly flooding her.

"Is it because of the photos?" She looked up at him, wanting to see his eyes when she asked. She wouldn't be able to stand it if he lied.

He recoiled as if she had hit him. "What? No, fuck no. I don't care about those, or the video."

His voice rang sincere, and she found herself believing him, relieved. But that left one other option for why he would turn her away. One she probably should have anticipated considering how they met. She pulled her hands away from him, and he only hesitated a second before letting her go. Min stepped back, wrapping her arms around herself. Her eyes drifted to the large, floor-to-ceiling window, the city lights winking at her through the dark, not able to look at him.

"Then it's me. You're just not… I'm not…" She took a deep breath, trying to calm herself and hide the rejection she felt. "I'm sorry, I didn't mean to throw myself at you. It was unprofessional and you deserve better. You've done nothing but make your feelings about me clear since we met, and I should've respected that."

She turned to the bed, intending to bury herself under the comforter and sleep away her embarrassment, but strong arms caught her waist, pulling her back into him, her head tucked under his chin and his grip so tight on her it trapped her breath.

"Hey, wait, no. That's not what this is."

She did her best to pull away, but he wouldn't let her. She held herself as stiff as possible, ignoring his warmth and his scent as it completely engulfed her. His words, when they came, were low, almost a growl, close to her ear as if saying them too loud would shatter the tension building around them.

"Min, I don't know what's happening, but you need to trust that I want you. More than anything. And I don't know what to do with that feeling, don't know how to express it or get rid of it or even what I want to do about it. Just know it's there, and I'm slowly losing the fight against it."

Her hands flexed on his chest. "I want you, too."

His grip tightened, and one of his hands slid up her side and settled just under her breast. This close, she could feel him swallow. Hard.

"You're hurt, sweetheart. I don't think fucking you as hard as I want to is really the best thing for you right now."

Warmth spread through her and pooled at her core. And she desperately needed him to do something about it.

"Could we at least try? Just to be sure?"

Breath rushed out of him, hard and fast. "Goddamnit, Min."

Hayden's other hand slipped lower, lower, until he was cupping her through his thin sweatpants. The possessiveness in his grip almost made her come right there. He froze, hard muscle pushing against her breasts as his hand at her core subtly clenched against her, almost as if he was testing something. Finally, his other hand caressed up, over her breast, landing on her neck. He grasped her there, turning her head toward him, their eyes catching each other and their lips a centimeter apart. He was so close she could see the silver threaded through his dark eyes as they went back and forth between hers, searching.

"Are you wearing my sweatpants without any underwear?"

She licked her lips, his eyes following the movement. "I didn't have anything other than the thong I was wearing. Have you ever tried sleeping in a thong? It sucks."

His eyes closed as if he was trying to steel himself, fighting for control. When Hayden opened them, they scorched her, his need and desire and a swirl of other emotions she couldn't identify shining through. Without saying anything, the hand cupping her moved higher, slowly pushing into the front of her sweatpants and sliding right back down toward her core. His fingers stroked her softness lightly, finding no barrier between them, exactly where she needed him. And she moaned.

"Christ, Min. You're fucking soaked for me." His voice was unsteady, his fingers still caressing her as if he couldn't stop himself. Min moved her hips closer, chasing their friction, chasing the sensations he was creating inside her.

"Then do something about it."

The side of his mouth quirked up, and then he was kissing her. And unlike their gentle kiss from before, this kiss was hard, consuming, devouring. As if he had thought of it for years and couldn't slow himself down. Which was good because she didn't want him to. She wanted him fast and hard against her.

She opened her mouth and his tongue slipped in, stroking her, biting her, marking her as his. Soon his tongue followed the rhythm of his hands, stroke matching stroke as he slowly circled, spreading her wetness, his fingers finding and surrounding her small bundle of nerves in a steady, consuming rhythm. Her hips pushed against him, grinding on his hand, needing more.

"Open your legs, Min."

She did as he commanded, widening her stance so he could feel more of her, his fingers sliding and caressing while the palm of his hand pushed right against her core.

And then his fingers circled her clit and pinched it.

She cried out, breaking their kiss. But he didn't stop, only continued to circle her, teasing her with his hand and flirting with her clit as her moans grew louder.

"Your pussy is so fucking soft. Can I feel you inside?"

She barely had time to nod before she felt a finger push into her, followed shortly by a second. His mouth captured hers again as he started pumping, his fingers sliding in and out of her, his palm rubbing against her clit as his tongue swirled inside her mouth. She felt the tension in her, felt how quickly her climax was rising, and fought it as best she could, not wanting to end this so quickly, not wanting to give him any reason to remove his hands from her body.

Almost as if he could feel her fighting it, his fingers moved with new urgency, curling inside her and rubbing a magical spot relentlessly. His hand at her neck tightened, securing her against him, hard and possessive. Min slowly lost control of her body, her knees going weak, everything centered and focused on what he was doing to her. Needing more.

"Fuck, Hayden, don't stop." She was desperate, barely aware of what she was saying, just knowing that everything good in the world started with him inside her.

"Louder, baby. I want the neighbors to complain. I want

everyone in this hotel to know how you scream when I make you come."

His words enflamed her, pushing her toward the edge of her orgasm, but she still fought it, not wanting the sensations to end yet. Needing him inside her forever.

And then the hand at her cheek slipped down, pulling down the loose neckline of her too-big shirt—*his shirt*—baring a breast to him. He grabbed her, hard, twirling her nipple between his thumb and forefinger in a way that she felt all the way down to her core, plucking at her and claiming her. Her body jolted as he kept up his rhythm, stroking her inside at that delicious spot he had found as his fingers pulled her nipple hard.

"Min, you are so fucking beautiful like this, in my arms, with my fingers inside you. I wish you could feel the way you're clenching against me, how tight you are. How fucking good you are. I can't wait to taste you."

Min heard herself moan loudly, her mind senseless to anything that wasn't his hands on her body. His hand went to her other breast, caressing in circles until his fingers found that nipple and twisted.

"Stop holding back, baby," he commanded, his voice hard. "Let me see you come."

Sensation ripped through her and she cried out as her orgasm took over, her body convulsing and spasming as he kept up his rhythm, stroking her and kissing her. He kept whispering in her ear about how he loved the feel of her shuddering against him, loved that he was the one to make her come. She wasn't sure how long her orgasm lasted, just that her body was made of lightning and was combusting, leaving her ruined.

Finally Min's muscles relaxed, tension leaving her as she

collapsed, limp against him. She wasn't sure she would be able to stand without Hayden holding her up. Her head landed on his shoulder, turned toward him, watching his face lazily as her heart rate slowed. She felt when he removed his hand from inside her, heard the wet sound his fingers made as they slipped out. As Min watched, he brought his fingers to his mouth, sucking the taste of her off of his hand.

She knew she should probably be scandalized. But with his eyes locked on her, his fingers in his mouth, she couldn't help but feel her nipples tighten. He made a small noise as he licked his fingers as if he had found the sweetest candy and was planning to eat it all himself.

When he was done, Hayden kissed her, his hips grinding against hers, igniting all the nerve endings she had thought were destroyed with her orgasm. His kiss was softer, less frantic, but claiming her in a way that she had begun to crave, branding her with his mouth. Min wrapped her arms around his neck as his hands found her ass and squeezed. Without warning, he lifted her until she was right where she wanted to be, his erection pressing into her core through their clothes as her legs instinctively wrapped around his waist. She rocked her hips against his, loving the pulse of him. His breath caught and his hands clenched on her ass, kneading. Min could feel his need pulse against her.

Min took one hand and slid it down his chest, lower, finding his hardness and grabbing him. She was doing her best to stroke him through the denim when he jostled her, knocking her hand away.

"Sorry, baby, we're still not doing that tonight."

She pulled away from his mouth, an incredulous look in her eyes.

"What? Why not?"

She was pissed, but he only smiled. He took slow steps forward, walking with her still wrapped around him, watching her eyes flutter as the movement had him brushing right against her clit.

"Because you're still recovering from your shock from earlier."

"That is such fucking bullshit—"

"And I don't have any condoms on me."

"Oh." That gave Min pause. She was usually the one demanding protection no matter who her partner was. It surprised her that with him it had slipped her mind. "The hotel probably has some."

"It's three a.m. and I don't feel like parading through the lobby with an erection."

She leaned forward, licking his neck from shoulder to his ear, and then biting him there, softly, just enough for him to feel her teeth.

"I'm on birth control. And I would make you feel so, so good."

"I know you would, baby, but I have other ideas on how good you could make me feel right now."

He dropped her on the bed, her ass bouncing against the mattress at the sudden movement. Min was sprawled on the bed, her legs spread and her hair wild when she glared up at him, outraged. She didn't want to admit how hot she was from his manhandling.

"What the fuck, Hayden?"

He chuckled, sliding a hand into her hair and tugging her close, just enough to bring her mouth back for a kiss.

"God, your fucking mouth, I swear. Someday I'm going to fill it so good, you won't be able to sass me."

"Why wait?"

Hayden paused, seeming to think about it, then shook his head. "Next time."

Min's pulse raced at the thought of a next time as he pushed her back into the bed. She flopped, ungraceful, and immediately came up to lean back on her elbows, watching him. Hayden's hands went to her hips, sliding her sweatpants off while his eyes devoured every inch of skin he exposed. Once they were off and in his hands, Hayden brought the sweatpants to his face and inhaled like a man short on oxygen.

Min couldn't hide her shudder of arousal, but she tried to play it off.

"I didn't know you were such a perv."

"Only when it comes to you, Min," he said with wonder in his voice, softly, as if he didn't realize he was talking out loud.

She squirmed as his eyes landed on her now bare pussy. Min kept it waxed clean, and she had just had an appointment before coming to the convention. Which meant he was seeing everything, on display, including how much she was dripping from her previous orgasm. Her blush snaked everywhere, through her whole body. But Min didn't cover herself, instead holding still while he silently memorized every one of her dips and curves. His eyes lifted to hers.

"Take off the shirt."

She moved quick at the command in his voice, whipping his shirt off over her head and letting it fall somewhere without a second thought. She was completely naked in front of him, but he was still fully dressed in his jeans and old tee. Hayden's hands clenched as she took a moment to just stare at him. Even through the shirt, she could see muscle. He was a good half a foot taller than her when they were side by side, which meant he was towering over her prone body on the bed. Min could feel herself melting. Something about her entire body being exposed, of him being able to see every nook and cranny and fold of her pussy while he was still fully clothed, made her feel wonderfully dirty. She let her legs fall open even wider, watching for his reaction.

Hayden's gaze rested on her breasts, then her face, then slid back down to her pussy as if he couldn't decide where he wanted to look first.

"Touch yourself."

Min didn't hesitate. She let herself fall back onto the bed, keeping her eyes on him, and brought her hand to her breast. She circled for only a moment before grabbing her nipple, pinching it, biting her lip to stop herself from crying out at the blaze in his eyes. Emboldened, she stroked her chest, circling down to her stomach, caressing her skin. His eyes followed her hand, absorbing everything.

As her hand lowered, he reached for her, grabbing her thighs and pulling them apart, pushing her knees to the bed, exposing her even more. Hayden then dropped to his knees before sliding his hands closer to her core and holding her open. Cold air rushed her as he leaned in and inhaled deeply. She almost came right then.

"Show me, Min. Teach me what you like."

His eyes met hers, and she swallowed hard. She had never done this in front of a partner before. It somehow felt more intimate, and she could feel herself hesitate. After all, they may have known each other for years, but they hadn't known each other in person until recently. Was she really going to do this with him?

As if he could feel her indecision, his thumbs lightly caressed up and down her exposed core. She could feel the sensation inside her.

"Baby, please."

It was the desperation in his voice that had Min's hand moving, sliding down to where he held her open. She could feel his sigh of relief right against her as she began to tease herself, running her fingers along the outside of her clit, frustrating herself enough to make her breath shudder.

"Yes. Just like that." Min could almost feel his voice vibrate against her, and she knew she wasn't going to be able to stand too much more. She finally brought her fingers to her clit, rubbing in slow, light circles, pressing harder with every caress. And then she felt his hand over hers, following the movement, learning it until it was just him, pressing and swirling and caressing and Min realized the moans she was hearing were her own. She was somehow close once again, ready to fall off the precipice when he pulled his hand back.

She didn't even have time to complain before he grabbed her thighs and yanked her to the edge of the bed, keeping her knees bent and pulled away from each other so that absolutely nothing was hidden from him. He licked his lips as his eyes glanced up at her from his kneeling position.

"I've been dreaming about this since I chased you into that elevator."

And then he lowered his head to her pussy and she stopped thinking altogether. He flattened his tongue and licked her once, slowly, from her opening up to her clit. Once there, he let his tongue swirl around her there, mimicking the movement she just taught him with her hand.

"*Fuck.*" Min couldn't stop herself from yelping. She squirmed, overwhelmed with sensation, still sensitive from her last orgasm.

Hayden held her firmly, pulling her legs over his shoulders and wrapping his arms around her to hold her down as he proceeded to devour her as if he was a starving man. Her hands went to his hair, sinking into the curls and she wasn't sure if she was trying to push him off or pull him harder into her. He stayed where he was, his tongue circling her, swirling around the sides of her clit but never quite hitting where she desperately needed him to.

"Hayden, god, please."

"What do you need, baby?"

She shook her head, unable to speak as he kept tormenting her. In response, Hayden slowed his rhythm.

"Use your words, Min. What do you want?"

She was sweating, her body slick as one of his hands slid up, caressing her stomach, on the way to her chest where he grabbed a breast and squeezed. When she whimpered, he pulled away from her, cool air rushing at her body. She yelled in protest.

"No, don't stop."

"Tell me, Min." His hands were still on her thighs, his thumbs caressing circles into her skin. Min shifted, trying to push his hands closer to her core, but he wouldn't budge.

"I need to come," she finally whispered.

"What's that?"

She would've thrown something at him if she could. "I need to come," she repeated, louder.

"And who can make you come?"

"You can make me come, Hayden. Please, you have to."

And then he was everywhere again, his hand on her breast, kneading, pulling at her nipple, his tongue finally swirling on her clit, and his other hand sliding up her thigh. It was only a moment before she felt his fingers push into her again, stroking her, reaching deep. He curled them into her, finding that spot inside where she needed him most.

She was babbling now, saying his name over and over,

moaning, begging, her nails scraping his shoulders in desperation, until he sat back for a moment, his eyes locking on her.

"Min, I need to feel you come on my tongue. And you better scream, or else we're doing this all night until we get it right."

"Hayden, please." Min had no idea what she was saying. Her hands were clutching his shoulders, her nails digging in. So close.

And then he leaned down and sucked her clit.

Min screamed as she exploded. She clenched everywhere, trapping his head between her legs as he kept licking and sucking, his fingers drawing out every last muscle spasm from inside her, his tongue lapping up every drop of wetness that it found. She hadn't thought she could come again, or if she did, she didn't think it would be as hard as the first one. But her spasms hit her hard, her back arching under the force of it as Hayden steadily rode wave after wave. When she finally felt herself relax down into the bed, Min felt a deep sense of dread as she realized every time with Hayden would be like this.

The thought had barely registered when he was climbing over her, pulling her in for a devouring kiss. She tasted herself on his lips in a way that she loved, his tongue diving deep into her. She wrapped her naked body around him, wanting his weight on her, for him to sink into her.

Min wasn't sure how long they kissed like that before Hayden pulled her up higher on the bed. He broke away to pull down the covers and then tucked her in. Suddenly Min was exhausted, could barely keep her eyes open, the events of the day hitting her all at once. She was drifting before Hayden even turned the light off, the faint feeling of his lips on her forehead settling every anxious thought in her head until she finally succumbed to sleep.

CHAPTER 11

HAYDEN

When Hayden finally pulled himself from the deepest, most restful sleep he had had in a while, the first thing he noticed was the hair tickling his chin. He blinked his eyes open and managed to look down at himself without moving to see Min wrapped around him, her head on his chest and a smooth leg flung over his thigh. He had managed to pull a shirt over her head before she fell asleep the night before, but now it rode up toward her hips, leaving a lot of leg exposed to his gaze, her skin practically glowing where it rested against his sweatpants.

And then the memories came flooding back. Min in his clothes. Min moaning, biting her lip. Min naked and touching herself while he watched.

His already hard morning wood stirred, which Hayden expected. What he didn't expect was the light squeeze to his dick, almost reflexive. Both of his hands were accounted for, one around Min and the other flung to the side, which meant Min's hand had apparently slipped into his sweatpants sometime during the night and groped him in her sleep.

Fuck, she was gonna be so mad. Hayden let himself smile with anticipation. He knew that she was going to wake up and be incredibly awkward. She may have been the one to ask him to hold her, but the fire that had overtaken them both had been overwhelming. None of Hayden's sexual experiences could even come close to it. But he didn't know where that left them. After his ex had tried to out his real identity and with the onset of his anxiety, Hayden had basically sworn off serious dating until he was done with his streaming career. He didn't trust easily, and that wasn't going to change overnight. This thing with Min had to be short-lived, a simple convention fling. Something between friends to let off steam. He couldn't let it be more than that, even if the woman plastered against him was slowly taking up a lot of his waking thoughts.

And if the thought of not seeing her after the convention left acid in his gut, he was just going to ignore it.

The head on Hayden's chest stirred, pressing deeper into him as if chasing the last remnants of sleep, and he felt a sleepy hum against his skin. He shook off his thoughts, instead bringing his hand up to slide through her hair, playing with it as he watched her very, very slowly realize where she was, and who she was with.

Hayden had suspected she would bolt. Instead, she blinked up at him, her brown eyes sleepy and curious. That close, with her walls down, he could see the moment when she remembered what they did last night. A blush overtook her, and he could almost feel the heat of it course through her body where they were touching.

"Um," she rasped, blinking at him, her body still soft against his. "Good morning?"

Hayden reached out and brushed her hair back from her face, keeping his eyes on her.

"Good morning."

"Is my hand on your dick?"

He bit back a smile. Sleepy Min was pretty adorable. "It is."

Her eyes moved to the curtained window where a few streaks of light came in, as if she couldn't believe they were there. Her hand flexed on his dick again. Hayden wasn't sure if she meant to, but before he had a chance to ask her hand was sliding away, pulling the comforter up until it covered everything but her eyes. She peeked at him, shy.

"I, um, might need some coffee."

He laughed out loud at that, dropping a kiss on top of her head before he released her, hopping out of the warm bed.

"Coffee can be arranged." He grabbed the phone on the nightstand, dialing up room service and pacing while he searched for the menu they must have tossed somewhere the night before. Min, meanwhile, stayed in the bed, cocooned under the covers. He felt her eyes on him as he paced. He had worn sweats to bed but had gone shirtless. He usually wore less, but last night he hadn't been sure how Min was going to feel waking up in his bed after last night and all they had done.

He turned to watch Min while the phone rang in his ear. She was starting to peek out from under her covers. Her hair was wild, auburn waves everywhere as she rubbed the sleep from her eyes. The comforter fell lower and she looked at the shirt she was wearing. She grimaced at the DeathsHead design, and Hayden couldn't help but chuckle. FlameThrower wouldn't be caught dead in her rival's merchandise, and it had to rankle Min. Her eyes flew to his and she turned beet red, flipping him off.

Hayden loved that he knew she blushed.

"Hey, yes, we're gonna need two coffees and some French

toast," he told room service when they answered. "Two orders."

Min, ever the lover of breakfast, sat up straighter, whispering.

"Eggs. Bacon."

He grinned. "Yes, with eggs and bacon as well. Thanks." He hung up and stared at her, taking in the dark circles under her eyes and the nervous set of her mouth.

There was silence for a moment, and Hayden knew she was trying to think of what to say. At a loss, she peeked at herself underneath the comforter.

"I, uh, don't have pants on."

"I could only get the shirt back on you before you passed out." His grin deepened, but otherwise he didn't move, deciding to enjoy her discomfort. Her blush hit new heights, her eyes darting away from his, and Hayden couldn't remember a time he had enjoyed waking up this much.

"Little help?" she asked.

He laughed at that, reaching into the dresser for a pair of sweatpants and tossing them to her. She quickly pulled them on under the covers, wiggling in a way that made the bed shake, and then pushed the covers down.

"The coffee is coming soon?"

"It'll be a bit since I'm sure they're getting a lot of orders this morning. Figured you'd prefer to stay in rather than fight over the last French toast at the buffet."

"Only because you know you'd lose."

She ran her fingers through her hair, trying to tame the crazy curls and frizz that must have resulted from going to bed with it wet. Hayden thought she looked gorgeous, remembering the feel of that hair through his fingers, but her glance made him realize she was feeling self-conscious.

"You gonna go shy on me now, Flame?" He grinned at her, teasing her, wanting to see that sass he knew so well.

"No, of course not."

"Good to hear. Because for a second, it looked like you were trying to hide as much of yourself as possible."

She looked down at herself, and he knew she was seeing what he was, her pulling the comforter back over her fully dressed body. She looked back at him with a challenging glare.

"Maybe this bed is just really comfortable and I don't want to move."

Relief flooded him as he saw her usual spark. Last night she had been so vulnerable. He didn't mind her leaning on him, but he didn't want to think she had lost some of her fire. He loved her fire.

Hayden walked toward her, slowly, wanting to push her. She sank back into the bed as he approached. Her eyes were on him as he leaned over, bracketing her between his arms. Hayden was close enough to see her pulse fluttering in her neck, to see her eyes run over his body, his forearms, his chest, his lips, before landing back on his face. There was heat in them now, a heat that he could feel reflected in his own. He reached up, placing the palm of his hand on her neck, gently, feeling her pulse stagger against his fingers.

"Do I make you nervous, Min?" He pitched his voice deeper, enjoying this, enjoying how nervous and twitchy she was, how her mind was clearly racing to figure out how to react to his nearness. Fascinated as she settled on a smirk.

"In your dreams, Hayden. Now, get off me so I can breathe."

He laughed at her, but pulled back, giving her the space she clearly needed. She tried to hide it, but he heard the deep breath she took once he stepped away.

Finally, she slid out of the bed. Hayden saw her wince and was immediately concerned.

"Are you hurt?"

"My feet are a little sore from all the walking yesterday. It's fine." She couldn't look at him when she told him. He relaxed a little, but still kept an eye on her. She made her way to the bathroom and shut the door behind her, probably needing a private moment to process the night before. Hayden didn't know who had managed to get into her room, or who would carry such a grudge that they would trash her things like that, but he hated that she went through it. Hell, he hated that she even saw the video of herself. Hayden knew women in the gaming world had it rough, but having it right there in front of you in what should be a safe space was shocking. He burned to catch whoever the fucker was.

There was a knock at the door, interrupting his thoughts of vengeance. He set about getting the food on the table and ready, finishing just as the bathroom door opened. Min's face was scrubbed and her hair was a little tamer, probably as much as she could do without her brush. She settled at the small table and practically melted when she saw the perfectly made French toast steaming and waiting for her. She inhaled deeply.

"I'm so glad you remembered."

"Minerva, a man remembers a woman threatening him at a buffet over French toast."

She smiled at him as he plunked down a cup of coffee near her hand, and dug into her plate. He settled across from her, watching her while checking messages on his cell phone. Hayden could feel her eyes on him.

"Big plans today?" she asked.

"I'm meeting someone for a business lunch, and then the tournament. But I'm free until then. You?"

"Nothing until the tournament but I'll need to shop for a different outfit this morning. Feels like I'm just giving the trolls fodder if I show up in the same outfit as yesterday, walk of shame style." Her tone was casual, but Hayden knew better. She had been severely shaken by what had happened to her room. He didn't want to pry, but he couldn't stop himself from asking.

"Can I ask what happened there?"

She shrugged, focusing on her French toast. He could feel her reluctance to look at him.

"It's exactly what I've said in my statements. I was in a relationship. That man apparently recorded us having sex when I was unaware and without my permission. I would never consent to something like that, not with him. We eventually broke up. And then he posted stills from the video in some sick move to get me canceled." She took a bite of her breakfast then, chewing carefully. "And he's succeeding."

"No, he's not."

Min's eyes flew to his. Surprised. But she shrugged.

"He is, actually. After the photos came out, my sponsors dropped me. Fans hated me, somehow thinking that I should only be chaste and pious while playing shooting games with other men. I've been getting non-stop emails, DMs, letters, you name it from people who want me to kill myself, who want to hurt me themselves. Being a woman on the internet was already scary. But now, I'm a target. And I don't know if I can go back to the way things used to be."

Without consciously thinking about it, Hayden reached out and laid his hand over hers on the table.

"These people don't own you, Min, and they certainly

don't define you. Your fans follow you because they like your content. You don't need to change anything to please them. The assholes who are threatening you are garbage. They're not worthy of your time and energy."

She shook her head, still not looking at him but he could see her eyes turn watery, as if she was fighting off the tears.

"I need this tournament, Hayden. It's my last chance to show that I'm more than what he's trying to convince them I am. Not to mention the money from winning and from the sponsorship."

"Then do it. If anyone can, you can."

She smiled at that. "Okay, but I'm going up against a rival who's very, very good at the game."

Hayden leaned forward, letting her teasing wash over him. "How good is he?"

"Good enough to not need me to stroke his ego."

"But would you stroke other parts of him?"

She sputtered into her coffee at that, and he laughed, letting go of her hand and standing up.

"Look, I'm not going to pretend with you, Min. That sponsorship and money would mean everything to me as well, so I'm going to fight you for it. Prepare yourself."

She snorted, shoving food into her mouth.

"You've never been able to scare me, Death."

"Maybe not, but I can make you scream."

She gave a surprised snort as he made his way into the bathroom, a grin on his face.

This was going to be fun.

After Min had eaten, showered, and donned her jeans from the day before with another one of Hayden's Deaths-Head tees tied up into a crop top, they headed downstairs. They hadn't discussed it, but Hayden was happy she wasn't objecting to spending the morning together. At the front desk, they learned that the police had finished with Min's room and that the housekeepers were going to give it a thorough cleaning before she got back. Min definitely looked relieved, even as Hayden felt disappointment twinge. He wanted Min to have access to her stuff and her own room, but having her in his room, wearing his clothes, was a treat he hadn't been expecting. He wasn't sure he was ready for it to end.

With that knowledge, they made their way to the con. A lot of people must have been hungover from the night before, so they easily made it into the first car for the trolley, with plenty of space to sit. The trip went fast, and the crowd outside the convention center was easy to manage.

They made their way to the exhibition hall and immediately headed for the small vendors section. Hayden let Min pull him from shop to shop as she chatted with each of the owners about their wares. For his part, he kept quiet, happy to simply drift near her. It was always a gamble to walk the floor and talk to anyone, always a not-so-small chance that someone would recognize his voice and blow his cover. But right now, walking with this woman and feeling her excitement, it was worth the risk.

The problem was, now he knew how she felt under him, how she tasted, the sounds she made when she was getting close, and how his name ripped through her when she came. He had been hard for hours after she had fallen asleep, her smell everywhere in the bed and filling his head. With sleep eluding him, Hayden had spent his time trying to work on his game from his laptop, making notes on things that needed to be tweaked and rewritten for when he saw Theo for lunch. They still had so much work to do before they could launch.

On any other day, Hayden would be buried in it, overwhelmed by his to-do list.

But for now, he let Min pull him along with her. She had claimed that her FlameThrower outfit was so she could blend in unnoticed as herself. But Hayden could see the interested eyes on her, watching her move through the crowd. Min didn't have to be in her persona to be admired. He did his best to stay close and keep a hand on her back, but the hall was growing more and more packed, worse than it had been yesterday, and pushing through it was difficult.

After some drifting, Min found herself drawn to a booth with corsets displayed in a rainbow of colors. She grabbed his hand and pulled him toward her, pointing.

"What do you think?" she asked him. He looked at the corsets, shrugging. They were bright, with a variety of laces and ribbons everywhere.

"Like a unicorn vomited all over this place."

She laughed as she started sorting through the various blouses and skirts.

"Exactly what I need."

Just then, they heard a rustling behind them. "Looking for something in particular?"

Hayden turned and froze. In front of him was at least six feet of man dressed to the nines in a corset, fishnets, five-inch heels, and a bright pink wig contrasting nicely against his rich, dark skin. It was hands down the best FlameThrower cosplay Hayden had ever seen. A glance at Min told him she was practically glowing. It was love at first sight.

"Oh my god I love your outfit," she gushed. "Are you FlameThrower?"

The man laughed at that, preening. "Thank you, and yes. She's my favorite streamer."

Min beamed at him. "She's my favorite, too."

The two were making googly eyes at each other, and Hayden had to fight back a smile. Min may like blending in, but she also loved being seen as FlameThrower, and she always adored her fans. Right now, she was smiling ear to ear, and Hayden could almost feel her joy.

She held out her hand. "I'm Min."

The cosplayer took her hand with a smile, possibly not noticing Hayden was even in the booth, he was so focused on Min. "I'm Randall. But if you call me Flame, I'll give you a five percent discount." He winked at her and she laughed, loving her new best friend.

Randall turned to Hayden, hand out, but the smile noticeably dimmed. "Randall."

"Hayden." They shook, taking each other's measure in the way men do, and then Randall turned back to Min.

"Now, how can you claim to love FlameThrower when you're standing in my booth wearing a DeathsHead shirt?"

Min grinned. "Would you believe I had no choice?"

"Well, then we need to fix that. What do we have to do to make you happy?"

Min leaned in as if imparting a secret. "I need an outfit FlameThrower would wear if she was about to crush Deaths-Head under her boot."

Hayden rolled his eyes, and Randall immediately turned to his racks of clothes to start searching for the perfect ensemble. Min took the moment to reach over and pinch Hayden's side. He jumped, grabbing her hand.

"Ow?" He pulled her a little closer, loving the feel of her against him.

"Be nice."

"You were ready to throw yourself at him."

"I appreciate a fan."

Hayden grinned at her, dark and filled with promises. "I guess I don't like competition, no matter where it comes from."

She smiled at him. "I know for a fact you love competition. That's literally your thing."

He leaned into her, speaking low in her ear so it wouldn't carry through the small booth.

"I love competing with *you.*"

She laughed at his admission. The sight of her made his stomach dip at the memory of her last night, naked and spread out on the bed and calling his name.

"Well, think of this as a growth opportunity." She patted his chest then turned to Randall, who had pieced together a number of items for her to try on in the small dressing room stationed in the booth.

She disappeared behind the curtain. Hayden looked around at the booth, studying everything idly until he looked up and froze.

"Now, what can I talk you into buying?"

Hayden turned to find Randall, now focused on him with his best salesperson smile. Before he could change his mind, Hayden pointed to the T-shirts above him on display.

"You got that one in my size?"

CHAPTER 12

MIN

Min tried on everything, from the classic look she was used to, to the more daring outfits that Randall was pushing her toward. She was thoroughly enjoying herself. Randall was hilarious and attentive and had an easy sense of style Min respected. Finally, she settled on buying hot pink sparkly fishnets, a unicorn corset top, and a number of colorful beaded necklaces. She figured she could wear her pink mini skirt one more time before the internet called her out on it.

Stepping out of the booth, she looked around, wondering if she had lost Hayden. She pulled out her phone to text him at the number he had programmed into her phone that morning, and then stopped herself—they hadn't said they would spend all morning together. And two orgasms didn't mean he had to report to her about his whereabouts, especially since she had fallen asleep before taking care of him last night. She bit her lip, trying to figure out what to do, not sure if she had the right to text but knowing she already missed him when two arms slipped around her waist and she was pulled back into a hard chest. She looked up and relaxed at the sight of Hayden's smile.

"Done appeasing your fans, Minerva?"

"Done. Where did you wander off to?"

"Just down the aisle to scope out what else they had for sale. Did you know that for fifty dollars you could purchase a statue of a naked Deadpool as a Simpsons character?"

"How many did you buy?"

His laugh rumbled in her ear, and he pulled away, but not before she noticed he was now carrying a small bag.

She pointed at it. "What did you get?"

"Don't worry about it."

Her mouth dropped open in mock outrage. "You're not going to show me what you bought?"

"Maybe it's a naked Deadpool. I wouldn't want to offend your delicate eyes."

"Wouldn't be the first one I've seen." She reached for the bag again, but he held it up, out of her reach. She glared at him. "Are you being serious right now?"

"Can't a man have secrets?"

"Not at con." She leaned toward him, attempting to jump to reach the bag, but was interrupted when he grabbed her mid jump and pulled her into him, his mouth finding hers. She gasped at the sudden kiss, and his tongue slid in, stroking inside her mouth in a rhythm she recognized from last night. She grew warm as his other arm, the one holding the bag, slid around her shoulders, pulling her closer into him, kissing her with everything he had in front of the entire convention floor.

Someone bumped into them, yelling, "Stop blocking the aisle!" Min laughed, breaking the kiss with Hayden even as she looked up at him. His thumb stroked her bottom lip like a promise, and then he stepped back, grabbing her hand and tugging her to follow.

"Come on, we're running behind."

"Behind?"

"For lunch."

Fuck, she forgot he had a lunch meeting.

"Oh no, I'm so sorry, I didn't mean to take so long—"

"Min, it's fine, it's just lunch."

She couldn't believe how casual he was being about it. She didn't know what the meeting was, but it was literally the one thing he said he needed to do today before the tournament. And now he was going to be late because of her.

But, wait, why was he tugging her along? She attempted to pull her hand out of his, but he kept his grip, not letting her go. She did her best to dig her feet into the cement floor. Finally feeling the resistance, he turned back.

"What's wrong?"

She gestured to the doors, then to where he held her hand, knowing she probably looked a little insane.

"Hayden, it's *your* lunch meeting. You'll get there faster if you don't have to drag me along."

"I want you to come."

Something fluttered near her heart, but she steeled herself to not look too closely into his words. They were enjoying each other's company at a convention. It didn't mean more than that. This was a con fling, something they'd forget about once they got back to Los Angeles. And though she usually avoided casual hookups, she found she wasn't ready to let him go just yet.

She tried again. "You said it was a business thing. I shouldn't just crash it."

Hayden finally stopped trying to pull her, instead coming

close, invading her space, and Min inhaled the scent of the aftershave he had used that morning. A little cedar mixed with clean man. His hand came up to grip her neck and tip her mouth up to his. Everything in her started to throb.

"I want you there, Min. Stop fighting," he said, his voice low and full of sin. Her pulse sped up, and she knew he could feel it from where he gripped her neck. He could continue just pulling her along. Lord knew he was strong enough. But he waited for her answer, staring deep into her eyes, simply letting her know that she was who he wanted with him. And she knew, without a doubt, she wanted to be with him, for as long as they could. So, with a nod, she gave in.

He pulled her out the doors to the hall and led her out of the convention center. They waited at the streetlight with the religious protestors, chanting into their bullhorns, making it impossible to speak. When the light changed, Min and Hayden made their way across the street, dodging past the other con attendees who were slowly meandering through the down-town area, searching for a meal. The restaurants were packed, their waiting areas overflowing. Min grimaced.

"I hope you have a reservation."

Hayden grinned back at her, tugging her to keep up with his long steps. "He's holding a table for me."

"You and your fancy friends."

"So fancy, babe. You have no idea."

They walked further down the street, losing some of the crowd but still surrounded by signs of the convention. Finally, he stopped in front of a high-end restaurant, the hostess at her stand outside on the sidewalk. At the sight of the sign, Min stopped in her tracks, yanking Hayden back to her.

"Hayden, this is Insatiable."

"Yeah?" He kept walking toward the hostess, and once again Min was dragging him back.

"This place is Michelin rated. It's one of the best restaurants in the city. In California."

The infuriating man just winked at her. "Hope they have good tacos."

Through the windows, Min could see that the majority of the patrons inside were wearing suit jackets, the women in skirts and heels. Min looked down at her T-shirt and ripped jeans, then back up at Hayden.

"I think I'm underdressed."

"Maybe everyone in there is just over-dressed."

"Try telling them that."

"Happy to."

He strode up to the hostess, still dragging her along, and Min cringed as she anticipated the setdown the hostess was about to give them for their lack of dress code.

But instead, the hostess looked up and beamed at them. "Hayden? I thought I saw your name on our books."

"Hey Jenny, it's good to see you."

"Glad you're here. He's been in a mood."

Hayden chuckled. "Was the farmer's market out of Brussel sprouts again?"

"Strawberries. Had to change his entire salad concept." She matched his grin.

"My god, I'm surprised he even opened."

"It was touch and go. C'mon, let's get you seated."

Jenny led them into the restaurant, and Min couldn't help but whisper to Hayden.

"Hayden, what the fuck?"

"What?"

They were at their table before she could demand answers.

The table they were given was tucked away in the back of the restaurant. No windows near them, but still beautiful, away from the main area of the restaurant and therefore definitely more private.

Hayden pulled out a chair for her, tucking her in before sitting next to her. Jenny handed them menus and left with a wink. Hayden turned to Min, who hadn't even bothered to open her menu yet, just gaped at him.

His mouth quirked at the corner. "Are you okay?"

"We are in one of the best restaurants in the state. A restaurant that books months ahead of time, especially for Kickoff, and we just walked in, ignoring the dress code, with you flirting with the hostess."

"I was not flirting with Jenny. She's managed this place for years, so I know her. And she's good at her job."

"You were flirting. And she was flirting with you."

"Minerva, this may be hard for you to grasp but some women simply find me charming." He was teasing her, but Min still couldn't wrap her brain around anything.

"Hayden, what the hell is going on?"

Before he could answer, a man dropped into another seat at their table, throwing his ball cap down in frustration. Dressed in a black T-shirt, loose white pants, and an apron, his long, dark hair pulled back into a no-nonsense man bun, his muscled arms were covered in tattoos from his neck to his hands. And the look in his dark eyes said he was ready to strangle someone.

Luckily, he was glaring at Hayden.

"Make this quick. I'm in the middle of a lunch rush and I know Jenny already told you about the fucking strawberries. I'm not in the mood for attitude from you."

Hayden just grinned at him, seeming not at all worried

about the thundercloud of a man invading their space. "Pull out your manners, Theo. We have a guest."

Theo pulled his hand away from where he had been rubbing his eyes and turned a bleary look to Min. Feeling awkward, she waved.

He turned back to Hayden. "Why?"

"Because."

"Will she be sympathetic about my strawberries?"

Min immediately nodded. "It's the worst thing that could've happened. I'm surprised you're even standing and not just in a bathtub listening to Taylor Swift."

Theo exhaled, loudly, beleaguered. "No one understands."

Hayden clapped him on the back. "Your food is always delicious. That's why you constantly overcharge."

"I already miss the time you weren't visiting me. Did you put in your order yet?" He was looking at Min when he asked, and she glanced down at her still-closed menu.

"Um, no, not yet."

"Good, I'll choose for you." He grabbed their menus and then he was gone, throwing his hat back on his head and striding back into the kitchen. Everyone in the dining room covertly watched him as he stormed away, and Min couldn't blame them. She looked at Hayden.

"What just happened?"

He smiled. "You just met Theo Phillips."

Min started. "Wait, *the* Theo Phillips? The one who almost made Gordon Ramsey cry? The one who keeps turning down TV shows because he says he just wants to cook? The one who dated that supermodel?"

"Okay, a lot of that is fake, but yes, that Theo Phillips."

"How the hell do you know him?"

"He's my brother."

Min's jaw officially dropped as a server came over to with a bottle of sparkling water. Her mind scrambled.

"I thought you said this was a business meeting."

"It is. He's my partner for my next project."

"And what project is that?"

Hayden hesitated, and Min was suddenly reminded that this man did not trust easily, did not trust at all, actually, and therefore probably wasn't happy with her questions. She immediately tried to backpedal. "I'm sorry, I'm being nosey. You don't have to tell me, it's your business."

Hayden glanced around the room, making sure they were being ignored and that his voice wouldn't carry.

"Theo's investing in the video game I'm trying to make."

Min's eyes widened. "Wait, you're making a video game? On your own? Holy shit."

"I'm trying," he nodded. "It's been challenging, but we recently hired a few new designers to help with the build. The whole process is moving slower than I'd like, but it's something I've been dreaming of doing for forever."

"Hayden, that's amazing. Like, truly amazing."

"Thanks. I'm keeping everything under wraps for now. I want to see what I can do on my own without getting Deaths-Head involved."

"Can you tell me about it?"

"Later, when we're not in public. I'm here with Theo to mostly talk financial stuff in between his lunch break. But he gets a little hyper-focused when he's cooking, so it may be a minute."

"It's incredible that he's willing to help you with your dream."

"Well, DeathsHead was an original investor in his restaurant, so you could say he owes me. But I actually just like working with him. He's an ass, but he's as big of a gamer as I am. And he's smart, with great ideas. Although he still lords it over me how he wins at Mario Kart."

"That's because you suck at Mario Kart." Theo once again dropped down into the chair, this time with a bottle of wine. He immediately poured for himself, then offered it to Min. She waved her hand.

"No, sorry. Tournament is today, and I have to be able to focus."

"Oh, are you involved in that, too?"

"Min is one of the pros they brought in," Hayden said, keeping vague about who she really was. She appreciated that he didn't just spill her secret to his brother, even though she shouldn't be surprised.

"Oh, do I know your stream?" Theo sipped his wine, idle curiosity as he stared at her, and Min paused, uncertain how to answer him… until his eyes widened. "Wait. You're not…?"

He looked over at Hayden, who shook his head, trying to shut down whatever was going on in Theo's head, but it was too late. Theo laughed, loud and booming and enough to make heads turn toward them. However quiet Hayden liked to be, Theo clearly lived loud and loved attention. He shook his head.

"You're her. I can't believe it. He's with you. He brought you here."

Hayden's jaw clenched. "Things have… changed."

"Amazing how fast things change when a beautiful woman is involved." Theo laughed once more at Hayden's discomfort, then leaned toward Min. "FlameThrower?"

She nodded, surprised. "I've never had someone recognize me out of outfit before."

"I've seen a lot of your stream, Min. This guy loves to have you on when he's visiting. Says you make some of the best gaming content."

Min raised her eyebrows. "Is that so?"

Theo nodded, serious, and Hayden groaned, not meeting her eyes but not denying it. Theo continued to ignore him. "Tell me, Min. What's the most embarrassing thing he's ever done on a stream with you?"

Min thought about it. "One time we were competing and made a bet on who would win. He lost and had to sing the *DuckTales* theme song at the top of his lungs. The chat loved it. It memed for weeks."

Theo delighted chuckle filled the space before he leaned toward her. "Tell me you have fantasies about dating a chef."

Min leaned toward him, her chin in the palm of her hand. "A sexy man who can cook? Say less."

Hayden grunted, knocking his brother back in his seat and crossing his arms. "We're supposed to be here for a meeting."

"We were, and then you brought me a present."

"She's not a present. She's an intelligent woman who's not going to fall for your horrible personality."

"She'd be the first." Theo winked at her, fucking with his brother in a way that made her grin while Hayden muttered something about being an only child. Min couldn't be sure, but she thought Hayden had moved his chair closer to hers. She was enjoying the hell out of this lunch.

Taking pity on Hayden, Theo began to talk shop as the first course came out, a salad with a distinct lack of strawberries that still managed to be the best salad Min had ever had in her life. She listened idly as Hayden and Theo went over the details of what was needed next for their game. While she didn't get the full description, from what she heard it sounded like a huge endeavor, one that would take a large studio at least two years to produce and at least twice as long for an established indie studio. It was astonishing to think that Hayden had worked so hard for so long on this project and that no one knew about it. Yet another example of how much DeathsHead valued his privacy.

By the time she was finishing her main course, some sort of shrimp scampi that tasted like heaven on a plate, Min was ready for a food coma. She looked at Theo, a dreamy look in her eyes.

"You're a genius."

He took her hand, kissing the back of it. "You are officially my favorite customer."

"Can you stop mauling Min for one minute?" Theo just laughed at his brother as Hayden threw him a disgruntled look, taking her hand out of Theo's and tucking it into his lap where Theo couldn't get it.

Theo's grin was wicked. "It's so good to see you. Bring her back."

"Not if you're just going to flirt with her."

"She likes me flirting with her."

Min beamed at him while she let a grumpy Hayden pull her up from her seat.

"You are very good at it."

Theo winked at her. "Good luck at your tournament, Min."

"I hope your strawberries are there tomorrow, Theo."

He kissed her cheek goodbye and then Hayden was tugging her away.

"Unbelievable," he muttered.

Min laughed. "Don't tell me you're jealous."

"Of him? Never."

Hayden had to hit the restroom, so Min made her way to the front of the restaurant to wait for him, pulling out her phone to check messages. She was warm from the good food and Hayden's attention, and she wanted to revel in it for a little longer.

"Min?"

She stopped in her tracks, her stomach dropping to her knees as she turned. She recognized that voice, and she wanted to scream.

"Alex."

Her fucking ex. The asshole that made the video. The absolute douchebag who leaked the pictures of her, and probably the one who trashed her hotel room. Her entire body froze with rage.

He already had a sneer forming when she turned to look at him. His blonde hair was neat, and he had clearly dressed for the restaurant, looking good and solid in his suit coat. Alex's blue eyes gave her the once over, from her messy hair that was threatening to fall completely out of the ponytail she had tossed it in that morning, to the tips of her scuffed old sneakers. He gave her the frown she recognized, the one that he always wore when he disapproved of something she did.

"They actually let you in the door like that?" he asked in disbelief.

Min steeled her spine. "Well, it helps that I don't look like some bag of dicks who crawled up from the sewer."

His eyes glinted, and she saw something like hate in his eyes. She had no idea what she had done to make him treat her with this animosity, but she was really fucking tired of it.

Alex smiled at her, but it was ugly. "I'm surprised you could afford to come to the convention. I heard all your sponsors dropped you."

She narrowed her eyes. "Guess not everyone was in the mood to blame the victim."

"Victim?" He snorted. "Is that the story you've been feeding people?"

"That's what they call it when your asshole ex films you naked without your knowledge or consent and then posts it on the internet."

His eyes gleamed, the predator in him loving that she was pissed.

"I had nothing to do with you being caught on camera. Although I certainly wasn't surprised, considering. Let me guess, you've already bounced into bed with a new guy."

"You mean did I quickly recover from mediocre sex with you and move on to something better? It wasn't hard, Alex. Literally, my hand is better than you."

"Keep telling yourself that, sweetheart."

"What the fuck are you doing here, Alex?" Min was shaking but trying not to show it. Alex had always made a big deal about how emotional she got when she was angry, so she had tried to train herself to be as calm as possible, even when she was raging. But she was pissed, her anger radiating through her, mostly at herself. What the hell had she been thinking staying with him for so long?

He smirked at her. "I'm here for the same reason you are, Min. The tournament. I was invited to compete. Of course, that was before I knew they were inviting has-beens—"

He didn't get a chance to finish his sentence before Hayden appeared out of nowhere, grabbing him by the throat and shoving him back, slamming him into the wall. People all over the restaurant gasped and pulled out their phones, but Hayden ignored them.

"You need to change how to talk to her," Hayden growled in his ear. Min was surprised and a little frightened of his swift violence, but also grateful. Alex had always made it his mission to intimidate her, and though she had never let him, she was still relieved to have Hayden there with her, supporting her.

Alex finally realized he was in trouble. He struggled to break Hayden's hold on him but failed.

"You don't know her, man. She'll leave you high and dry for the next cock that comes around."

With the hand still around his throat, Hayden yanked Alex forward, and then slammed him back again, harder, the wall shuddering under the impact.

"Talk about her like that again and I'll break your fucking neck." Hayden's voice was low, dangerous, glittering with anger.

Alex clearly got the hint and backed down, realizing that Hayden wasn't going to let him go. "Sorry, mate. Not here to step on your territory, just surprised to run into an ex. Don't worry, she's all yours."

Hayden still held him there, his eyes scanning Alex from head to toe and back. Min could see the truth hit him with Alex's ugly words.

"You will not talk to her. You will not approach her. You will keep her name out of your fucking mouth. As far as you're concerned, she doesn't exist. If you act otherwise, I'll make sure *you* don't exist. Understand me?"

Alex nodded, and Hayden slowly let him go, Alex gulping oxygen while he stared at Hayden. Hayden, meanwhile, turned to Min, touching her cheek with one hand, worry in his eyes. His mouth opened, probably to ask if she was okay, but Alex interrupted.

"Do I know you? You sound familiar."

Hayden froze, a flash of something in his eyes that Min saw and made her want to shrivel up into nothing. It was one thing for Alex to ruin her life, but she wouldn't let him ruin Hayden's. Which is why when Hayden turned back to Alex, she grabbed his arm, pulling him with her.

"We should go."

Hayden was torn, not wanting to get recognized but also not wanting to leave Alex there.

"Hayden, *please.*"

With much reluctance, he finally let her pull him toward the door, but Min suspected it was only because Theo had come out from the kitchen to see what was going on. If Hayden was going to trust anyone to deal with Alex, it would be his brother. He was already approaching with a thunderous expression on his face, which Min could only assume meant Alex was soon going to be stuck with lunch from a vending machine.

Min breathed a sigh of relief when they stepped outside the restaurant, but stiffened when she heard Alex call to her from inside.

"See you at the tournament, Min."

Min and Hayden walked back to the convention center, both of them silent. Min wasn't certain what to say, but was also desperate to know what was going through Hayden's mind. Her ex had almost recognized him. It was literally the worst thing that could happen. The more she thought of it, the more she regretted bringing Hayden into her orbit, however inadvertently. He had told her from the get-go that the most valuable thing he had was his privacy. Running into Alex threatened that. She couldn't let him get that close again.

And so as they made their way back to the convention center, the time of the tournament drawing near, Min did the only thing she could think of.

She pulled away.

"I'm gonna head to the center early. Get ready, get in the headspace." She pulled her hand from his, not looking at him, not able to meet his eyes. But she could feel his stillness, could sense his eyes on her as if he could easily guess what was going through her head.

"If that's what you need." His voice was neutral, the warmth of his gaze on her face, and she just couldn't stop herself from gulping.

"Great. I'll, um, see you later. Thanks for everything."

She was gone before he could say anything, striding away as fast as her legs could carry her. He let her go, probably feeling relieved that she was walking away, that he didn't have to attach himself to someone so dangerous, someone who could ruin his privacy and his life with one wrong slip of the tongue. He deserved better. Hell, they had never even talked about this going further than the convention, so really, she shouldn't be so upset about it.

Really.

At least that's what she kept telling herself as she walked further and further away from him, losing herself in the crowd that once brought her comfort.

CHAPTER 13

HAYDEN

"I look forward to washing your blood off my hands."

Hayden's deep voice echoed in the arena right before the shot rang out. His opponent, a lesser-known streamer, screamed as the head of his avatar exploded with the shot, the body falling to the floor. From his secret streaming bay, tucked away into the back hallways of the convention center, away from anyone who would bother him or recognize him, Hayden grinned at the sound of the cheers echoing loudly even all the way back here. People loved to see DeathsHead win.

He watched his ranking move up his screen, declaring him the victor of his latest bracket. A voice came over his headset, the player he had just killed in cold blood.

"DeathsHead, I'm going to be paying you back for that."

Hayden smiled. "Good game."

"Good game."

Hayden clicked out of his screen, disconnecting his mic and turning his attention over to the other brackets, searching until he found her.

FlameThrower. Dressed in the outfit she bought today, her

pink wig without a hair out of place, her fuck-me mouth pinched in concentration as she hunted the last of her prey. Hayden drank in the sight of her, beautiful even when she tried to completely hide herself in the over-the-top outfits. She wasn't the loudest streamer competing today. But she was definitely one of the best.

As he watched her in her element, Hayden's thoughts wandered back to the restaurant and their run-in with Min's ex. The fucking nerve of that guy. Approaching Min in public like that. Talking to her with such disrespect Hayden's hands flexed, wanting to pummel the guy. But Min didn't want that, had pulled him away from violence, and Hayden had to respect her choice. But given the chance, he would make sure that asshat never came near Min ever again. Hell, he had texted Theo to make sure the dick wasn't allowed back in the restaurant. It didn't take a huge leap of logic to assume this was the guy who had made the video and most likely leaked the photos. Hayden hoped Min's lawyers were ready to fight dirty. Because he sure was.

He smiled as Min's avatar tossed an improvised bomb at her opponent, completely obliterating him. He couldn't help but laugh as she publicly celebrated the win, pumping her small fists and bouncing around her streaming bay. One of the best things about FlameThrower was how deeply she loved the game, and it was always a joy to watch.

Her scores flashed over the screen, and her ranking came up. She'd be participating in the final round. Against him. His blood heated at the thought. She was one of his favorite opponents in the game, her creativity and skill making the challenge worth everything he threw into it. Although this time, they both had more on the line. They both had reasons for wanting the money, for needing the sponsorship. So while he hated the idea of standing between Min and what she wanted, he was still ready to fight her for the win. And he knew she was ready to do the same.

She finally signed off her stream with a wave, probably heading to change out of her FlameThrower gear. Hayden pulled out his phone to text her.

HAYDEN: So… what are you up to tonight?

She didn't text back right away. Hayden tried not to let it bother him. He had sensed her starting to pull away after lunch. Hayden was willing to give her a little time, but there was no way in hell he was going to let her push him all the way away, especially not over her fucking ex. He didn't know where this thing with her was going, but he knew he wasn't ready for it to end. Not yet.

Hayden left the building, making sure the hallways were still empty, so he didn't run into anyone. So far the company had delivered on its guarantee of his privacy, but Hayden could never relax his guard. Especially not at the convention.

He made it outside, taking a deep breath before heading away from the center, not sure where he was going. Soon, he found himself at the bay, wanting to take in the water and relax. Sometimes people got so caught up in the con that they didn't notice they were right next to the Pacific Ocean. The convention center had one of the best views, but you had to take your head out of Kickoff long enough to see it.

After a few minutes, Hayden checked his phone again. Min still hadn't responded to his text. Without thinking about it, Hayden pressed the call button and brought the phone to his ear.

She answered on the second ring.

"Hello?"

"You avoiding me?"

He heard her hesitation. "No. I just wasn't sure how to respond."

"Don't think that hard about it. What are you doing tonight?"

"A few friends invited me for a drink at the Waterfront."

"What kind of friends?"

"The kind who know me in both my personas."

There was a pause, and he let it hang, wondering what was running through her mind, wondering if she was just going to shut him down or if she was going to—

"You could come. If you wanted. Only if you were comfortable." The words rushed out of her, almost like she wanted to get them out before she thought about it too much.

"Why wouldn't I be comfortable?"

"Because it's people you don't know. The Waterfront will be packed. We'll probably be out late. It's a lot of things you don't like."

"You'll be there?"

"Yeah."

"Well, I like you. So I'd love to join. If you're okay with it."

He heard the catch in her voice and felt like a fucking king.

"Yeah, I'm okay with that."

"Then I'll see you soon."

He was smiling by the time he hung up, shaking his head. Whatever was happening between them, Hayden suspected that Min was feeling it, too.

CHAPTER 14

MIN

Min couldn't look away from Hayden as he made his way through the overly crowded bar. She had known he was tall but hadn't realized how much he towered over others until he was using his solid shoulders to push his way through the packed room. He had thrown on a dark button-down shirt under his usual black hoodie, the sleeves pushed up to his elbows to show off the forearms she had secretly spent time fantasizing about. He had probably tried to do something to tame his curls, but the dark locks licked the air around him, creating a halo of dark energy. But his mouth was what caught her attention. It curved up on one side, almost imperceptibly. No one glancing at him would notice, but she had spent too much time studying his face since they had sat together on the train. There was something about that mouth that sent heat shooting up her spine.

Although, now that she shot a glance around the room, Min realized a lot of people had taken notice of him. In an interested way that made something curl in Min's stomach. One woman in particular reached out in the crowd and let her hand stroke his arm as he walked by. Hayden didn't even stop, just shook his head at whatever she was offering, his eyes on Min across the room. Her breath caught at his intensity. Breathing was overrated, anyway.

Brittany turned, following Min's gaze, and even over the noise, Min could hear her wolf-whistle.

"Who is *that*?" Brittany's boyfriend, Robbie, turned to stare, as well as his brother, Gus. And now Min felt self-conscious, worried Hayden was going to feel all these people staring at him and hate it. She pulled her eyes away, tugging her hair nervously, jangling the bangles on her wrist. Her brain scrambled to think of how to explain Hayden to Brittany. Brittany had been her roommate in college, and they had immediately bonded over how much they both hated their RA. They had been best friends ever since, had both started streaming at the same time and had supported each other's channels in a number of ways. Brittany was a fashion streamer, so she was always dressed to impress, changing her outfit to match the mood. Tonight, she had gone for the bombshell look, her winged eyeliner and low-cut blouse sending off enough Marilyn Monroe vibes to inadvertently cause a few breakups in the room.

The problem was, Brittany knew her too well. When the pictures of Min leaked, Brittany had called her demanding they go set Alex's house on fire, her inner arsonist requiring a sacrifice. Luckily, Min had talked her into settling for getting drunk and burning his hoodies that he had left at Min's place. But Brittany was loyal, cared fiercely about Min and would be instantly suspicious of men around her for a while. Min wasn't sure she'd be able to lie to her.

But hell, she was going to try. "That's... um... a friend?"

She cringed at how her words came out. Even she would think she sounded suspicious.

Brittany's eyebrows shot up as she realized how much Min was hesitating. Min could feel Brittany's energy heighten as her curiosity took control, like she could sense the torrid details Min was keeping from her.

"Excuse me, are you saying that man eye-fucking you right now across the bar is a 'friend?'"

Luckily, Min was saved from having to think of an answer when he was suddenly there, leaning next to her on the table, not quite touching.

"Minerva." She tried to hide the shiver that ran through her at the sound of his deep voice, but he probably saw it anyway. God, had she just been with him at lunch? Because her body was reacting like it hadn't seen him in months. She stood straighter, forcing herself to turn and catch his eyes, finding he already had a small smile on his lips.

The loud clearing of a throat had Min remembering that she was, in fact, in the middle of a group of friends and couldn't just sit there and stare at this man she was slowly becoming obsessed with.

"Sorry, right. Hayden, this is Brittany, Robbie, and Gus. Friends, this is Hayden." She left it at that, not even wanting to try to define her and Hayden's relationship. Brittany was already dying for more information and would probably corner her in the ladies' room later to demand answers. Which meant that unless Min wanted to face the inquisition, she was going to have to slow her drinking.

Hayden shook hands with everyone and then settled next to Min, not touching her, just leaning on the table. She felt a little disappointed at that but tried to shake it off and remember that she was the one who wanted to keep distance between them. She didn't want him wrapped up in her drama with Alex. It was for his own good.

She told herself that even as she could feel her body leaning closer to him. God, she was fucked.

Robbie, Brittany's boyfriend, threw Hayden a friendly smile. "Good timing, I was just gonna get a round. Whatya drinking?"

"If there's a decent bourbon, I'd appreciate it." Robbie turned to the bar, not bothering to ask the others since he already knew their drinks. Brittany homed in on Hayden, a predatory gleam in her eye that Min knew far too well. Min felt herself tense.

"So, Hayden. How do you know our Min?" Brittany kept her tone polite, but Min could hear the tension, the warning in her voice. Brittany was like a dog with a bone if she wanted information. It was one of the things Min loved about her. Just maybe not in this particular moment.

Hayden didn't appear to sense the danger he was in. "We met at a business meeting in LA. Ran into each other on the train down here." Brittany nodded, and Min was impressed. Everything he said was true, if vague, and still kept both their identities secret. He needn't have bothered with Brittany, since she knew almost everything about Min, but still. It was nice to know he could keep her secret.

"You enjoying the con?" Brittany asked.

Hayden shrugged. "It's definitely had some high points."

Min looked away to sip the dregs of her drink, trying to hide the blush she knew was blooming on her cheeks. She could almost feel Brittany's eyebrow raise.

"And what high points would those be?" she asked.

Min fought the urge to roll her eyes. Brittany's question would sound innocent to anyone who didn't know her. But

Min recognized it as the same tone of voice Brittany had used when she found out Min knew the RA was cheating on her boyfriend and hadn't told her immediately.

Min was going to have a lot to answer for when they were alone.

Hayden, however, didn't seem to know the danger he was in.

"The hotel has excellent French toast," he said blandly. Brittany's eyes flew to Min, wide. *WTF??* Min pretended to take a sip out of her empty glass and ignored her. Hayden continued, "How has your con been going?"

Min managed to elbow Gus in the gut. Robbie's older brother was always quiet, preferring to listen rather than to engage. But he was a good person and knew how to take a hint, thank god.

"We've been enjoying the floor. Hit a few panels, talked with some streamers, and then were watching the tournament. It's always a lot, but it's nice to run into people out here, the ones you don't see every day, you know?"

Hayden nodded. "Definitely."

It's then that Robbie came back, dropping off all the drinks he had been carrying with the skill of a working bartender. He slid Hayden's bourbon toward him while handing Min her rosé. He then pointed to a spot across the room.

"Some seats opened up, but we need to move fast."

Brittany was off like a shot. The competition for seating at Kickoff was fierce no matter where you were, from panels to restaurants. Min tracked Brittany's blonde ponytail until she got to the small table right before another couple and slapped her hand on it with victory. She didn't even blink at the other couple's disappointment, just turned and waved the rest of them over. Brittany was competitive, and her favorite thing in the world was winning.

"Holy shit, she's fast." Hayden was clearly impressed.

Min smiled. "She's got many skills."

The group slowly made their way toward her, but as they got closer Min's stomach dropped. There were only three chairs.

"Um, guys?"

Robbie had claimed a chair and Brittany had already plopped into his lap, taking a sip of her cosmo. She waved a well-manicured hand.

"Min, just pick a lap. It's fine. The boys won't mind."

Min wasn't so sure about that. She looked at Gus, who had a sparkle in his eye that said he was enjoying her discomfort. She had known him for about as long as she had known Robbie. He and Min had always been friendly when they hung out, thrown together by Brittany and Robbie's relationship. Whereas Robbie was friendly, the way a golden retriever was, Gus was more of a lone wolf type. Classically handsome, with olive skin, a hard jaw, and well-kept dark hair, Gus was steady and reliable in a way that could often go unnoticed if you didn't pay attention. Min had always wondered if he actually enjoyed hanging out with Robbie and Brittany, considering how extroverted they both were. But he always showed up when invited, and he seemed like the kind of guy who wouldn't be anywhere he didn't want to be.

Before she could say anything she was tugged, hard, losing her balance and landing right in Hayden's lap, her hand automatically going to his chest for balance. She blinked at him, shocked.

"Hayden, what the fuck?"

His face was closer than she had expected, so his eyes were

only inches from her, blazing with a darkness that took her breath away.

"If you think you're sitting in another guy's lap right in front of me you are severely asking for punishment." He was speaking so low he was practically growling.

Min was caught, couldn't look away, his heat and the smell of his clean aftershave surrounding her. In a possessive gesture, one of his hands slid from her knee up to her outside thigh and tugged her closer to him, settling her. Her side burned as it came into firm contact with his chest.

"Punishment? Like you'd put me in time out?" Her outraged voice was barely a whisper.

His other hand had been on her back, but now it slipped lower, down her spine to the top of her buttocks, and he gave her a quick smack that jolted straight through her.

"Among other things."

Min felt her mouth gape open but he was apparently done talking about it, turning instead to her friends, who barely seemed to notice Min and Hayden. Brittany, however, gave Min a look that made it very clear they were going to have some words about this.

But Brittany was soon distracted by the menu. She was someone who took food very seriously. "I need something hot and fried. Min, want to split some fries?"

Min tried to pull herself out of whatever haze Hayden had created around her, but she was slow. "Um, sure."

Hayden grabbed a menu and held it up for them both to stare at, but Min couldn't read anything. She was too focused on every single part of her body that was touching every single part of Hayden's. Her breathing turned uneven with the memory of everything that body had done to hers last night, and she squirmed a little. In response, his hand on her thigh gripped her tighter.

"Stop."

"Your legs are going to fall asleep."

His voice again rumbled in her ear. "I'm more worried about what body part you're going to wake up if you keep moving like that. In case you couldn't tell, we're not really in a place for me to be able to do something about it."

Min froze, staring at him, and he stared right back, not at all bothered that he was apparently talking about his erection to her in a packed public space.

Brittany, thank god, saved her. "Min? What about you?"

Min turned to find the server patiently staring at her. She panicked.

"Chicken fingers?"

The waiter turned to Hayden, who ordered the same, and then left. Luckily, Brittany was chatty and quickly filled the table with cheerful stories about how their con adventure had been going so far. Her friends pulled Hayden into conversation, and Min could feel him loosen a little, that their openness and lack of guile was letting him put his guard down just enough to hopefully enjoy himself. When the food came, there was some awkward shuffling as Min turned, adjusting herself, now straddling one of Hayden's legs, facing the table, her back to his chest. She tried to give him as much personal space as she could, but he just splayed a hand on her stomach and pulled her ass flush to him.

And fuck, she could feel how hard he was.

A light laugh tinkled from across the table. Min's eyes flew to Brittany, who was sitting with a smug look on her face smirking at Min while she inhaled french fries at an ungodly rate. Gus tucked into his salad and Robbie took a bite of his burger before turning back to Hayden.

"So, Hayden, who are you rooting for in the Bleeding Sword tournament?"

Min froze mid-bite. Her curiosity was burning.

"I've got a few favorites, but probably DeathsHead."

Brittany snorted, rolling her eyes with derision. "Ugh, that guy. There's no way. FlameThrower is going to tear his ass up and hand it to him."

Hayden chuckled, and Min felt it all along her back. "I don't know. He's pretty good."

"He's arrogant, but he's careful," Robbie said, thoughtful. "He knows Flame is there, so his best bet is to not get over-confident."

Hayden grinned. "I don't think Death would ever approach FlameThrower with anything but caution."

Brittany was still riled up at his answer. "He's gonna lose, and he's gonna lose hard. Min here can't stand him."

Min could feel Hayden's eyes on her, and she sure didn't want to get involved so she just shoved as much chicken finger in her mouth as she could.

"Really, Min, I about died when I saw you wearing his shirt. The shirt of the enemy. How could you?" Brittany shook her head in disgust, and that made Min grin as she swallowed. Brittany was, among other things, exceedingly loyal. It was one of the many things Min loved about her.

"I didn't have a lot of choices. Someone broke into my room yesterday and vandalized my stuff. I had to make do." Min took another bite as three pairs of eyes focused on her, shocked, and she remembered that she hadn't actually mentioned that yet. Whoops.

"What the fuck Min? Is that why you called me last night?

When I asked you about it you said it was just a pocket dial. Are you okay? Do you have a place to stay? Do you need clothes? How could you not tell me?" Brittany was in full mama bear mode, throwing down the fry she was holding and looking ready to leap across the table and either hug Min or strangle her. Or both.

Min waved her down. "The hotel is cleaning my room, and I picked up some clothes today on the floor. It's fine."

Gus chimed in. "If you had to wait for the hotel to clean your room, then where did you stay last night?"

Min opened her mouth and then quickly shut it, remembering the actual answer that she absolutely did not want to tell a table of her friends out in public at a bar. She felt herself heat up, an entire body blush taking over her as her eyes glanced behind her, no idea what to say.

Hayden stepped in. "She crashed with me."

Silence took over the table as her closest friends realized there was more to Hayden than Min had mentioned. Brittany sat up straighter.

"She crashed with you? A guy she met once before running into on the train here?"

Hayden didn't look away from Brittany, meeting her eyes with a challenge.

"Yes."

That was it. *Yes.* As if that would calm down Brittany's sudden suspicion and big-sister protective urges. Min's brain came crashing back to earth, realizing she needed to work fast. Brittany was only about five foot two, but her punch could knock a grown man out when she was mad enough. Min had seen it happen.

"We knew each other before. From online. We only just met in person in LA. He's staying in the same hotel, and he offered, so it made sense. Besides, your hotel room is always packed with your entire wardrobe. I didn't want to spend the night cuddling with your socks."

Brittany was a fashion streamer, which meant when she traveled, she brought almost every item of clothing she owned in order to show her followers how to put together different outfits for various situations. And though tonight she was channeling Marilyn, her tense shoulders and her glare made it clear just how fast her stilettos could become weapons.

Min looked at Robbie, trying to psychically convey that he needed to get his girlfriend in line. Robbie, dense as ever, completely missed it, but luckily Gus saw. He set his beer down with a louder clink than necessary.

"Leave Min's sex life alone." Min groaned, not really what she had been expecting. It didn't do much to calm Brittany, but she at least looked less likely to slash tires. She turned her glare to her boyfriend's brother.

"Min's sex life is my business." Brittany then turned back to Min, pointing with a perfectly manicured coffin-shaped gel nail. "And you. Next time someone trashes your hotel room you *tell me*."

Min nodded. "Yes, mother."

Brittany made a face at her, but laughed, the tension breaking. They settled into the night with the conversation flowing. Hayden was quiet at first, but Min could feel him relax as the evening went on. The drinks were, in turn, helping her to relax, sinking into Hayden, his arm still wrapped around her as he sipped his bourbon. During a lull in conversation, she felt his mouth at her ear.

"How you feeling, babe?"

"Like I'm having the best time. You?" She tensed, waiting for his answer, worried that he secretly hated her friends. If he did, she would have to get off of her new favorite spot on his lap. And she really didn't want to do that.

Hayden immediately put her at ease. "I'm having fun, don't worry. I meant more how sober are you feeling? Out of curiosity?"

She turned fully to look at him, seeing his eyes flare at her movements, desire, and possession and something else in his gaze making her lose her breath.

"For curiosity's sake?"

He nodded, his grip on her thigh tightening.

"I've only had two drinks and was going to switch to water. Buzzed enough for a good time, but sober enough for, um, consent purposes. In theory."

"In theory," he echoed, and Min could feel the sparks between them growing, igniting, her hand rising to his cheek seemingly of its own volition. Their mouths inching closer to each other.

"Ugh, get a room already."

A french fry hit Min in the head, and she jumped, turning to Brittany, who was simultaneously trying to look mad and hide the urge to laugh.

"Did you just throw a french fry at me?" Min asked, outraged.

"Yes, because you're ignoring me. We're gonna head to another bar downtown. It apparently has themed alcoholic slushies that all taste like sweet battery acid. Wanna come?"

Min could feel Hayden's eyes on her, but he didn't say anything, letting her take the lead. She knew if she agreed, he would come with her to what sounded like a gimmicky bar with terrible drinks. But he was letting her make her choice. Finally, she shook her head.

"No, I think we're gonna head out."

They all stood up, hugging Min goodbye while Hayden shook the guys' hands. Brittany held her too long, whispering in her ear.

"I expect to hear every dirty detail that you've been keeping from me. I'm talking length. Width. Number of orgasms, location of hands at all times—"

"Get off me, you pervert." Min was laughing as she pushed Brittany away, blushing even as she let Hayden take her hand and lead her to the door. Brittany yelled after her.

"I'm not fucking kidding, Min!"

Min laughed the whole way until finally they were outside. The cool night air and the sudden silence came as a shock to her overheated senses. Hayden kept walking, glancing back at her.

"What was that about?"

Well, there was no way she was actually telling him, absolutely not.

"Just Brittany being herself."

He sent her a look, like he knew she was hiding something, but instead of calling her on it he just pulled her next to him, wrapping his arm around her shoulders. She felt his lips in her hair.

"How was your tournament?" he asked. Min poked him in his side, hard.

"You finished before me, don't act like you didn't watch." She held her breath, hoping he had watched, hoping he stalked her just as much as she watched him. He laughed.

"I may have caught the end."

"Were you impressed? Scared? Turned on?"

"Would you believe all three?" He looked at her then with such affection that Min didn't know what to do, what to feel. When Hayden looked at her, like he was trying to commit everything about her to memory to play over in his head later, she could feel herself melting.

"Yeah, DeathsHead!"

Min jumped, turning to see the group of guys that were walking past them, heading toward the bar they had just left. They all cheered when they saw her shirt, a few showing off their own DeathsHead shirts. Min gave them a weak thumbs up, which made the guys cheer.

"He's gonna kick FlameThrower's ass tomorrow! She doesn't stand a chance!"

They all cheered, and Min's smile froze on her face. She felt colder than she had the entire weekend. She could feel Hayden's eyes on hers, studying her. She started to pull away, but his grip tightened on her shoulder.

"Don't."

Still, Min stepped back, wrapping her arms around herself. She found herself staring at the wall behind her, the street, anything but him.

"Don't what?" she asked, knowing she was being a brat.

"Don't pull away. Tell me what's going through your head."

She shook her head, her emotions zigging and zagging all over the place, leaving her unable to pinpoint them enough for her to explain.

But she tried. "Hayden, we're competitors."

"So?"

She gave a sad laugh at that. "So, what's going to happen tomorrow? I don't know how I'll feel if I lose, Hayden. I know that sucks. I know it's immature of me, but I need this money. I need the sponsorship. If you beat me... I know it's unfair to say this, but I don't know how I'll feel."

"Are you saying you want me to throw the tournament?"

She immediately shook her head. "Hell, no."

"Then you want me to withdraw?"

"No, you should be there. You're one of the best players, probably *the* best player, you can't not be there. It won't feel like winning without you."

She still wasn't looking at him, but she felt him move closer, his hand going to her neck, wrapping around her and tipping up her chin, forcing her to meet his sharp gaze.

"Min, the money from the tournament would bring me that much closer to making my game a reality. Making my *dream* a reality. I've been working on this for years. I can't just walk away from this opportunity."

She closed her eyes, unable to take his intensity. "I know."

"Look at me." Her eyes flew open, once again caught in his as his thumb stroked her jaw. "You are the best player I've ever competed against. I won't go easy on you. I won't let you win. I'm going to make you earn it. You better come ready to give your all, because that's what I want. That's what I've always wanted."

She gulped, hearing the honesty in his voice. "That's what I want, too."

"And when it's over, no matter who wins, you and I are going to talk and figure this out. Because if you think you're walking away from me after this weekend, then baby, you haven't been paying attention."

He kissed her then, hard, anger and desperation mixing as he tried to convince her with his kiss to keep fighting with him, but also to keep fighting for them. Min did her best to try and answer his kiss with her own, letting her tongue slip into his mouth, wanting to claim whatever she could for as long as she was able.

He was the one to pull away first.

"Min, the things I want to do to your body are not for a public street."

"Then why are we still here?" He smiled at that, kissing her one more time before grabbing her hand and tugging her after him, urgent to get back to the hotel. And she couldn't blame him, doing her best to keep up because she was on fire and if she didn't have him soon she was going to destroy everything.

They somehow made it to the trolley, Hayden shoving his way in and pulling her with him. Min found herself sandwiched between him and over a hundred other people, everyone shoved into everyone else's space, people everywhere. There were no seats available, standing room only as Min found herself trapped in the middle of the car next to one of the balance poles. She only had time to wonder if she'd even be able to find the room to breathe when the doors to the trolley shut, sealing them all in together. She tried to shuffle to get a little space, but there wasn't really any to be had. Any direction she moved, she bumped into people.

Hayden's arm came around her from behind, pushing her toward the pole while also pulling her so tight against him she could feel his hardness against her ass. His other hand landed on the pole in front of them, keeping them stable.

"Relax," he whispered in her ear, his hand on her stomach as he anchored her against him. She grabbed the pole in front of her on instinct and glanced around them. No one was paying them any attention. Hell, no one was even able to see anything below their shoulders, they were all packed in so tight. She leaned back to whisper to him, praying her voice wouldn't carry through the trolley.

"How can I relax when I can feel you?" She wiggled her butt for emphasis, not able to stop herself. His hand flexed on her stomach, the friction of his jeans on her backside feeling so perfect through her skirt that she bit back a frustrated moan. He froze, and Min could feel his mind working, like he was figuring something out. A soft chuckle hit her ear, sounding evil and seductive and delighted.

"Oh, Min," he whispered. "I think I know one of your secrets."

And then she felt his hand on her stomach slip lower.

She couldn't see his face—there was no room to turn around, no room for any sort of movement. But his chest was pressed into her back, and she was so close the sides of his open hoodie came around her, pulling her deeper into his warmth. She sent another glance around her, reassured that everyone on the train was caught up in their own lives, chatting with their friends, singing nerdy songs, deep into several cocktails, and paying her and Hayden zero attention.

She cleared her throat, staring at the pole in front of her. "What are you doing?"

He didn't answer, simply commanded. "Hold your backpack in front of you."

She shifted her bag, realizing as he must have that it was big enough to block whatever movement his hand was about to commit from anyone who actually managed to see through the bodies pressed tightly together in the car. Combined with the sides of his hoodie engulfing her, even if anyone looked at them, they wouldn't see more than a couple cuddling on the train. Min felt herself shiver as her imagination ran wild. She tried to grasp on to her quickly fleeing common sense. There were rules against something like this, right?

"Hayden, we're on the trolley. There are a ton of people here."

She felt his hot breath as he pressed his lips to her ear. "No one can see. They're not paying us any attention, completely caught up in their own worlds. Not knowing that I'm over here dying to feel your pussy."

His hand slipped even lower, more bold with her backpack covering him, and she felt his fingers attempt to tickle the inside of her thighs below the hem of her skirt. She instinctively held them close together, clamped tight with her desire and nerves.

His lips caressed her ear. "Baby, you need to help me out here."

"Hayden…"

His voice dipped even lower as his hand stroked her thigh.

"Min, spread your fucking legs for me. Now."

She felt her legs move before it registered what she was doing. His exhale of relief hit her ear as his hand finally slipped between her thighs, caressing her possessively as they moved higher up her body.

"Good girl," he whispered in her ear, and she shivered.

His fingers softly brushed against her underwear before dipping inside to stroke her lightly with one finger. She bit her lip, her eyes everywhere as she tried to make sure no one was watching them.

"Goddamnit, Min. You are so fucking wet."

She wondered vaguely if she was out of her mind for letting him touch her like this. But she also knew she wouldn't stop him. Hayden's touch was everything she craved, and a very surprised part of her brain told her that she trusted him. That was astonishing enough, considering she would never have agreed to something like this with Alex. But Hayden was different. He knew all about what her shithead ex had done and still wanted her with a need that pulsed through her. Last night she had felt how important it was to him to take care of her. Even here, on the trolley, with his hand in her panties, she felt cherished. Worshipped.

His fingers moved, stroking her slowly, the movement barely noticeable except on her clit, where he teased her with a rhythm that was driving her out of her mind. She shuffled her feet, bracing her legs even wider, clutching her bag in front of her like a lifeline. She stared at where his hand was gripping the balance pole, keeping them steady, and she licked her lips at the strength she saw in his hand. God, she had it bad. There was no real way to turn to look at him, but she could just imagine his face, the fake bored expression he was wearing to hide what they were doing. Her breath hitched as his hand stroked deeper.

"Min, you can't come here. Not if you don't want everyone knowing what we're doing." Even as he warned her, Min felt him slip a finger inside of her, stroking until he found a spot that made her nerve endings come alive. Attempting to look as innocent as possible, she pressed herself harder into his hand.

"I can be quiet," she lied, and could feel his deep chuckle against her back as it rumbled through him.

"No, you can't. You like to scream, and it makes me hard just thinking about it."

"Then stop touching me so I can calm down." She didn't mean it. She'd probably let out a scream if he pulled his hand away, which would definitely turn heads. But he was being such a jerk about it that she couldn't help but challenge him like she always did.

In response, he added a second finger inside her and increased his rhythm, pushing in and out of her so incrementally she thought she'd die. "I don't want you calm, baby. I want you crying my name like a prayer. I want you on fire."

Hayden's fingers kept up their rhythm while his hips

pushed her from behind. The feel of his erection had her biting her lip to keep a moan from slipping through. He kept rubbing, slowly, and a wave of arousal rolled through her entire body, landing on her center where he was stoking her flame. Her insides clenched, making her light-headed.

"Hayden—"

The trolley car took a hard turn, jolting the crowd. Hayden pushed Min harder into the pole to keep her steady, his cock grinding into her ass through his jeans as she struggled for balance. Luckily, she managed to keep her backpack in front of her while they jolted. Once the car settled into its normal rocking rhythm, Hayden let go of the pole, letting her anchor them, letting his hand trail up her arm until it gripped her neck. The possessiveness of the gesture made her gasp, and she shuddered as her orgasm hit her, doing her best to bite her lip to keep quiet as she spasmed against his hand. He was holding her still, so hard against his chest to hide her jerking movements, his lips on the pulse at her neck as she came apart.

The trolley rocked as it slowed down for a stop, people jostling, and Hayden's hands left her, their sudden absence making her groan. His hand went under her shirt to her stomach, wiping her wetness there, and something about it had her shaking, needing more, needing him to use her body and fill her so tight and hard that she broke into a million pieces. She turned to stare at him, their eyes so close she could see the strands of silver near his pupils. Hayden's gaze devoured her. People moved around them, some exiting the trolley, some just finding a more comfortable spot. But Min and Hayden stayed right where they were, his hand on her stomach, hers on the pole, still holding her bag in front of her. She licked her lips and his eyes followed the movement so intensely that she couldn't help but squirm.

"Stop," he warned. "Or else everyone here is going to see how hard I am for you."

"Don't threaten me with a good time."

He kissed her then, softly, behind her ear, and she melted at the tenderness of it, rocking into him as the trolley started moving again. His hand slid against her, this time heading up, caressing her skin until he was tickling the lace of her bra. She didn't even bother glancing around, didn't really care who was watching as long as he kept touching her. But he stopped right under where she really wanted him, gripping her around the ribs as his thumb idly brushed the underside of her breast.

"Tonight, I'm going to put my mouth on every fucking inch of you, Min. I want to taste you everywhere until you're exploding and screaming my name."

She shuddered at that, the words sinking into her soul, her thighs even wetter.

"Why the hell did we stay so far from the convention center?" She sounded desperate even to her own ears and cringed. She felt him smile against her, his thumb still caressing her lazily.

"Privacy, Min. I want you all to myself."

The doors to the trolley opened then, and Min realized they had arrived at their stop. Hayden placed one more kiss to her ear before pulling back and grabbing her hand.

"Come on, baby. I have plans for you."

CHAPTER 15

HAYDEN

Hayden wasn't sure when during the evening he had lost his mind, but if he had to guess, it would be around the time he saw Min across the bar. Since then, he had been fighting this pulsing need to drag her away from prying eyes and claim her in a way that would leave them both completely ruined. Even now, after discovering the exhibition kink she kept well-hidden and making her come in the trolley, he was already missing his hands on her body. The only thing he could think now was that he needed Min, upstairs, naked in his room, before he combusted. His blood was hot, pumping, all heading down south and leaving very little for critical thinking as he practically dragged her into their hotel by her hand. He was pulling her behind him and making a beeline toward the elevators.

"Oh, Ms. Hayes?" The voice barely registered to Hayden, but he felt Min tug on his hand, stopping him. He turned and frowned at her, and she rolled her eyes, heading to the front desk, leaving him no choice but to follow. The hotel staffer waiting threw her a big smile.

"I'm happy to tell you your hotel room has been thoroughly cleaned and is back to how it should be. Your things, as they were returned by the police, have been stored inside. We've also gone ahead and had the lock reprogrammed. I have your new keys here."

He slid a little paper across the counter to Min, which she picked up. Hayden had never hated a hotel key more. But the staffer, clearly not reading Hayden's vibe, or maybe just completely ignoring him, went on.

"I'm again sorry such a thing happened. We've submitted our security tapes to the police and are cooperating to the fullest."

Min cleared her throat. "Did you find anything? In the tapes?"

He looked at her with sympathy. "Someone in a large dark hoodie with their face covered."

"So could be anyone, is what you're saying." Hayden could practically see her deflate at the news.

"We're leaving that up for the police to deal with. They mentioned they would send you the footage to see if you recognized anyone, so you'll probably be hearing from them tomorrow. Meanwhile, we've also stationed a security guard on your floor for the duration of your stay. Please let us know if there's absolutely anything else we can do to assist you during your time here with us."

Min bit her lip, looking down at her new keys.

"Thanks."

She stepped away as the staffer told her to have a good night, still staring at her new keycard until she was standing right in front of Hayden. When she finally looked up, there was uncertainty in her eyes that Hayden hated. Here he was, practically burning for her, and she was clearly rethinking everything. Now that she had her own room, the energy between them had changed. And although he would probably go blind beating himself off in the shower if she changed her mind about him, he couldn't blame her if she needed to decompress from the convention and everything that had happened by herself. In her room. Alone.

But he fucking hated it.

Without talking, they walked to the elevators and got in, joining an older couple wearing matching Batman shirts who looked extremely exhausted and a little drunk. Hayden hit the button for their floor, and he leaned against the wall, Min leaning on the opposite wall.

He hated that, too.

He stared at her over the heads of the other couple, noting that she was a little pale. Her mouth that had been smiling all night was now pinched into a flat line. And her eyes were distant, like she was caught in her own thoughts. Hayden used the quiet in the elevator to remember the night they had shared, to run through everything they had said and done, and he realized that, besides last night when she had kissed him, he had always been the one to instigate, always been pulling her toward him. Hadn't been able to help himself. But now, thinking about it, maybe she had been trying to pull away and he had been too far gone for her to realize. That wasn't like him. His heart tried to reject his new theory, but here they were, her with her room back and him without a way to convince her to stay.

He just... wanted her to. Desperately, if he was being honest with himself.

But that wasn't fair. Especially after everything she had been through before they had met, after everything that fuckhead Alex had done. Hayden found that if she didn't want to stay, he wasn't going to try to change her mind. Her last lover had taken a lot of choices away from her. Hayden could at least give her this.

The elevator dinged, and they were suddenly there, on their floor, the promised security guard seated in the lobby area, nodding at them before he went back to his newspaper. Hayden followed Min down the hall toward their rooms, the walk feeling both too long and too short at the same time. Once there, she froze, turning toward him but still not meeting his eyes. Her mouth opened a couple times, then closed, like she couldn't figure out what she wanted to say. The silence, once awkward, was now deafening. Hayden couldn't stand it anymore.

"Look, I get it. It's been a long day, especially for you, on top of how tiring the con usually is. Plus, the final tournament is tomorrow. We both need to be on our A games. If you want to call it a night and just… well, I get it." He couldn't even look at her when he said it, infusing as much nonchalance into his voice as he could, all the while hating the taste of the words in his mouth even though he knew they were what she was wanting to hear. "It's up to you."

Her eyes were on him then, but he couldn't figure out what she was thinking. Only that Min was holding back. She exhaled a long breath. "Okay. If that's what you want. Can I… can I just grab my stuff from your room?"

Hayden closed his eyes and turned, unlocking his door and opening it for her. She walked in, her scent of apple and promises hitting him like a punch to the gut as she entered. He took a deep breath in spite of himself. He let the door shut behind him, leaning against it as he watched her grab her clothes, her leggings, her bag of things she had managed to save from the vandalism. It wasn't a lot, and he was disappointed at how quickly she managed to completely erase her presence from his room.

But then he watched as she shoved everything into her bag a little too violently, the movement jagged in a way that he wasn't expecting from her. When Hayden dared to look at her face, he found her eyes were flashing with anger. She was practically vibrating with it. *What the hell?*

"You're mad." He kept his voice neutral, not sure why she was mad, but needing any excuse to keep her here, talking to him, for even a little bit longer.

"Yeah, Hayden. To be honest I'm fucking furious." She looked up at him then and he almost recoiled with the fire he found there, all aimed at him. He couldn't hide his surprise.

"Why?"

"Look, if you're not interested, I'd prefer if you'd just, you know, act not interested all the time. This hot and cold waffling, one minute pushing me away and the next treating me like I'm fucking precious—"

"You *are* precious."

The words slipped out of him with no thought from his brain. He couldn't have stopped them if he tried. But that clearly pissed her off even more.

"Fuck you." She finished zipping her bag with a violent swipe and swung it over her shoulder. For a second, Hayden wondered if she was going to hit him with it.

"I'm gonna need you to walk me through this, baby, because I'm lost."

She pointed an accusatory finger at him. "Don't call me that. Not when you're in the middle of kicking me out."

A jolt of lightning went through Hayden's body, and he jerked up, no longer leaning against the door. His heart started beating again, loudly. She could probably hear it.

"I am not kicking you out. You're choosing to leave." He was cautious, not wanting to get too hopeful but hell if this woman's temper didn't ignite him.

"After you told me to, Hayden. What do you expect me to do?"

"I didn't tell you to leave. I gave you the option. You're the one packing."

"Well, fuck you, because I don't want to leave." She stormed up to him, barely coming to his chin even in those ridiculous heels she was wearing, and she poked him in the chest so hard he was sure there would be a bruise. In fact, he hoped there would be.

He stood straighter, looming over her, bringing himself so close he could feel her breasts against his chest. Could feel her nipples harden against him in a way that had him fighting for calm.

"Good," he told her, his voice dropping several octaves. "I don't want you to."

That statement somehow seemed to let the air out of her tires, the fire leaving her eyes, replaced by confusion.

"You don't?"

"Of course not. I just don't want you to feel like you don't have any options other than to stay with me. You haven't been treated well in the past, Min. It makes me crazy to think about." His hand came up to cup her face, and he leaned closer, inhaling her. "But I want you. I want you so bad my fucking teeth are rattling with it. If you want to leave, I'll respect your choice. But if there's a chance you'll let me inside you, then, baby, I'm willing to beg."

Hayden was close enough to watch her pupils blow wide, her gorgeous brown eyes swallowed by the darkness of desire. He could feel her breath come faster, her chest heaving against his, those fucking lips so close he wanted to drown in them.

She rattled out a breath as she ran a shaky hand through her hair. "You talk too much."

The words were barely out of her mouth before Hayden was on her, his mouth slamming against hers, his arms wrapping around her, scooping her up against him. When Min wrapped her legs around his waist, holding him tight and hot, he was fucking lost. There was no coming back from this.

Not breaking their kiss, he walked them the few steps to the large, floor-to-ceiling window before letting her feet down on the ground, making sure to slide her down his body to torture them both. She moaned in his mouth as his tongue stroked hers. His hands slid up her body, needing to touch every part of her, frantic to memorize the shape of her. Hayden caressed her arms locked around his neck before pulling them away, pressing her wrists against the tall window behind her. The curtains were wide open, and the glass felt cool where it brushed his hands, but his entire focus was on Min as she pulled back, her eyes flaring with confusion.

"Gee, this feels familiar." Her tone was sardonic and it had him smiling, his mouth already watering for another taste of her. Hayden couldn't resist giving her one small peck on her nose before he grabbed her hips and spun her, quick, wanting to hear her gasp of surprise. He slid up to her hands again, setting them on the window on either side of her head, pushing her into the window with his hips.

"These hands don't move from this window." He could feel her shudder, could see the goose bumps racing down her arms and he loved it, loved having her under his hands and so turned on she couldn't think straight.

"And what if I do?" she challenged, her voice low and

husky with desire. He grinned into her neck, his hands sliding down her arms to her torso. He found her breasts, gripping them, massaging them through her shirt, through her bra. He took a moment to put his mouth to her ear and gently bit her lobe at the exact moment his fingers circled her hard nipples and pinched them. She squealed.

"I don't recommend it, baby girl." He loosened his grip, letting his fingers tease her sweet nipples, relishing her moans. Finally, Hayden let his hands slide lower, gripping her thighs through her hot pink miniskirt and yanking her back against him. He leaned into her neck, planting a kiss right where it connected with her shoulder before nipping her, biting, wanting to leave his mark for everyone to see that she was his. At the same time, he pulled her skirt up, pulling her hips further back toward him so that she leaned into the window, her hands bracing her weight, leaving her body completely open to the window. They were in one of the highest buildings in the city, so the chances of them being seen were low. But after the trolley Hayden couldn't help but love the idea of the city going about its business, unaware that they could look up and watch Min writhe and moan just for him.

Her skirt bunched at her waist, Hayden stepped back to take in the view, admiring Min's round ass. The underwear he had only felt before he could now see was a thin, hot pink silky thong, cutting straight through the beautiful cleft of her ass. His cock practically jumped at the sight. He took a moment to adjust himself in his jeans and to think desperately of rotten food, of sports statistics, of literally anything that would help him find his control. Hayden needed for this to last, for this to be good for Min. He couldn't risk losing it and scaring her.

Her ass wiggled with impatience. "Um, you getting bored back there?"

He answered her with a loud smack, loving how she jumped at the contact on her ass. Fascinated with how red it turned from the impact.

"Just considering my options. Christ, Min, you're so fucking beautiful."

"I can't believe you just spanked me." Hayden smirked. Her words were outraged, but he could hear how aroused she was, could already see how wet it made her.

"Min, I never want to hear you imply that I'm bored with you. Not when I'm staring at this gorgeous pussy debating whether my tongue or my cock is going to be inside you first."

He slipped his hands into the sides of her underwear, slowly peeling them down her legs, letting them fall and leaving her bare. Hayden's hungry eyes absorbed the sight, grabbing her ass and massaging the cheeks before pulling them apart so he could study every inch of her. The sight of her, her tight pucker right above her sweet pussy ripped a groan straight from his chest.

"Hayden, touch me, please." She sounded desperate, as desperate as Hayden felt staring at her. He glanced up, seeing her reflection in the window, biting her lip, bracing herself.

He took a deep breath. "Don't move your hands from that window."

And then he dropped to his knees, his palms keeping her spread as he finally, finally buried his face deep into her. His tongue lapped, pressing, slipping in between every barrier she had, her taste, everything he remembered and more, a taste he had fantasized about all day and already couldn't wait to have again. She pushed back against him, silently urging him on, and he gripped her tighter, keeping her still, wanting her so still while he did everything he had been dreaming about doing to her. He felt like he had been starving, ravenous for her, and now that he had her she wasn't going anywhere until he had his fill. His thoughts were wild, racing over memories of what they had done and mixing them with every fantasy he had ever had. His need made him pause to take a shaky breath. Grasping for control.

"No, don't stop," she told him, desperation and desire and something else in her voice, something that he felt tug through his chest and grip him. He vaguely noticed her legs were trembling, but one glance showed him that she had kept her hands on the window, not daring to move them even when she was gasping with need.

Good.

"What do you want, baby?" He said it near her, into her, letting her swallow his voice and feel it inside. She was shaking, attempting to push her hips back into him. But he kept himself back, simply laying sweet kisses on her thigh, her lips, ghosting a kiss over her clit that he could feel made her clench. He wanted to hear her say the words.

"I need…" She stopped, attempting to grind back into him, but Hayden pulled further back.

"Use your words, Min. Tell me what you want."

"You, Hayden. I want to feel you inside me." Satisfaction ripped through him, and he pressed into her, devouring her, his tongue pushing inside her with a rhythm he felt in his soul. At her broken cry, he brought a hand around, pressing her back against him, letting his fingers find her clit and swirl. Her knees buckled, but he held her tight.

"Fuck, Hayden. Fuck." He felt her tighten, felt everything in her clenching, and he pressed the heel of his hand against her, rubbing her, fierce, needing her to find oblivion.

"Now, Minerva. I need to feel you shatter."

And she did, her entire body shaking as he held her tight against him, his tongue and hand continuing their work as he held her up, her cries filling him in a way he hadn't even known he was empty. His entire body was on fire for her as she shuddered and moaned his name and drenched his mouth with her orgasm and he knew without a doubt that he would never be the same.

CHAPTER 16
MIN

When Min came back to earth after the entire body meltdown she just experienced from her orgasm, Hayden was laying gentle kisses on the back of her thighs while his hand lightly caressed her pussy. His rough possessive touch from before was now soothing, petting, and she relaxed against him. She opened her eyes and it took her a moment to remember she was staring out a large window over a dark city.

"First the trolley, and now in front of a window. For someone so hellbent on his privacy, you sure seem to love making me come in public places."

He placed a gentle kiss higher up on her thigh, his hand still caressing her lightly.

"And you love it," he said into her skin. "You should've heard your breath when I touched you on that crowded trolley. I had you shaking and wet within seconds of getting my hands on you. I'm going to have a hard-on every time I take public transportation from now on because of you."

Min's breath caught at his dirty words. "That's... that's ridiculous. I've never... I've never wanted—"

Hayden cut her off. "Yeah, you have. My guess is that you've just dated assholes who you didn't really trust to play with. But I'm here now, baby girl, and if it gets you dripping for me then I'm more than game."

A shudder ran through her body before she could stop it, and his satisfaction was almost a physical entity she could feel.

"Well, we'll have to agree to disagree. Can I move now? Before someone gets their telescope out." She tried to sound tart, but her words came out weaker than she had expected.

Min felt him smile against her. He laid one last, lingering kiss on her core before pulling back, letting his hands run up her body as he got to his feet. He slid his fingers under the shirt she was wearing—*his* shirt—and pulled it over her head. The bra was gone in another moment, her skirt following it, and then she was standing naked in front of the window with her hands still pressed against it. Min heard him step back and she shivered, immediately missing his heat, a little bereft at the loss of him. She started to drop her hands but his harsh voice stopped her.

"No."

Confused, she turned to look at him, their eyes meeting as she registered the wild, feral look as his gaze slid everywhere over her body. She must be a sight, naked except for her heels, slightly bent over with her bottom sticking out, everything exposed just for him. She stepped her legs closer, rubbing her thighs together, annoyed with him even as she could feel how turned on she was from his stare.

"Hayden?"

His eyes ran over her, landing on her pussy, and it was like she could feel it there, caressing her.

"You're so beautiful, Min. Standing there, wrecked and bent over, presenting yourself just for me. I want to imprint this moment on my brain."

Min realized he was still dressed, leaving her feeling vulnerable and excited. She dragged her eyes down his body, lingering on his crotch for so long his hand went there and tugged.

Hayden took in a ragged breath. "Min, I swear to god, sometimes I think I could come just from how you look at me."

Her eyes met his. "Take off your clothes."

His shirt was gone before she finished her sentence. His hands went to the fastenings of his jeans, flicking the button open, teasing her, watching her watch him.

Min's mouth went dry. "Hurry."

He grabbed her chin then, pulling her up so their eyes locked, suddenly so close she couldn't breathe.

"Let me assure you, Min," he told her with that deep, deep voice she would dream about for years. "Hurrying is the absolute last thing I plan on doing."

God, she could feel herself get even wetter at that, her eyes on his as he slowly stepped back and stripped off his jeans, taking his boxers with them until he was completely naked in front of her. Her eyes engulfed him as his hands went to his cock, stroking it with a rhythm Min could feel pulse inside her.

He was massive. Thick and long and beautiful in a way that she had never considered cocks could be. His large hand stroked himself while he stared at every exposed part of her, stirring her in a way she had been certain moments ago wouldn't be able to happen for at least an hour. But the breath she sucked in was shaky as she watched his hand run to the head of his cock, swirling there in the wet precum that was waiting, before stroking back to his base. She was usually a one-orgasm girl, something her previous lovers had appreciated. But staring at Hayden, she knew one wasn't enough, that he wanted everything from her. And her treacherous body was ready to hand it over to him.

Somehow, her mouth was still working. "If you tell me you still don't have condoms, I'm going to fucking kill you."

He chuckled at that, his hands leaving his cock long enough to reach into his bag and pull out several foil-wrapped packages. She would have cried with relief if she wasn't so turned on. She turned to look back out the window as she heard him rip the foil, staring out into the night, suddenly feeling how exposed she was here, naked up against this large window, the lights on behind her.

And then she felt him, his heat radiating at her back, such a stark contrast to the cool glass under her hands that she moaned. His hands came around her, pulling her into him, her back against his hard chest. His hands came around her, grabbing her breasts and kneading in a way that caused sparks behind her eyes. This close, she could feel his hardness pressed right against her, rocking into her slightly as he pushed her closer to the glass, her eyes sliding shut at how good he felt. She wanted to lose herself in him, in the pleasure only he could bring. She craved it.

"Eyes open, baby girl."

Her eyes flew open at the command, finding his in the window's reflection. One of his hands came to hold her around the neck, firm, keeping her still. He pushed her forward, her breasts now pressed against the glass, the chill of it making her shiver. She realized in this position, her entire body was on display in the window. Their hotel was taller than any of the other buildings around them, so there was no chance of a neighbor just glancing over and seeing what they were doing.

But if anyone had a telescope aimed at them, they would see every single part of her, from her tight nipples flat against the glass to her bare pussy. His voice rasped against her ear.

"I'm going to fuck you against this window, Min. We're going to leave a mess here that the hotel staff will see and immediately know what we were doing. That I was deep inside you making you scream my name with the entire city below us not realizing how fucking dirty we are for each other."

He tightened his grip on her neck slightly, just enough to make her gasp, as his other hand slipped down, cupping her, possessive.

"But the neighbors will know. And they'll know I'm the one making you come with how loud you're screaming my name. They'll know without a doubt that this pussy is mine. Do you understand?"

She nodded, not certain her voice would work right now, but it wasn't enough for him.

"Say it, Min."

Her hand slid down, covering his with her own as his grip tightened on her core.

"I'm yours, Hayden," she whispered. "Fuck me already."

The words were barely out of her mouth before he spun her around, his mouth crashing against hers in a kiss so wild it would bruise her, mark her soul as his. Not breaking the kiss, she felt his hands slide to her ass, gripping her and lifting her against him, her legs parting, wrapping around his waist as he pushed her back against the cold window for leverage. The contrast of the cold at her back and his heat at her front made her moan. In response, he pushed against her, his cock sliding between the lips of her pussy, rubbing against that most sensitive part of her while he covered himself with her juices. She ground against him, seeking out the friction he was causing and wanting so much more.

"Hayden," she whimpered, her body on fire and desperate for him to flame her higher. Instead of listening, his mouth moved from hers, kissing her neck, her collarbone, down and down until his mouth found her breast, loving it with his tongue. He groaned into her.

"God, I have been dreaming about these breasts."

He was caressing and circling and teasing her as he moved around her hard nipple, but didn't touch it, driving her crazy. Frustrated, Min dragged a hand into his hair, pulling, hard, her mouth not able to say what she wanted but her body insisting that he stop teasing. And it must have worked, because finally he was there, his tongue swirling on her nipple, sucking on it, biting it. She could feel that bite all the way between her legs where he was still grinding against her, his length rubbing her clit and making her blood pound.

He moved from one nipple to the other, giving it the same attention, one hand coming up to knead the breast now wet from his ministrations. The feeling was wonderful but it wasn't enough. He was large and hard and she wanted him inside her, filling her. Her hands slipped down, grabbing his ass, her nails digging in. He pulled away from her breast with a lick, breathing hard.

"Slow down, baby girl."

"No," she said, one of her hands slipping between them, finding his cock and rubbing it, stroking it as it slid against her. "I need you, Hayden. Now."

His breath shuddered against her. She could feel him fighting his desire, fighting her, so she stroked him with as firm a grip as she could, feeling it shoot through his whole body.

"Please."

The desperation in her voice, along with her grip on his cock, seemed to finally break through whatever barriers he was trying to use to slow them down. The next thing Min knew he was lifting her up higher against the glass before slamming her down on his cock in one long, hard thrust.

"Hayden!"

Min savored the feeling of him inside her, finally filling her and stretching and claiming her. She let out a shaky sigh of relief. Dazed, Min felt her inner muscles clamp down on him lightly as her muscles ticked with the invasion.

His pupils were wide, staring down at her so intensely she wondered if he could see her soul, how hot it was burning for him. Finally, he exhaled, forcing the tension out of his body and he finally rocked up into her, hitting a spot that had previously lay dormant and now made her eyes roll back into her head.

He pulled back, thrusting into her again, the spot he found making her cry with every thrust, calling his name, begging him to fill her, harder and faster. He stayed close, even as he built his rhythm, even as he drove into her harder and harder, his mouth at her ear egging her on.

"Just like that, baby girl. You're so fucking tight, so fucking wet. I want to bury myself inside you and never leave." He thrust even harder at that, her cries going louder, and then he pulled a little away, putting some distance between their torsos, her upper body suddenly cold with the loss of his heat.

"Eyes, Min. See what we look like."

She opened her eyes, having no memory of ever closing them. She followed his gaze down to see where he was inside her. The sight was the most erotic thing she had ever seen. His cock was so large she sent a wave of gratitude to her body for being able to take him. While she watched, he pulled out, slow, her mouth watering with the sudden desire to taste him.

And then, just as slow, he pushed back into her. She felt him inside her, pushing to invade, demanding that she take him fully, and she felt her orgasm rise even closer to the surface.

"You did this, Min. You make me so fucking hard, make me forget my plans to go slow, until all that's left is your wet pussy and my cock dying to slide into you, begging to make you come so I can feel you grab me and hold me inside." His voice was deeper than she had ever heard it, wild with need and heat. But she was beyond words, her moans getting louder and louder as he pushed all the way inside her, demanding everything.

Hayden kept driving into her, each thrust harder than the last, her moans turning to cries as he pushed deeper and deeper inside her. He lifted her higher, a hand going under one of her legs and lifting it up to his shoulder, widening her, changing the angle so that he was now hitting a new, delicious spot, and she heard herself scream as she let go. Her body spasmed, her pussy clamping on him as he shouted, his thrusts becoming frantic and uneven as his own orgasm rose to meet hers, both of them reaching oblivion together.

Her head was on his shoulder when she came back to herself, both of their breathing loud and harsh. His hands were running up and down her back, into her hair, caressing her ass, petting her. When she managed to lift her head, he was already there, kissing her deeply as he kept his arms around her. Vaguely, she felt him shift her weight and pull her away from the window. It was only a moment before the room shifted, and he gently laid her on the bed. His cock slipped out of her when he pulled away, leaving her empty.

"No." She started to sit up, not wanting him to leave her, but he gently pushed her back down, planting a sweet kiss on her jaw.

"Just a minute, baby."

Min stayed on the bed, her legs spread from where he had just been, and felt absolutely no desire to ever move again. She heard him get rid of the condom, heard him splashing in the bathroom until he came back to her.

He scooted her higher up the bed, tucking her under the covers before climbing in next to her. There was some shifting and adjusting until Min found herself draped against him, her head on his chest, one of her legs between his. She had never felt more secure, more cherished than she did in that moment. His heart was beating under her ear, loud and strong, and Min lay there, content to listen to it until it slowed.

"Hayden?" she whispered, not wanting to break the moment.

"Yeah?"

"What the fuck?"

He chuckled, his muscles loose as he pulled her even closer.

"I don't know. But I think I'm starting to figure it out."

She listened as his breath evened out, feeling his body against hers, and felt herself relax, giving in to the exhaustion overtaking her as she was caught against this man who had somehow invaded her life. She barely felt his lips in her hair before she drifted off into sleep.

Min woke as sunlight started coming through the window, realizing too late that neither of them had remembered to close the curtains after they had made love. She stayed still, taking inventory of everything, Hayden's body underneath hers, one hand in her hair, holding her close, one of her legs wrapped around his waist. And something else. Being careful not to jostle him too much, she peeked under the covers. She stared at Hayden's body, studying it in a way she hadn't been able to last night, adjusting her leg so that she had a better look.

He was gorgeous. His hard chest was showcasing muscles Min didn't know a professional gamer could have. Which meant Hayden was a gym bunny, something she was absolutely going to give him shit about when he woke up. Her eyes traced the sharp lines of those muscles, following them down until they landed on his semi-hard cock. Memories of everything they had done last night flit through her mind. As if it could read her thoughts, Hayden's cock grew in front of her eyes, becoming so hard and thick it took her breath away.

"What time is it?" His voice was even deeper in the morning. Min didn't take her gaze away from his cock since it was clearly loving the attention of her watching.

"Still early."

"Mmmm…" was his only answer, but Min could hear the anticipation there, and felt a matching thrum inside her core.

The covers moved as Hayden pushed them down, his erection now casting a shadow in the morning light coming from the window and Min was licking her lips before she could think. She slid a hand down his chest, letting them roam over those abs.

"So. You go to the gym."

"I have a home gym."

"Oh god, you're one of those." She shook her head mockingly.

"A guy with a garage and a set of weights?"

"A gym rat. You probably flirt with girls by telling them what you bench."

"The only bench I want to tell you about is the one I want to bend you over."

She lost her breath. Her hand moved down, tracing the light trail of dark hair marking a path right to where she wanted to be. She slid further south, her touch light as she caressed his full length.

"Fuck, Min."

He shifted, and she felt empowered, loving how quickly he lost it with her touch, how it took only one more light stroke before his tip was wet with precum. She touched it with her finger, bringing it to her mouth for a taste, and his groan vibrated the bed. She looked at him then, her finger still in her mouth, to find his eyes hot on hers, drowning with fire and desire and desperation.

Min sat up, still naked from the night before, and pushed the rest of the covers away. On her knees beside him, she took one of his hands, guiding it to her head. With her encouragement, she felt his fingers clench in her hair near her scalp, holding her firmly. And then she leaned over, her breath hot against him as she slowly, so slowly, licked his cock from base to tip.

"God*damn*," Hayden whispered, almost to himself. His legs shifted and he shook his head, clearly trying to bring himself under control in a way that had Min smiling. "Min, you don't have to do this. I don't want you to feel pressured—"

"Shut up, Hayden." Her command was direct, fierce, her eyes never leaving his cock but she could feel it twitch when she spoke. "This cock is mine, and I'm hungry. So the only thing I want to hear you say is my name as you fuck my mouth."

And with that, she took him, pushed him into her as far as she could get, wrapping her hand around the base for help as she focused on loosening her throat. She heard her name rip out of him as she came back up, trying again, taking him deeper the second time and humming with satisfaction. She brought her hand up to his balls, gently cupping them, massaging him, and could feel Hayden's hand on her head, pushing her down further, loving how desperate he was for her, wanting to take as much of that huge cock as she could. She felt powerful, alive, as she brought this huge, sexy man to frantically cry out her name.

"Min, I'm coming." He bit out the words and Min sucked him harder, her cheeks hollowing, loving the sensation of him in her throat, and she felt when he let loose, his hands hard in her hair, fucking her mouth, his hips jerking wildly against her, his hot sperm hitting the back of her throat as she swallowed as fast as she could.

After several long moments, he relaxed, going soft in her mouth and she sat back, still lightly licking and sucking every drop of him before sitting back in satisfaction. He caressed her hair, his eyes hooded and sated.

"You destroy me, Min. I've been fantasizing about your mouth forever."

She smiled, his words delicious, and she let him pull her toward him for a kiss, falling into the heat of him until they were interrupted by the loud, angry yell of her hungry stomach.

"Um… I'm going to need some breakfast soon."

His eyes twinkled at her as she blushed. "I think so. Should we shower and hit the buffet?"

She nodded. "First dibs on the French toast." He chuckled at her, standing up from the bed, and she sighed as she admired how truly wonderful this man's ass was as he strolled to the bathroom. When Hayden disappeared inside, she shook her head, trying to bring her mind back from the gutter it lived in permanently and reached for her phone. The sound of the shower turning on filled the room as she unlocked her phone, seeing that she had several notifications. Her heart fell into her stomach as a sense of horrible déjà vu raced through her.

She had almost a hundred messages—from friends, family, strangers on social media. All commenting on some sort of pictures. Holding her breath, she clicked the link her sister sent with five question marks and read the headline of the article, her body going cold.

'FlameThrower At It Again: disgraced streamer seduces tournament official before final round.'

Her eyes raced over the words accusing her of using sex to win the tournament, her heart pounding in her ears. She didn't even know the tournament officials, had only been introduced to the PAs who would signal her when it was time to start. All the players were isolated from the officials running the tournament and making sure they all played fair. So where had the story come from?

And then she saw the photo.

It was from the Waterfront bar last night. A zoomed-in, somewhat blurry shot of Min without her FlameThrower outfit, on Hayden's lap. They were looking at each other, ignoring everyone nearby, his arms tight around her. It would be clear to anyone how much they wanted each other.

The article went on to list her real name, as well as to post more pictures of her actual face pulled from old social media accounts she had previously deleted. The identity she had worked so hard to keep out of the public eye was now front and center, revealed for anyone to find and google.

Min couldn't stop the tears from coming, all her hard work over the years to keep her streaming life and real life separate, all ruined in one article. Not only had they accused her of something awful, they had basically doxxed her. She would never be able to go back to simply being Flame-Thrower.

A thought hit her, and she poured over the article again, true fear in her until she had read it three times. There was no mention of the name of the man in the photo with her, and no whisper of DeathsHead. The pictures of his face were blurry, only recognizable if you knew him. Hayden's identity was still a secret. At least for now.

Just then the bathroom door opened, and a freshly showered Hayden walked out with a towel wrapped around his waist. He froze when he saw her, and she wondered what look she had on her face.

"What's wrong?"

Wordlessly, she handed him her phone and showed him the article. He read it, his eyes darkening, his jaw clenching. He zoomed in on the photo, on their smiling faces so close to each other. Min's eyes watered at how happy they looked, even as he glared down at it.

"Who took the photo?"

"I don't know. There were hundreds of people crammed in there."

His eyes came to hers, a little cold, and she could feel part of her heart shrivel.

"But it had to be someone who knew you, the real you. Otherwise, they wouldn't think to take your picture without your FlameThrower look on."

Min shook her head. "The only people I saw there that I knew were sitting with us."

"How many people know?" His voice was hard, and something in Min was starting to spark.

"I don't know. A handful." She took a deep breath. "I'm sorry, Hayden. I know this is your worst nightmare. I'm sorry I've dragged you into my mess, however inadvertently."

"Don't be," he said. "It's my fault. I shouldn't have…" His voice trailed off and something inside Min went very, very still.

"Shouldn't have what?" she asked, carefully.

He shook his head, not wanting to finish whatever that thought was. But Min could feel the implications of it in her heart.

"I need to call my lawyer and get her on this. You should call yours. We'll need a statement from the tournament confirming that the guy in the picture does not work for them before the final round today." Hayden was already scrolling through his contacts, clearly itching to start damage control, and he suddenly felt farther away from her than he had ever been.

"The internet won't believe the tournament, Hayden. Not until they know your name."

"Not happening." His was voice hard, cutting.

Min let out an exhale, feeling everything crumbling around them, the tentative connection they had found completely destroyed in the aftermath of the false accusation.

"Okay. I'll head to my room and call my lawyer. I'll release a statement simply stating that you're a… friend I met here, not employed by the tournament."

There was an awkward pause, so awkward that she could feel her skin crawling as he slowly met her eyes. They were devoid of all the heat and affection they had built together, and Min's heart broke at the sight.

"That would be best."

Min turned, no longer wanting to see him, sliding into her clothes, grabbing her bag and walking out his door without either of them saying another word.

Min was proud that it wasn't until she was in her own room, now cleaned up of the graffiti and mess, that she cried.

CHAPTER 17

HAYDEN

Hayden hung up his phone, pacing through his brother's empty restaurant while Theo slouched at a table, sipping wine. Hayden envied his calm but also hated him for it. Ever since Min had shown him the pictures of them, all over the internet no less, his anxiety had been spiraling, dark and threatening to overwhelm him. This was everything he had always worried about, what kept him up at night. He had worked damn hard for his privacy, and now he was on the verge of losing it.

Theo interrupted his panicked pacing. "What did the lawyer say?"

Hayden ran his hand through his hair, frustration in every cell of his body.

"She's already working with the tournament people on a statement that I don't work for them and never have."

"Did she mention any fallout from the tournament itself?"

Hayden shook his head. "There shouldn't be, considering they know the story is false and that I don't work there. The lawyer's also in contact with the internet news site that published the story to begin with, but they're claiming the pictures were sent anonymously from an IP address belonging to a library computer here in town."

"Sounds like a shitty source. Will they retract the story?"

"They're standing by it. And they made it clear that they're going to pay good money for whoever can give them the identity of the mysterious man in the photo with Min. Fuck, this is a disaster."

In the past, Theo was the hothead and Hayden would work to calm him down. But now Theo just sipped his wine, their roles reversed. "It can't be that bad. Who really gets invested in streamers?"

Hayden thumped down into the chair next to his brother. "The article itself was picked up by every gaming website in the country, as well as a few mainstream media outlets. And has been trending top five on Twitter all morning."

"So your picture is everywhere." Theo still sounded calm, and for some reason, that really pissed off Hayden. He glared at his brother, simultaneously knowing he needed Theo to talk him down and also wanting to yell at him.

"Yeah, everywhere. I'm lucky if I get out of this mess with my identity intact."

"And how's Min doing?" Hayden heard how carefully he asked the question, how deliberately neutral he was, and grew instantly suspicious.

"Why did you ask it like that?"

"Because you've been here for an hour pacing and panicking and bitching and on the phone yelling at people and I haven't heard you mention one word about the woman you brought here. The one you couldn't stop staring at who is once again being forced into a scandal, this time doxxing her."

Theo's tone was mild, but Hayden felt like he had been

punched in the gut. Hayden drummed his fingers on the table, his mind racing. How was Min doing? She was pale when she left, and it had felt awkward. And he hadn't stopped to check on her before he came here. She was also living a nightmare, a repeat of one that she had just started coming out the other side of.

And Hayden hadn't even checked on her.

"Fuck," he said. "I don't know."

"Have you seen her since the article came out?" At the look on Theo's face, Hayden knew he was seeing right through him. "Shit, you were with her when she saw it this morning."

"That is… none of your business."

"You were with her and saw the article and then proceeded to only think about yourself. You are such a fucking dumbass." Theo looked pretty pissed, which was a surprise. His brother was usually on his side no matter what, ride or die. That's when it really hit Hayden that he must have royally fucked up for Theo to be this mad about something other than food.

"It was a lot at once. You know my anonymity is a big deal to me." Hayden heard how defensive he sounded and felt like shit. Lower than shit.

"Yeah, I know, and I respect that, and the anxiety you deal with. But do you really think Min values her anonymity less than you do yours? She's being accused of cheating at the one event that was supposed to help her get her career back. And now it's all exploding in her face—again—and the guy she thought liked her is acting like the situation is all about him." Theo shook his head in disgust. "Men. No wonder they hate us."

The truth hit Hayden, hard. He sunk his head into his hands, overwhelmed with how terrible he had handled that morning.

"God, I'm truly the worst asshole."

"You are."

Hayden was frustrated, his mind racing in several directions at once. The only way to publicly refute the claims that he worked for the tournament were to out who he was, giving up his own privacy. But doing that would only create more of a frenzy around him and Min, not to mention completely destroy his anonymity.

"What am I going to do, Theo?"

Theo shook his head, finishing his glass of wine and standing up, clearing the table. "I don't know, Hayden. This is a complicated situation and there are no simple solutions. All I can tell you is yesterday you were in here with a girl, looking at her like she hung the fucking moon, ready to break my fingers for flirting with her."

Hayden opened his mouth to argue but found he couldn't. "We've only known each other a few weeks," he tried, sounding weak even to his own ears. "We hated each other for years before that. We never even hung out before this weekend."

"I saw the photos, Hayden. Whoever that girl is, you don't hate her. I suspect it's actually the opposite."

Hayden worried he was right. But still. "It doesn't work that fast."

Theo shrugged. "I knew the moment I held a knife in my hand that I wanted to be a chef. And I was six."

"That's because you're certifiably insane."

"All I'm saying is, whatever's going on between you two, it isn't just a con fling. You're not going to forget about her the second you get home and fall back into your cave. I get that your privacy is important to you, and I respect you for that. But you're using streaming as a way to hide, Hayden. If you really don't do anything to help her with this, you don't deserve her."

Theo walked into the kitchen, leaving Hayden to stew on his own, and he couldn't help but feel the words hit him like a freight train. Min was important. The thought of leaving her out to dry for this, for photos of them together, left him feeling nauseous. Maybe she would forgive him for it, but she would always see him as yet another person who dropped her at a low point in her life. And Hayden found he couldn't stand that. He was slowly realizing that he didn't want to be just another person in her life. He wanted to be *the* person. And that was terrifying.

His phone beeped an alert and Hayden glanced at it, then froze. He had an alert notification telling him another article about Min had dropped. He opened it, skimming, finding more of the same information already published, but stopped as he scrolled further down. There were new photos, this time from LA, when both he and Min had been leaving the Bleeding Sword corporate office after that first disastrous meeting. It looked like it was shot from across the street, but they were both in it, talking to each other, standing close. Hayden could remember the moment before they had walked separate ways to their cars, when she had said a begrudging "thanks" before storming away from him. Peering at the picture, Hayden thought they certainly didn't look as loved up as the ones in the bar did. But there was no mistaking that he was the same guy from the Waterfront photos.

How the fuck did someone get these? It was one thing to see Min across a bar at a huge fan convention, but on a busy LA street? The first time his and her paths had ever crossed? There was something going on here, something Hayden was missing. But he sure as fuck wasn't going to stop until he figured it out.

CHAPTER 18
MIN

"Okay, here's what we're going to do. You go off and win your tournament and make everyone rue the day they were assholes to you. While you're doing that, I'm going to take a quick trip back to LA and set his house on fire. I'll be back in time for dinner. I'm feeling tacos."

Brittany was moving around her hotel room, on a mission. Min vaguely noted that the room looked like Brittany—her clothes everywhere, a camera set up in the corner with a patterned drape so she could stream her "Getting Dressed" content for her channel. Brittney doled out fashion advice for every budget, and her fans loved her for it. On her channel, she was chipper and bright and the personification of sunshine.

But in real life, Angry Brittany was an anarchist waiting for an excuse.

"You're not going to set his house on fire. It's not his fault." Min could feel how exhausted she was as she lay on the bed in Brittany's room, almost completely burritoed in the comforter. She had come here after crying her eyes out in her room alone, when it had gotten to be too much and she needed a change of scenery, needed a friend to help calm her down before the tournament. Although now that she thought about it, Brittany wasn't really anyone's first choice to calm down a situation.

At Min's words, Brittany whirled around, pointing an angry finger at Min. "Don't you fucking dare pretend like he's innocent in this. He's a fuck-up and a loser and he doesn't deserve you. And maybe he knows that, but he'll definitely know it after I put tampons in his gas tank."

Min groaned. "Brittany, we're not going near his car."

"Why the fuck not?"

Brittany paced, hands on her hips, fire in her eyes, and for the first time, Min realized Brittany was in goth girl mode—leather jacket she probably found at Goodwill, tight ripped jeans, and an old worn-out Dashboard Confessional shirt. Brittany dressed with her mood, and her current mood was to destroy. Min took a deep breath.

"I like him, okay. I like him a lot. And yes, he's being a dick, and yes, he needs to be punished for it. But he also has things going on that I can't tell you or talk about that make his reaction to this situation understandable and even sympathetic. So, until I sort through my own emotions and figure out how I want to handle everything, nothing is going to be set on fire and gas tanks are going to be left alone. Is that clear?"

Brittany's boot tapped on the carpet as she stared at Min, searching. Finally, her shoulders loosened and she dropped onto the bed next to Min with a sigh.

"You never let me have fun."

A laugh almost escaped Min. "Is Robbie aware of what a pyro you are?"

"Of course not. I already terrify him. He couldn't handle it if I showed him the real me." Brittany said it with a laugh, but something about her tone had Min raising a brow.

"Um, should we unpack that?"

"Absolutely not. So, what are you wearing to the tournament tonight?"

Leave it to Brittany to focus on the fashion. "I don't know. I'm not even sure if I should go. Everyone's pissed, saying that I'm trying to cheat. Before that, someone trashed my hotel room. I'm feeling like the universe is sending me signals, and I should probably start paying attention."

Brittany snorted, throwing an arm around Min and pulling her into a hard hug. "Bullshit. That's not the universe, that's men who are garbage trying to tarnish you. How did they find your hotel room? I didn't even know where you were staying, and I'm so deep in your business I'm practically a butt plug."

Min laughed at that, but after a moment she quieted. She hadn't thought about it before, since she had spent quite a few months convinced the universe was against her. But this one didn't make any sense.

"No one knew where I was staying," she said slowly, her brain trying to connect dots that didn't make sense. "That was part of the deal. Hayden and I would stay apart from the other streamers for privacy. No one but the company knew what hotel we were at, and they had signed an NDA."

"Okay, that's suspicious. Did the cops ever send you the security footage?"

Min bit her lip. "They did, but there wasn't much. Just a guy covered in a large hoodie. He did a good job of disguising himself."

Brittany stilled, serious. "Do you think it was Hayden?"

"No, Brittany, Jesus." Min's heart clenched at the thought.

Hayden had disappointed her, had hurt her, but he would never do something so awful.

"Don't give me that. I'm here with my friend who just had her fucking heart broken so I'm going to assume the worst about this asshole who kicked you down after all this shit happened *again*."

Min's mind was still spinning, trying to see the connections. It was almost like…

"Someone doesn't want me here. Someone who knew where I was and what I was going to do. Someone who knows my real identity."

Brittany flopped back on the bed. "Okay, but who? You know it wasn't me or Robbie or Gus because we love you. And you're adamant it wasn't Hayden. So, who?"

"Alex," Min said slowly. "Alex is here. He's competing in the tournament. He knows who I am, and he has access to all the tapes since he fucking made them in the first place. Someone must have told him where I was staying. Someone who really doesn't want me competing."

Brittany threw her a sly look. "And what do we do when some asshole tries to stop us from doing what we want?"

Min smiled, feeling right for the first time since she left Hayden. "We crush them beneath our boot heel."

Brittany leaped up, jumping on the bed, knocking Min around so much she laughed.

"Fuck yes! You're going to win this stupid tournament and then take that trophy and shove it up their assholes!"

"There's no trophy, Brittany."

Brittany leaned over, glaring at Min with a lot of malevolence that told her Brittany would be bringing a lighter to the tournament. "But the rest is going to be true."

"Damn straight."

Min felt like throwing up.

She was fighting the urge, since she was in a rideshare and the driver was already looking at her suspiciously, like he could sense she was about to violate his sedan with her vomit. Min tried to ignore him and focused on taking deep breaths while staring out the window.

She could feel her newfound determination to win the tournament being tested with every passing moment. Everything had gone from bad to the toilet drain. The photos from the Waterfront were terrible enough, but now there were new photos of her and Hayden everywhere from the day they first met. Min knew it was only a matter of time before people figured out who he was. And she was terrified.

Hayden was going to hate her. If he didn't already.

The first thing he had made clear to her, from that very first day in the elevator when he pushed into her and demanded to see her phone, was that he didn't want to reveal his identity to the world. He had told her over and over again how important his privacy was to him, how overwhelming his anxiety was about the issue. And now here they were, with Hayden caught up in the shitstorm Alex had thrown her in, a victim of the slut-shaming mob that had already ruined her career. They wouldn't stop until they knew who he was.

On top of that, everyone thought she was cheating at the tournament, a tournament she desperately needed to win. She needed the sponsorship to help relaunch her career as a streamer, needed the money to help cover Devery's medical bills. The people running everything had already released a statement claiming that whoever the man was, he didn't work for them, and that Min's performance in the tournament was based solely on her ability to play the game. Min was grateful they had backed her up. But of course, the internet didn't believe any statements that had been put out, calling it a conspiracy as if this was somehow all working in Min's favor and not completely destroying her life. Now, even if she won, there would always be some doubt about her performance.

And then more pictures had leaked, this time of Min and Hayden in LA the day they met. Min didn't know how anyone got those, unless her ex had taken to stalking her around the city. Which, when she really thought about it, she couldn't discount. And now the world knew FlameThrower's real name, knew what she really looked like. Her days of blending into a crowd were over.

As her rideshare pulled up to the venue, she saw a crowd of protestors waiting outside, all with hate on their signs telling the tournament to disqualify her. Her driver whistled at the sight.

"You sure you want me to drop you here?"

Min took a deep breath. "Wouldn't be my first angry mob."

The cab driver shook his head. "If you say so."

Min handed him his money, tipping well, and stepped out onto the street. She was in her normal clothes, just jeans and a plain T-shirt, no makeup, and her auburn hair thrown in a ponytail. She had dressed as plainly as possible, keeping everything she needed in her bag to become FlameThrower. But the internet had done its job relentlessly, and the crowd recognized her the moment her feet hit the sidewalk.

Min was instantly swarmed. People she didn't know shoved their way close to her, screaming into her face that she needed to quit the tournament. One larger gentleman called her a slut. A woman across the way was screaming something unintelligible at her. As Min pushed her way through them, slowly, trying not to instigate, she found she couldn't hear anything, could barely think. So, she just tucked her head down and strode as best she could for the entrance. Luckily, the crowd didn't seem intent on physically hurting her, just following and yelling obscenities—a small favor. When she neared the entrance, security was waiting for her, pushing back the crowd to let her slip through the door alone.

She sighed at the sudden quiet of the building, a relief after the yelling from the street. Min already felt a headache forming and was trying to shake it off when she heard footsteps behind her.

"Ms. Hayes?"

Min turned to find Dylan, one of the businessmen who had originally arranged for her to join the tournament. He smiled at her, but Min couldn't help but notice that it didn't reach his eyes. Dylan indicated to a room behind him. "Could I have a word with you before you prepare for the tournament?"

Her heart sank as she joined him in what turned out to be a small conference room. She sat at the small table and braced herself. She didn't know what he wanted to talk about, but after the day she had, she could only assume it was going to be awful. She tried to hide her nerves, clasping her hands in her lap. She wanted to appear unbothered, but it was too soon after a crowd was just calling her names to seem completely unaffected.

Dylan started. "So, obviously it's been a bit of a day. The company has been under fire since the photos leaked, and we've been doing what damage control we can. I'm sure you saw the statement refuting that the man in the photos with you ever worked here. We're ready to stand behind that. But in reality, unless Mr. Phillips is prepared to step forward, there's going to be a shadow on this event."

Min nodded, agreeing with what he was saying. "I don't believe Hayden is going to step forward. He's worked for years to keep his privacy private. This would ruin that for him, and I can't ask him to do that."

Dylan shook his head. "Then we're in a bit of a pickle. There's concern the other players could file suits against the company. Obviously, that's something we would like to avoid."

He paused there, giving her an expectant look that confused Min. Did she miss a question? Whatever it was, she wasn't figuring it out on her own.

"Sorry," she said. "I'm going to need you to spell whatever this is out for me."

Dylan tensed, even as he plastered a fake smile on his face.

"Ms. Hayes, we appreciate your situation. And we're so happy that you've been able to participate in the tournament. While we won't ask you to remove yourself from the competition—"

Min's heart stopped. "Wait, what?"

Dylan soldiered on as if she hadn't interrupted. "—I think you can understand when we suggest that if you do happen to win it would be best for you to announce you won't be keeping the money."

Min blinked. She couldn't help it. She was stunned. "Give back the money?"

"To mitigate the fallout if you do manage to win." Dylan's voice was so even, so bored, that it sounded like he was ordering bread for the table, not ruining her life.

Min's jaw dropped. She couldn't believe what he was telling her. "But I can't. I need the money. My sister was in a car accident making her unable to work. This tournament, the winnings were supposed to help pay for her bills. I'm not some rich streamer, I'm just a woman trying to make ends meet doing what she loves."

Dylan shook his head, appearing sympathetic in a way that made Min's skin crawl. "Ms. Hayes, you're free to do what you'd like if you win the money. But there is going to be a massive investigation when all of this is over. Your behavior has made it impossible to declare this a fair game without it."

Min is taken back. "My behavior? I had a drink at a bar with a friend. Hayden was there, too. Are you going to talk with him about his behavior?"

"Unfortunately, that looks different when you've already been involved in some less than PG photos circulating the internet. And besides, Mr. Phillips is in a different position than you."

Her mind raced, trying to understand what he was really saying. And then she realized.

"DeathsHead is a bigger deal than me. I'm here because he's here, otherwise, I wouldn't be. So, you won't be holding him to this standard of punishment. He's going to walk away as if nothing happened, while I take full blame. As if I did something wrong. Which I didn't."

"That's not exactly what I'm saying."

"Not in those words, but it's what you meant." Min crossed her arms, willing herself to speak as coldly as this douche.

Dylan sighed, sounding almost annoyed with her, and Min couldn't believe she had signed a contract with this man. Couldn't believe she was once again in this position, getting blamed for pictures she didn't consent to, having her career taken away yet again. Sure, this time she was fully clothed, but in the world of competitive gaming, cheating was a death sentence for a streamer. She wouldn't come back from this.

Dylan knew that. And he didn't care. "The fact is that the

company has signed a number of NDAs in order to work with Mr. Phillips, which means there's little we can do to refute his position in the tournament."

"Meaning you can't force him to give back his winnings?"

He stood up, apparently finished with this conversation.

"You're free to do what you'd like, Ms. Hayes. Just know that no matter the outcome, there will be an investigation that may get uncomfortable for some involved. I encourage you to remember that, should you win."

He turned to leave, and Min felt bitterness rising in her, the unfairness of the entire situation. She had done nothing wrong, she had not consented to any photos, hadn't flaunted her relationship with Hayden, had done nothing but try to compete in the tournament and win money to help herself and her family. And now he was telling her that no matter what, she couldn't win.

"I'll think on my choices," she told him, letting her voice go cold. "But you should think about who knew both me and Hayden were going to show up to your office around a similar time. Who would know to be ready with a camera to snap a few shots? Because I didn't tell anyone, didn't even know he would be there. And I would bet all my future winnings that Hayden hadn't told anyone, either. Which means the leak came from you."

Dylan had turned back when she started talking, and now the asshole was frowning at her like she was a bug he had just squashed under his shoe. Secretly, she wanted to crumple up into a ball and hide, but there was no way she was going to let that show. She forced herself to smirk at him.

"In fact, you and your company were the only people who knew where I was staying for the convention. But somehow, someone knew where I was, what room I was staying in, and managed to break in and trash the place. Feels like there's only one place that person could've learned that information. Am I right?"

Dylan's eyes narrowed at her. "Bleeding Sword was obviously distraught to hear what had happened to your room, but if you're implying there's a breach in our protocol, I'm going to assure you that we had no involvement."

"You were the only ones besides Hayden who knew."

"Are you implying that we were behind the damage to your room? I hired you, Ms. Hayes. Why would I do that?"

A calm came over Min, grounding her and sending her clarity that she had lacked before this very moment.

"The company never wanted me to win. I'm a bad image for you, thanks to those fucking pictures. You just wanted me here to go up against DeathsHead. The problem is, I am damn good at this game. Probably the best, if I'm being honest. So maybe you had to do something to be certain I wouldn't win and tarnish your precious competition. Nothing big, just something to scare me enough to drop out. Am I right?"

"That's slander. I'd be careful repeating that to anyone."

Min's eyes ran over him, seeing the disgusting slime of his soul that he hid behind tailored suits.

"If I were you, I'd look into how ironclad that non-disclosure agreement is that you signed, because I know my lawyers will. And my guess is Hayden is going to have strong feelings about it when the truth comes out."

Dylan looked at her with a calculation that Min knew in her bones he usually hid from people. He wasn't going to concede anything, wasn't going to admit anything, and she just had to deal with the fallout from this situation she had absolutely no control over.

Min took a deep breath and then gathered her bag. She had

just enough time to change into her FlameThrower look before she had to report to the green room for the final bracket of the tournament. She steeled her spine and gritted her teeth, letting her anger power her.

Fuck Bleeding Sword. Fuck Dylan. Fuck whoever took those photos. And fuck Alex.

Min was going to win the tournament. She was going to keep the money, and pay for her sister's medical bills, and get her life back in order. She was tired of men walking over her and calling the shots. It was time to take control, starting today.

And whatever happened, she would make it up to Hayden. Even if he never wanted to see her again.

CHAPTER 19

HAYDEN

Hayden strode into the convention center like a man on fire, Theo's words been ringing in his ears. He had been pissed when he saw the crowd of protestors outside the usual entrance for the players in the tournament. Imagining how Min had felt seeing those assholes and their stupid fucking signs made his stomach churn. So, Hayden had ducked around, using a different entrance that was less populated, and then wound his way into the tournament area, heading for his private streaming bay. He kept his eyes open, noting the halls were empty and he was the only one there. He hadn't run into anyone either time he had come here, but Hayden was always cautious.

When he finally approached the door to his bay, one with a simple "PRIVATE" sign posted outside, he stepped inside with relief. The company had kept their promises so far about keeping his identity secret, but there was always the chance that a quick encounter with a stranger could turn into a disaster. Since the pictures had dropped of him with Min, Hayden was paranoid that he could feel eyes on him at all times, his anxiety burning in his chest so hot his hands were tingling. But what felt worse every moment was the memory of Min's face when she had told him about the photos. How stricken she had looked when he had shut down. How pale she was when she gathered her clothes and left, taking all her warmth and smiles and scent with her.

God, Hayden felt like an ass.

Distracted by his thoughts and self-loathing, Hayden didn't notice until he was already in his bay with the door shut that one of the Bleeding Sword execs was there waiting for him. Dylan. The slimy one that made Hayden feel like he needed a shower. This was the last thing Hayden wanted today. He leaned his back against the closed door, crossing his arms, shooting Dylan a look full of nothing but poison.

"What do you want?" Hayden let his voice be cold. He didn't like people in his space on a good day, much less this guy in his streaming bay where he was about to compete.

Dylan held out his hands as if to look innocent and instead ended up looking like the definition of a douchebag.

"Just checking in on you, big guy," Dylan joked. "Hope you're ready for this last round of battle."

Hayden's eyes narrowed. Something was up, and this Dylan guy was going to hedge around it until he could pass blame. Hayden didn't like it. Didn't like this man who pretended to be on the up and up and in reality wasn't.

"I'm ready," was all he said in response.

"Good, good. Should be a pretty easy victory from the looks of it, all things considered." Dylan tapped his fingers to a rhythm that only annoyed Hayden more.

"What do you mean?" Hayden kept his voice even, knowing that he could unnerve people with it easily. Dylan seemed not to notice, which was stupid on his part.

Dylan guffawed. Actually guffawed. "Well, since the new photos came out, I'm guessing Flame doesn't have her head in the game, and she was really your only competition. Should be smooth sailing from here. I've had the lawyers start to draw up the contract for your sponsorship with Bleeding Sword."

"I haven't won yet."

"Only a formality, let's be honest. I saw Ms. Hayes a moment ago and she certainly did not look like her heart was in this tournament. What with all the scandal she's caused around the actual event, she's lucky to even be here." Dylan smirked then, as if he and Hayden shared a secret, as if Hayden was somehow part of this venom Dylan was spewing. And Hayden felt sick.

Dylan continued. "Besides, you're the bigger draw. The shareholders weren't very interested in sponsoring someone with her reputation. They took a lot of convincing just to let her enter."

Hayden felt himself go still. "FlameThrower is one of the best players of this game you have. She is absolutely committed to this tournament. Some asshole leaking photos isn't going to stop her."

Dylan, the idiot, just waved his hand dismissively. "Yes, but we both know that doesn't really matter. Sponsoring DeathsHead will be an amazing partnership, one I'm looking forward to cultivating. Already, we've broken several Esports streaming records. Millions of people have been watching the tournament. Even more are already logged on and waiting for this final round. We've made history here." Dylan rubbed his hands together like the cartoon supervillain he was, and Hayden knew he was going to lose it.

Hayden wanted to punch something, wanted to scream at this asshat so loud the walls shook, but he forced himself to breathe and think. In the quiet, his mind made connections and put facts and events together that hadn't been clear before. Suddenly, Hayden was seeing the situation from higher ground and realized the problem was even bigger than he thought. When the truth hit him, it felt like a physical blow.

"You did it. You took the pictures. Or you bought them and had them leaked anonymously. You set us up."

Dylan shook his head, denying it even while smiling, the bastard.

"No way, man."

But Hayden knew he was full of shit. "Those photos that came out today were from the first meeting. You're the only ones who knew that we were both going to be there, that I was going to be there making a personal appearance. You had a photographer ready."

Dylan, starting to realize how intensely pissed Hayden was, began backing away slowly, which is when Hayden realized he had been stalking closer, towering over the weasel.

"Hey, no, man, seriously, that wasn't us. The company wouldn't do that."

Hayden was dismayed to find that Dylan wasn't even that good of a liar. Somehow that made it all worse.

"The company wouldn't, but some asshole looking for a promotion or a big payday streaming event would."

With Dylan's face turning red, he started scrambling for anything that would get him out of this situation, as if he finally realized how truly pissed off Hayden was. And Hayden was glad, glad to have his anger and betrayal acknowledged because he was desperately fighting to keep himself as calm as possible.

"Hey, wait, no," Dylan tried to spin, all blood draining from his face in a way that Hayden found immensely satisfying. "I was just… that's not what this is. The company is extremely interested in sponsoring you as DeathsHead, was all I was saying. You're a big deal, and we're excited that a partnership appears to be on the horizon."

Hayden ignored his words. They didn't matter, anyway. "The company, including you, signed several NDAs saying you would not reveal my identity. Which you should've thought about before you had those photos plastered all over the internet. Let me guess, you thought you would just blame it on Min's asshole ex who leaked the last ones?" Hayden was officially squared up, in Dylan's space, in his face, using his height to intimidate in a way he usually hated. But this guy, this shitstain of a human being, deserved it and more.

Dylan sputtered, not a good look for him, but it told Hayden everything he needed to know.

"Here's what's going to happen," Hayden told him softly. "We're going to play out this tournament. Whoever wins, wins, and gets all the prizes they're due. And then my lawyers are going to draft a breach of contract suit so airtight that I will basically own you and the company you work for because of all this bullshit you pulled. Now get the fuck out of my room."

Dylan was gone before Hayden finished his sentence, and Hayden slammed the door behind him. He felt like such an asshole for not seeing the truth about Dylan, about the tournament.

About Min.

Min had been hurt so many times. By her ex, by Dylan. And what Hayden found was making him crawl out of his skin was knowing he had been the one to hurt her the most. His initial reaction when she had shown him the photo leak had been to retreat, to hide, to run to his brother and lawyer up and figure out how to make his privacy wall stronger. But all of that pushed Min away and left her alone. Vulnerable. The exact opposite of how Hayden wanted her feeling when they were together.

Fuck, he was an idiot. He'd let down Min. He'd fucked up the tenuous relationship they had been building, a relationship that even he had to admit had started the first time they had streamed together and she had called him obscenities when he'd blown up her avatar with a proximity mine. And now they were barreling toward this tournament and he didn't have time to find her beforehand, to apologize and tell her the truth about Dylan. About the bullshit he was trying to pull.

Even if Dylan didn't want it, even if the company didn't want it, Hayden knew Min wanted this win. Hell, at this point Hayden was ready to throw in the towel and let her have it. He could work for a few more years to earn the money he needed to complete the game. He and Theo could wait.

But Hayden also knew Min would hate being handed a win. She wanted to fight for it, wanted to earn it, not only for herself but for every troll on the internet that had attacked her after the first photo leak. She had to prove she was more than what they called her, even though Hayden already knew that better than most.

But it was what Min wanted. Which meant it was what Hayden wanted.

He had to be prepared to give it his all. Because if he did anything that made her feel he wasn't trying his hardest to defeat her, she would be so fucking pissed. More so than she probably was right now.

Hayden straightened his shoulders and settled into his streaming bay, pulling his headset on and his microphone closer. If Min wanted a fight, and he knew deep down she did, then he was certainly going to give her one.

CHAPTER 20

MIN

Min finished the last swipe of her lipstick and stood back, checking herself over to make sure she didn't miss anything. She had taken her time getting ready, making sure her outfit was perfect, her makeup perfect, her wig well placed. Making sure FlameThrower was in her element, the persona worn like armor for what Min knew was going to be a fight in more ways than one. The crowd outside the convention center made it clear that she would have no fans in the audience to cheer her on. The comments online in response to the latest pictures were full of false accusations and hate that would follow her forever. This may very well be the last time FlameThrower ever made an appearance, so Min wanted to savor it. Savor this person she had created so she could do what she loved and share it with the world.

Knowing this was probably goodbye meant that Min was even more determined to go out on a win. The Bleeding Sword guy had thrown her, had tried to intimidate her and scare her into backing down. But once she put on her wig, her corset, her ridiculous fake lashes, Min knew she wasn't going to be giving up like they wanted. She was going to win. And then she'd deal with the fallout.

She caught sight of her own eyes in the mirror and knew she was full of shit. The morning with Hayden, the perfect morning after the absolute perfect night with him, was there under the surface, breaking her heart when she remembered how shell-shocked he had been when she showed him the new pictures. She knew his story now, knew how used and vulnerable he would feel, and she hated it, hated that she was involved in making him feel that way, even if she wasn't the one who took the pictures.

But she also felt a spark inside her, one that was burning with indignation. Hayden knew her, knew how hurt she had been, what she had gone through since the first photo leak. She thought he knew her enough to know she would never do something like this to him, but she had seen the look on his face. Whether or not she took the pictures, he blamed her. And she couldn't stop herself from hating him a little bit for not trusting her. For not being there for her. With her. She knew she deserved better than this. And she was done accepting worse.

With that in mind, Min decided at the last minute to forgo her heels and keep her large boots on. She needed the strength from them, and the comfort if she was honest. Throwing one last layer of lip gloss on, Min stepped out of her dressing room and headed for the green room.

The room was quiet when she arrived. A few TVs were set up around the space to watch the tournament. The screens were currently showing the commentators bantering back and forth about probabilities and skill levels of each of the players who were set to compete in this final bracket. Min's eyes cast about to find only a few other streamers she didn't recognize, lounging on couches with their headphones on, getting into their heads before the last round of the tournament. Hayden was nowhere in sight, but Min didn't expect him to be. She knew he had a private streaming bay somewhere in the building, and she wondered how he was prepping for their last tournament. They would be against each other this time, and with everything that had passed between them, Min felt her heart ache a little at the thought that this would be the last time they'd stream together. As much as DeathsHead had driven her crazy when they played, he was still her favorite opponent.

She was so lost in thought that she jumped when she heard the cold voice behind her.

"I'm honestly surprised you even showed up."

She turned, eyes already narrowing on Alex's stupid handsome face, his mouth twisted in a forgery of a smile as he looked at her with every ounce of hate she felt for him.

"Thought the crowd outside would've made it clear how unwanted you are."

She glared at him. Min still found it hard to believe that she had missed all the signs of how toxic he was, but she had. When they had first started dating, he had been thoughtful and kind, always letting her set the pace of their relationship, never pushing her for more than what she was willing to give him. Min had been on dates where the man had been a little too enamored with her FlameThrower persona, but Alex never once gave off those vibes. He was content to date a streamer with a higher audience than him and hadn't batted an eye when she had gently turned him down for streaming together. She never liked to mix her personal life with her streaming, and he had seemed to understand.

And then he changed.

It had been slow at first. A comment here, a bitter look there. And then she had woken up one morning with the knowledge that he really didn't like her success, didn't like how much more popular her channel was than his. She had felt guilty at first, as if she had been doing something wrong by simply making the same gaming content she always did. She had blushed when he started criticizing her outfits, claiming she was "whoring herself out for likes." Min knew he was wrong, and the fight they had after that comment had made the walls shake. He had apologized, and it had seemed sincere at the time, so she forgave him. All couples fought eventually, right?

When he had first asked her to let him video them together, she thought he was just being adventurous with their sex life, which had never been much to brag about to begin with. And to be honest, she had been a little intrigued. But she had said no, explaining to him that it was too risky for her, that it was too easy for anyone to hack a phone nowadays and she didn't want to gamble. It was after she had said no that he had changed, becoming short with her, more cutting, colder. By the time she had broken it off, his negativity started to seep into her in a way she hated, and she knew she had to leave before his toxicity affected her permanently.

No, she wasn't sorry they ended. She was just sorry that she had taken so long to end it.

With that in mind, she worked hard to hide her feelings. "Why did you do it, Alex?"

He cocked his head, playing dumb. "Do what?"

That pissed her off. "We broke up. The relationship had run its course. Hell, by the end of it, I didn't even think you could stand being in a room with me. It wasn't the end of the world,

for us not to be together. But the video, those screenshots…
how could you?"

She truly didn't know. The entire situation bewildered her,
even now when she'd had months to process beyond the
initial hurt and betrayal. She knew she had done nothing to
deserve his anger, his bitterness. His retaliation. And yet even
now she could see how incredibly angry the question made
him, even as he covered the anger with an arrogant smirk.

"Of course, our breakup wasn't the end of the world. If
anything, you did me a favor, leaving me before you got
caught up in the consequences of your actions. Before
revealing to the world your true self."

She shook her head. She wasn't going to let him dictate this
conversation, or gaslight her into thinking she had done
anything wrong. That part of her life was over.

"You recorded us without my consent after I had specifically told you no. And then you took screenshots and leaked
them online for everyone to see. You ruined my career. You
hurt me. How could you do it?"

"I had nothing to do with any of that," he lied, straight to
her face, somehow smiling. "But you need to know, women
don't just break up with me. I'm a fucking catch, and they're
lucky to find themselves in my orbit. Understand? Women
don't say when we're done. I say when we're done."

He was aggressive, moving closer and closer to her,
looming over her, but she stood her ground, no longer willing
to let him intimidate her. She glared up at him.

"We're done, Alex. You're a loser who wasn't worth my
time, and I should've realized that much, much quicker. I don't
know why you dropped the pics, or why you broke into my
hotel room, or why you're following me around and trying to
rig the competition. But I'll tell you right now—you are not

going to win. You're up against the best. You haven't been able to run me off, and you won't be able to scare me. You better get ready to have your ass handed to you on a live stream. Because I don't know anyone who deserves it more than you."

Their eyes locked, hating each other, and Min vaguely wondered if he would actually become violent with her when a PA ran over to them, interrupting.

"Alex, thirty seconds."

Alex nodded at him, then glared at Min as he stepped back.

"By the time this tournament is over, FlameThrower will be nothing but ash under my boot. Have fun trying to get any sort of career after this."

He strolled out to the exit, stepping out as he was announced and Min could hear the audience screaming for him, cheering. He wasn't the best player, but he had a loyal fan base, and they had shown up for him here at the convention. She watched him enter on one of the nearby TVs, his smile much what it used to be before she knew the truth about him, a sweet grin hiding how fucked up he was. Min wasn't a violent person in real life, but right then she wouldn't have minded if a piano appeared out of nowhere and fell on his head.

"FlameThrower, thirty seconds."

She nodded, moving toward the door herself. Knowing this was going to be bad. But also knowing she was going to get through it. Somehow.

"Please welcome our next challenger — FlameThrower!"

The announcer had used the same voice as she had with every other player, but the reception was vastly different. Min stepped out into the arena to almost dead silence. She glanced up at the audience, noting that the place was packed with people staring. Some were actively glaring at her, but others seemed just curious, like she was the latest gossip and they wanted to be there to see how it went. Her boots echoed through the quiet arena as she made her way to her streaming bay, making sure to keep her shoulders up and back.

And then she heard it. Someone cheering.

She paused, wondering if she was hallucinating, and turned back to the audience. Her eyes scanning until she found Randall. Standing and towering over the rest of the people seated around him, dressed in an impeccable Flame-Thrower cosplay, Randall cheered his head off for her, his yelling and whistles echoing through the room. He was shortly joined by Min's friends, Brittany and Robbie and Gus, all losing their minds screaming for her. She smiled, waving, feeling the love and a little emboldened even with her mostly quiet reception. It wasn't the welcome Alex had received, nowhere near, but as Min waved at Randall she could have cried at the sweet moment. She had support. She could do this.

She kept walking to her bay, settling in, when the announcer picked up again.

"And streaming from a secret location, please welcome: DeathsHead!"

Min almost needed to cover her ears, the crowd's screams were so loud. She glanced up, several screens above them flipping through the players' streams just in time to see Deaths-Head's avatar join the game. Her heart flipped at the sight, even as she tried to keep a straight face, knowing the camera would capture her reaction. Her and DeathsHead's rivalry was legendary, after all. A lot of people were here not only to root for him but to watch them battle each other.

And to watch her lose.

Min schooled her face, concentrating. She needed to win this. She'd figure out the rest, including Hayden, after.

The final round of the tournament involved dropping the remaining players onto a brand-new player map, one that would be uploaded to the regular game following the tournament for worldwide players. It was a great promotional tool for Bleeding Sword, and a great way to keep the competition fair for the remaining players.

Min loved the anticipation of a new map.

As per usual, there were ten of them left, all the best of the best that the company had either recruited or auditioned. Min was only familiar with Hayden and Alex—the others were new to the tournament and were probably skilled, unknown streamers hoping to make their big break. Luckily, Min knew the ratings from the tournament in previous days already must have boosted the new players' audience, so no matter what the noobs were coming out winning.

Min's avatar spawned on top of a building, and she took a moment to both take in her surroundings and admire the game. The under-appreciated part of video games was often the artistry behind it. The art of the locations themselves could take Min's breath away, and from the looks of it, the team at Bleeding Sword had outdone themselves with this new map.

It was large, larger than any of the previous maps, and looked to be modeled after a medieval castle, one that was crumbling with age. The detail, the atmosphere, everything was beautiful in a way that made Min want to savor it, to take screenshot after screenshot so she could admire it later. Min had spawned in the woods surrounding the property, hidden in the dense trees and foliage. She immediately had her avatar crouch behind a thick tree and began to systematically search for items and weapons, while keeping an eye out for her fellow competitors. There was no knowing where the game had randomly spawned them, or where any NPC zombies could be hiding, so she had to be careful not to get caught by surprise.

Min's careful efforts paid off after a few minutes, locating a few low-level firearms, as well as a combat knife. Nothing to get excited about, and certainly nothing that would sway the game in her favor, but enough to hold her own if she happened to come upon another player. She circled the castle, searching for an entrance other than the large drawbridge that was currently half open as if trying to seduce a player into revealing themselves to open it. But Min wasn't dumb, so she ignored the bait in favor of looking for an entrance with more coverage. She was guessing the castle itself held the best weapons, and she needed every advantage she could get.

The other players were in her headset, joking and talking trash, but Min ignored them. Chances were that they were all doing exactly what she was doing, searching for weapons and a solid location to claim for home base. She kept an ear out in case they were dumb enough to let slip their positions, but she figured if they had all made it that far into the tournament, then they were smart enough to keep quiet about things like that. Alex, she noted, was talking enough to fill the whole stream, probably so in love with his voice that he couldn't imagine letting anyone else get a word in edgewise. The other players were egging him on, eating it up, but she and Deaths-Head stayed quiet. From experience with playing against him, she knew that meant he was in the middle of plotting something terrifying, and her blood thrilled with the thought.

Another few minutes of searching had Min switching out her shotgun for a machine gun and she smiled. She had a high-level weapon. She had her infrared goggles. She was still lacking med kits, but she couldn't wait any longer. It was time to get the real game started. It was time to find her opponents.

A heat signature through the trees told her she was close to someone, and she froze, uncertain if the other player had spotted her. The name hovering over the avatar showed it was a player she was unfamiliar with, so she had her character crouch, readying her gun as she slowly, so slowly, crept up behind him.

In a blink, she realized she had misjudged—the player had known she was there—and when an unfamiliar voice in her ears yelled, *"Eat metal, FlameThrower!"* she couldn't stop the grin on her face as she fired—hitting the guy's character right in the chest with her bullets. She took damage, but he only had a handgun, whereas her machine gun tore through him. His avatar fell to the ground and dropped his items around his body. She quickly scooped up what she needed, ignoring the yellow warning flash of her health. All that mattered was that she lived.

She vaguely heard the guy complaining over the comms that he had been hoping to last longer, and then his voice came through just for her.

"FlameThrower, it's an honor."

She smiled, not expecting the tribute—most male players get an attitude playing with women, especially losing to them. And since Min was considered a pariah right now, she certainly hadn't expected any sort of respect from the players she didn't know. It was a nice gesture on his part, one that touched her in a way she wasn't expecting.

"Come find me on stream in the future," she told him. "I'll be happy to plaster you with more bullets."

He didn't respond, and she assumed his mic had been cut off since he was officially out. She focused instead on her search, knowing she needed a med kit fast.

A while later, she heard another male voice taunting.

"Don't tell me you're afraid to face me, Death."

A deep, dark laugh that she knew she would always feel in her bones came through her headset. Despite herself, she felt her ears perk.

"Never. Usually, people are afraid to face me."

The comms went quiet for a moment in anticipation. And then there was nothing but gunfire, the other man yelling into his comms, almost screaming with the bullets, until suddenly the feed went silent. Min held her breath.

"Goddamnit, DeathsHead."

"Sorry, Gargletoon. I have a final opponent in mind, and you just weren't it."

Min shivered at that. The deafening sound of the audience around them cheering for DeathsHead filled her with pride, even though she knew she had no claim on him. Hayden was good at this, and Min loved that he was good at this game she loved, that he took it as seriously as she did.

Min pushed her avatar to limp around, searching desperately for healing, wondering if this new map meant that the med kits spawned less often. Probably, if it was considered a map for advanced players. It wasn't until she wandered into her third location to do a scan that she found it.

A door into the castle.

It was hard to see, covered in overgrown plant life and hidden unless you angled your camera just right. Even the path up to the door was non-existent, with no clear sightlines for snipers that Min could see.

If med kits were anywhere, they were going to be inside. So that's where she was going.

Min kept her camera moving, trying to have eyes everywhere as she approached the door. Soon she was inside, wedging the door closed with a nearby large stone that had fallen from a wall.

She made her way carefully down a maze of hallways, all while admiring the space. She was in what must have been made to look like a servant area, with close walls and long hallways. She found several doors, some wedged shut, some with nothing but empty rooms. She considered setting traps, but she needed healing first. That was the priority.

Min turned a corner of a hallway and found herself at the open doorway of a large room. It was maybe a ballroom, with high ceilings and a second floor that looked down onto the floor she was currently on. It was fancy, fancier than she had seen thus far in her search, but what had her freezing was what lay in the middle of the room.

A med kit.

All by itself. Her infrared goggles didn't show any heat signatures, but that didn't mean anything. In the game, for every boost there was another item to counteract it, meaning that for all that she had infrared goggles, someone could be in this room with stealth gear. She had to be careful.

But she was in the yellow for health. She needed the kit. Even if this was a trap, she had to go for it.

Searching again and seeing nothing, Min circled the kit, keeping the door behind her in sight. Her instincts were screaming at her that someone was in this room, waiting to make a move. But nothing happened, even as she inched closer and closer. So she kept moving, growing more and more anxious.

And then she heard the telltale click of the trap.

A curse escaped her, exploding onto the otherwise quiet comms and making her other opponents laugh. Min ignored them as she watched her avatar yanked up by the snare trap that she had failed to see. Now she was trapped, upside down, her foot in the air, her vision swirling in a circle until the physics of the trap settled. Min was pissed at herself. She knew this was a trap, she should've seen the snare. This was a rookie mistake. She knew she was better than this.

"You make it so fucking easy, Flame."

Min froze at Alex's voice, at the hate and menace infused in it. The crowd cheered, thinking it was just one of their favorites facing her, probably not even registering how vindictive his voice sounded. When her avatar finally stopped spinning from the physics of the trap, Min adjusted her camera, spotting his avatar on the balcony above her. He must have found the stealth gear after all. Fuck.

Not hesitating, she pulled out her knife and started sawing at the snare, trying to move quick as he came closer to her. A single shot rang out, and her health went down into the warning zone, her knife dropping out of her hand. She was a sitting duck waiting for the timer of the snare to run out and release her.

"You should've dropped out, Flame. No one wanted you here. No one thinks you deserve to be here."

There were cheers from the audience at that, supporting him and his hatred of her. And that hurt, more than Min was really expecting. She knew she wasn't loved, knew the vast majority of the audience was here to watch her fail. But still, the reality of it, of listening to them cheer on the man who had ruined her career with his pettiness made her anger grow, the unfairness, the hurt, the lies, everything coalescing in her heart and burning with the fire of a thousand furnaces.

"I have just as much right to be here as you, Alex." She bit off the words, hearing the rest of the chatter from the comms die down as the other players eavesdropped. Even the audience was silent. Min had stayed quiet for the most part so far, and everyone wanted to hear how she would handle this situation. Were practically holding their breaths to hear more.

"Yeah right." Alex laughed, bitter. *"Everyone knows how you 'earned' your place in the tournament, Min. Couldn't keep your fucking legs closed, even after getting called out on the internet."*

Min shouldn't have been surprised he would go there, that he would be so crude in his accusations and even call her by her real name, but she was. At one time she had trusted him, so for him to speak about her like this, knowing that he had set her up, knowing that nothing he said was true, made her sick. And she was done protecting him.

"You really want to do this here, Alex? Because I'm happy to talk about what really went down, and who the person was in the photos. Because it was the same person who leaked those photos. The same person that trashed my hotel room two days ago, although I don't have the proof yet. And I suspect was one of the people responsible for the very false allegations that came out today. So, if you really want to do this here, then we fucking will."

"You lying bitch!" Alex exploded over the comms, his avatar aiming his gun, the shot ringing out, and Min knew she was done. She didn't have the health to survive a shot at this close range from any weapon. The fucker had won.

Except....

"What the fuck?" Alex was practically spitting into his comms, his avatar on the ground on one knee. Min spun her camera, searching, to find another player had entered the room without either of them noticing—someone named TeddyBear-Hugs. It wasn't anyone she recognized, which meant he was one of the lesser-known streamers.

As she watched, the avatar pointed his shotgun at her, and

with a boom, Min watched her avatar fall to the ground, now free of the snare.

"Hey, Flame. I'm a big fan."

Min exhaled, not believing what was happening. "Hey Teddy," she said, trying to keep the shake out of her voice. "I'm going to be really sorry to kill you later."

"Looking forward to it."

Teddy gave her an emote—a salute—and then turned and left the room. Min was now alone with Alex's avatar, who was still on his knees, his weapon nowhere to be seen. Min could hear Alex frantically smashing the buttons, trying to get his character up and moving. Min didn't hesitate, racing toward where she saw the nearest weapon had fallen. But Alex was quick, his avatar up and running next to hers. Shit.

They both scrambled for weapons. She figured his health was probably now as low as hers—shotguns had terrible range, but TeddyBearHugs had been close enough to Alex to do real damage with it. Min got to her machine gun first, sprinting over to Alex's avatar to get a better shot. He tried to dodge, tried to hit her, but she was faster, and with one press of her button, his avatar was down. Alex was out of the tournament.

Min watched, a little stunned, as Alex's avatar fell to the ground. She had thought she would feel vindication, relief, karma, something at this moment, but she didn't. Instead, she was hollow, as if all the conspiring and hate had taken up too much of her. Now that the moment was over, she was left wondering if there was anything left.

Slowly, Min became aware that someone was yelling, not over comms but in the actual arena. She slipped off one of her headphones to listen and immediately recognized the voice. It was Alex, and he was pissed. The mods had already shut off

Alex's comms so the streaming audience couldn't hear him. But that didn't stop Alex from screaming his outrage to the live audience, the officials, to anyone who could hear him.

"You fucking bitch. You think you can kill me? You think you can just dump me? Do you know who I am? You don't fucking deserve anything, you fucking whore."

There was a scrambling of movement around her bay, and she heard the audience yelling, booing, and then the game came up with a pause screen, tournament officials freezing gameplay. Which meant Alex was causing a huge scene. When Min looked up, it was to see Alex pushing his way through security guards to get to her. His eyes were dark, pissed, and he looked completely unhinged in a way that Min had never seen before.

"You're a fucking whore, you hear me, Min?! And everyone knows it now! No one wants you to win because you're a fucking disgrace. You should've stayed the fuck away like you were supposed to."

He kept yelling, security finally managing to pull him away from Min and toward the exit. His voice bounced through the arena, screaming obscenities at her, calling her names, but none of it registered. No matter what she had done, this reaction was off the wall—even the audience that supported him could see that. When security finally got him through the door and away from the cameras, Min was shaking. She had never been the focus of such hatred, not really, and gave thanks to herself that she had broken it off with Alex when she had.

The arena was silent in the wake of Alex's exit. Min took some deep breaths, trying to steady her nerves, knowing the cameras were on her and that her face was probably plastered on every screen. She knew she couldn't let them see how much his words hurt, how much she hated the destruction he had caused in her life.

And then a deep, gravel voice came through the comms.

"Nice shot, FlameThrower."

It was like the sun had finally come out after a rainy day, what his voice did to her. The approval there. She shook her head, already smiling. "Thanks, DeathsHead. Can't wait to put a bullet through your skull."

His laugh shivered down her spine. *"Stop flirting with me, baby. I got a tournament to win."*

Her screen flashed with a countdown, showing the game was restarted as the audience began to cheer. She forced herself to focus. She and Hayden had a lot to talk about after this tournament, but for now, she had to win. She gave herself a moment to revel in the cheers, in the countdown, in the anticipation. Min had missed playing the games, had missed streaming, but she had also missed playing against DeathsHead.

No matter what happened, she was going to enjoy this.

Their avatars respawned in new locations, all back to full health, and Min focused on her search for weapons, items, and players. It was a while later that she heard yelling back and forth, and she realized Hayden had cornered the last player left, taking him out swiftly. The audience cheered, and a now-familiar voice came over the comms.

"Give him hell, FlameThrower."

Min laughed. "Will do, Teddy. That is definitely the plan."

TeddyBearHugs signed off, and it was now down to just Min and Hayden. The audience was losing it, cheering for them both. This had been the draw for a lot of fans, a final match between FlameThrower and DeathsHead, and Min knew the streaming numbers must be through the roof.

"Well, FlameThrower? Feel like giving up?" His calm voice rasped in her ear, heating up her blood.

"Can't say that I do, Death."

"You really gonna make me find you?"

"Not if I find you first."

Min kept searching, and she knew he was doing the same. She found some stealth gear and equipped it, hoping to get an advantage to sneak up on him. They kept their banter up, always considered the audience's favorite part, only this time with a lot more meaning to it, at least for Min.

"How do you want it, baby? Fast and hard? Slow and painful?"

Not one to back down, Min bit her lip. "Well, Death, I know you have trouble making anything last too long, so I'm guessing I don't have to worry about a slow burn."

"Don't lie to the fans, Flame. You know I could make you burn for hours."

"I guess we'll never know since I plan on whipping you the first chance I get."

"I'm gonna hold you to that promise."

Min loved this, loved that he was clearly planning on giving this fight his all, loved that there was no backing down for either of them. She felt her adrenaline rush through her as she spotted movement way across the map—him running around a corner. She checked her weapon to make sure it was loaded.

"I see you, Min."

A pause and she considered if she should bluff. But she couldn't. It was just the two of them, exactly how Min preferred. She was ready for this showdown, whatever happened.

"Come get me."

CHAPTER 21

HAYDEN

"Come get me."

Hayden felt a hum under his skin at her words, at her dark as sin voice practically purring at him through his headset. It didn't matter that they were doing this in public, didn't matter that millions of people were streaming and watching them. This was how they had started, this was how they met. And as far as Hayden was concerned, this is who they were.

And now they were going to prove who was the best.

He ducked behind a short wall for cover and rechecked his weapons. He had his usual favorite machine gun, as well as a few smoke bombs. His Beretta was low on ammo thanks to Teddy, but it would do if he was in a pinch. He reloaded the machine gun with a button, then turned back to the room... it was time to find Min.

He had his avatar peek around the cover to where he knew she had been, only to find the room now empty. *Fuck.* Hayden spun his camera, searching for movement, but he couldn't spot her. The room itself had half a dozen exits—she could be anywhere, especially if she found stealth armor. He switched over to his heat signature goggles for a scan, just in case.

"You went all silent on me, DeathsHead. Are you giving up?"

Hayden pushed his avatar to stay undercover, sneaking toward the first door he could reach. Most likely she had left through the far door, but Hayden was betting on all the exits connecting somewhere.

"I would never give up on you, Flame." He heard her quick intake of breath. Hayden hadn't thought about the words before he said them, but he knew they were true. And he suddenly, very fiercely, hoped she knew that as well.

"You better not be getting sappy on me now. I'm getting really tired of men and their sensitive feelings."

His doorway had led to a hallway, and Hayden would bet money the hall wrapped all the way around the large room he had just exited. Several doors lined the hall, and Hayden ducked into the first one, scanning for Min and finding it empty. He went back out in the hall. He needed to get his head fully in the game, needed to focus. Which meant he needed Min to be a lot more worried than she currently sounded.

"I've been considering the best way to kill you, Flame."

"You and your unrealistic fantasies."

Hayden let his chuckle fill the space, the arena.

"I'm just saying, we've been here before, several times. How are we going to top ourselves?"

"Well, I'm going to crush you beneath my boot, so that will be nice."

"Now who's talking about unrealistic fantasies?"

Hayden ducked into the next room, something made to look like an old pantry and was about to exit it empty-handed when he saw the marker. He spun his camera to get a better angle, and almost lost his breath as the crowd in the stadium started cheering, able to see exactly what he saw.

A grenade launcher.

Hayden quickly picked up the weapon, checking the data. It only had one round loaded, which meant he had one chance to use it on Min. He'd have to lure her somewhere to get the shot. He didn't have to be exact, but still. Min was smart, and after the stunt Alex pulled with the med kit, she was going to be wary of another item trap like that.

As Hayden tried to plan, the crowd started cheering again, louder than when he found the grenade launcher, and Hayden grinned.

"Find something good, Flame?"

"Not sure what you mean, Death. I'm just a lonely, defenseless girl trapped in this castle. How ever will I survive against such a strong, Alpha male as yourself?" Her voice dripped with derision, and Hayden knew she must have either found a good item or was setting a trap for him. The question was what, and how was she going to use it.

And just as the thought registered, he heard a growl behind him.

"Fuck."

"Sounds like you got company."

Hayden quickly equipped his machine gun and spun just in time to see the zombie, dressed in rotted and rusted armor, push a large shelf out of the way and enter the once empty room. For a second Hayden had almost forgotten the game wasn't just about defeating each other. He also had to survive the damn zombies.

He fired, killing the dead knight with a head shot just as three more emerged behind him. Hayden quickly had his avatar sprint toward the door, slamming it shut behind him before heading further down the hall. Through his headset, he heard the faint sounds of gunfire.

"Don't tell me you're having a party without me."

"You're totally invited. In fact, I have a few friends I'd love you to get a bite with."

Hayden laughed as he searched the next room. His ammo was low for his machine gun, and his Beretta was down to three bullets. His best bet was to locate Min and wait her out, letting her use whatever new item she had found to save herself from the zombies.

"Fuck fuck fuck fuck—"

"Min, this is a family stream."

"The game is rated MA, asshole."

Hayden reached the end of the hall and slowed to peek around the corner. He wasn't sure where Min was, but he could hear her emptying her ammo on those zombies. Her weakness was how she always wanted to fight, hated running away, and that had gotten her into more trouble than anything. But right now, it worked in Hayden's favor because he could tell what room she was in. He readied the grenade launcher as he heard her unloading her gun into the zombies somewhere ahead of him. Slowly, making sure he kept to the walls in the hopes that any heat signature he gave off could be hidden by the zombies around her, he crept closer.

Finally, he approached one of the last doors in the hall. Min had gone silent over her microphone, but her gun was letting off round after round of ammo. She must be surrounded.

Hayden had his avatar reach for the door, slow, knowing he had to be ready to aim and shoot within nanoseconds of it opening. He took a deep breath.

"Always remember," he said, stepping back. "There's no shame in being second best."

The words were barely out before his avatar kicked down the door. The door shattered on impact, and he found himself staring at a mass of zombies. His eyes darted all over the screen, his camera spinning—*where was Min?* And then he saw it. Her uzi was on the ground. She had found a way to rig it to fire without her.

She had set a fucking trap.

"I'm glad you feel that way, DeathsHead."

He spun, noting that her avatar was now holding something and wearing a backpack, a weapon Hayden hadn't seen in the game before. No time to think, Hayden pulled up the grenade launcher and fired… right as Min dropped to the ground. The round went high, flying down the hall and exploding far, far away from Min.

Hayden angled his camera down to look at Min's avatar where it was crouched, the weird weapon aiming at him and he realized right before she pulled the trigger.

"Is that a fucking flamethrower??"

Within half a second Hayden was showered in flames, his entire avatar engulfed. As she sprayed him, he reeled back, his gun flying up as his arms came up to block the flame. He stumbled back, right into the arms of the zombies that were waiting for him. He was grabbed, bitten, pulled to the ground while on fire, his health meter quickly falling to yellow, then red, then to a flat line. His avatar screamed as the entire room caught fire, and Min's laugh filtered through Hayden's headset filled with delight and satisfaction.

"Gotta say, Death, you make a great torch."

Hayden couldn't even laugh, couldn't do much but stare at the screen in shock. "Where the hell did you even find a flamethrower?"

"It's always in the last place you look."

CHAPTER 22

MIN

The audience was screaming so loud Min's ears were ringing. She stood from her bay, her hands shaking, her whole body shaking, as she looked up at the screens above her, not believing her eyes.

She had won.

Min looked at the audience, her eyes finding Randall and Brittany and all her friends screaming, cheering, jumping up and down. She waved at them, elation and victory running through her veins. The crowd kept cheering, and then for some reason got even louder. Min scanned the room, the screens, trying to figure it out, and then she saw him.

Hayden had come out onto the floor. His eyes swept the room until he found her, and then he was pushing through the crew to get to her. Her eyes widened as she realized what he was doing—he was in front of cameras, his face on the screens around them, everywhere.

And then she saw what he was wearing.

A FlameThrower shirt. Bright pink, with her logo and a hell of a lot of sparkles, the same shirt she had seen in Randall's booth. Her mouth dropped. She was certain Hayden didn't own a single piece of clothing with color on it, yet here he was, basically proclaiming himself a fan, the entire arena and internet watching him stride straight to her.

And then he was there, his hands going to her face, his forehead dropping to hers.

"You did it, baby."

His voice echoed everywhere, and it hit her that he was still wearing his mic around his neck. Her eyes widened as she realized he had just revealed who he was to everyone, his voice too deep and distinct for anyone to have doubts as to who he really was. Literally everyone watching them now had their phones out, filming them, taking pictures. She tried to pull away, but he caught her, pulling her close.

"I'm sorry," he said, quieter than before but still into the mic. The arena got quieter, everyone holding their breath as they took in the real DeathsHead. "I shouldn't have let you deal with the fall-out yourself. I'm an ass. Forgive me?"

She shook her head, not believing what he had done, that he was out there clearing her and holding her.

"Nothing to forgive, DeathsHead."

He wrapped an arm around her waist, pulling her close, his other hand on the nape of her neck, his lips now only a breath away from hers.

"The name's Hayden."

And then he kissed her. If the crowd was loud before, they were about to bring the roof down watching their two favorite streamers make out in front of them. And Min found she didn't care, she just wanted to be wrapped up in Hayden, feel him everywhere, and not let him go.

He broke the kiss, pulling her tight and lifting her up in a bear hug that she felt in her bones. And then he kissed her, quick and possessive, before letting her go, keeping her hand in his. She turned a dazed look around them to see the judges and officials approaching her, the large ridiculous check already signed with her name on it, and Brad there to shake her hand. Dylan, thankfully, was nowhere in sight.

Min looked at Hayden, nothing but joy in her every cell. She gripped his hand tight as he smiled at her.

"You're insane," she told him.

He smiled back. "Insane for you, babe."

CHAPTER 23

HAYDEN

Hayden had spent years imagining what it would be like when his real identity was revealed. Sometimes it was a nightmare, his face suddenly on a stream for everyone to dissect and judge and find wanting. Sometimes it was a defiant action, he revealed himself just before dropping out of streaming forever, going to live off the grid in the woods like a recluse. Sometimes he just exploded into nothingness, as if revealing his identity made him cease to exist. So, it was safe to say that this was nothing like how Hayden thought this would go.

And he wouldn't have it any other way.

After their public display in the arena, Hayden pulled a dazed Min into the green room. Already, the TVs there were playing her win on a loop, including the footage of him running out to meet her. The sound wasn't on, but Hayden could read the chyrons confirming his identity, both as Deaths-Head and the man in the recent pictures with Min. He stared at the picture they splashed on the screen—his own face, with his name underneath. Everything he had fought against for years. He waited for his anxiety to take over, to feel the panic or numbness that always came when he faced a situation even remotely resembling this.

But there was nothing. He felt fine. A little relieved, to be honest.

He felt a squeeze on his hand and looked down to find Min's wide eyes, still wearing her pink contacts that were filled with concern. For him.

"How you feeling over there?" She whispered it to him, but he could still hear the shake in her voice. "Any regrets?"

He was already smiling. "My only regret was letting you walk out of my hotel room."

"You were in shock."

"Doesn't matter. I should've handled it better. There's no excuse. I'm sorry."

She leaned into him, and he was grateful for her weight, for her trust that she could lean on him.

"I can't believe you did that. Everyone knows. I may vomit."

He chuckled. "Don't? Min, when it comes to you, I don't care who knows. I don't care what trends on social media, what trolls have to say, any of it. All I care about is you, by my side, kicking my ass on stream."

A smile finally appeared on her face, and Hayden felt like he won the lottery. "I do love stomping you in front of an audience."

They're interrupted when a PA approaches them, looking both starstruck and nervous.

"Um, FlameThrower, and um…" He stopped, gulping, eyes large as he stared at Hayden clearly not knowing what to call him. Hayden held out his hand.

"Hayden."

The PA shook his hand, then looked at it like he may never wash it again.

"Right, Hayden, yes. They're asking for you in the conference room. For both of you."

The PA pointed across the way toward an open door. Even from here, Hayden could see Dylan looking like the cat who ate the canary, full of himself, as if this was his victory. Hayden looked forward to disabusing him of that notion.

Keeping Min's hand in his, they made their way toward the conference room, stopping a few times as other streamers came to congratulate Min on her win. There were several people just staring at him, which would normally make Hayden's skin crawl. But right now, with her hand in his, Hayden found he just didn't care.

Once in the conference room, Dylan clapped Hayden on the back and shook Min's hand as if he wasn't the biggest douchebag alive. Brad was already at the table, smiling and standing to shake both their hands. Hayden and Min sat across from him at the table, and Hayden had a sudden flash of the first time he met Min, sitting at a table much like this, agreeing to this tournament because he had been such an ass. He looked at her then, seeing the same moment in her eyes. And Hayden had to admit, even then, he probably would've done whatever this woman had asked of him. They had been rivals for years, and he had been an idiot to not realize there was something behind their chemistry. He had a lot of time to make up for.

"Truly amazing game," Dylan started. "The streaming numbers are in the millions. We broke records today, thanks to you two." He clapped his hands together with glee, his eyes darting back and forth between Hayden and Min as if waiting for them to celebrate with him.

Min leaned back in her chair, crossing her arms. Glaring.

"If you're going to tell me I can't keep the money, I'm ready to fight you in court."

Hayden's head whipped toward her at that. "Wait, what? Why would you not get to keep the money?"

"Dylan here told me before the game that due to the new pictures that were leaked of us, any win I managed would be tainted and would launch an investigation into the tournament as a whole."

Brad turned at that, his face paling. "Dylan, did you really say that?"

Dylan's smile didn't falter, but there was a panicked gleam in his eyes. "I was merely warning Ms. Hayes of the possible repercussions from the unfortunate recent pictures. I wanted her to be as prepared as possible."

"That's bullshit and you know it."

Hayden felt pride fill him as Min called Dylan out on his crap.

"You told me that DeathsHead was the draw and that in order to keep him as the winner and score a sponsorship with him, I would either need to step back or just give up the money. You also implied that the company never had any intention of letting me win, thanks to the pictures Alex had leaked."

Brad didn't seem to know who to believe, but there was enough suspicion on his face for Hayden to think that he suspected the answer. Hayden sat back, enjoying watching Min destroy this man.

Dylan tried to backpedal. "I'm sorry if that's what you thought I was implying—"

"Save it for your deposition. I know you're the one who told my ex where I was staying. My guess is you encouraged him to do something to distract me from the competition, maybe even drop out. Stupid of both of you, really. Alex should've warned you I'm too stubborn to quit."

"Look," Dylan tried. "I'm not going to lie. Bleeding Sword was very excited about the possibility of a long-term working relationship with Mr. Phillips."

Hayden snorted. "For the record, I wouldn't go into business with you or your company for anything. Not after seeing how little you did to help with the fallout of those stupid pictures. And definitely not after hearing how you spoke to Min."

Dylan's eye twitched. Hayden knew he was going to blow, it was just a matter of when. Brad, meanwhile, cleared his throat, trying to get control of the situation again.

"Dylan," he finally said. "Can I ask you to step out and give us a minute?"

Dylan's head whipped around to glare at his colleague. "I am a vice president at this company, Brad. I should be included in all the important meetings."

Brad didn't even raise his voice. "I'm also a vice president, Dylan, and I believe that any positive outcome from this meeting will not come if you are present in the room. So. You need to give us a minute."

Dylan looked ready to breathe fire. He sat for a long moment, staring at Brad. For his part, Brad stared back, not backing down. Finally, Dylan stood up.

"We're going to talk about this."

"We sure will," was Brad's only reply as Dylan stormed out of the room. Once the door was once again shut, Brad exhaled and turned back to them.

"Ms. Hayes, I must apologize for my coworker's conduct. It was never discussed on our end that you wouldn't be able to keep your prizes should you win, not even after today's unfortunate news cycle. If you'll still have us, Bleeding Sword would love to sponsor you for the next year. And of course, the prize money is yours."

Min didn't let anything show in her expression. "I'll think about it."

Brad nodded. "That's all I can ask." He then turned to Hayden. "Mr. Phillips, I want to apologize to you as well. The company is going to work to track down who leaked the information of our initial meeting. It's obvious that's the only way someone would've known to be in place to capture your photo."

Hayden wasn't in the mood to make this easier on the executive, even if he was less douchey than Dylan. "You'll be hearing from my lawyers about your breach of our NDA."

Brad nodded. "That's to be expected."

They all stood, and Brad took a moment, seeming to steady himself in a way that made Hayden curious about what he was thinking.

Brad looked Min in the eye. "Ms. Hayes, on a personal note, I am a big fan of your stream and have been for years. I'm deeply embarrassed and ashamed that this is your first experience working with me. I'm so sorry."

He meant it. Hayden could tell it was eating him up that Dylan had pulled such a stunt. Min must have seen his sincerity as well because she simply nodded.

"I appreciate that."

Brad knew that was all he was going to get, but he still seemed relieved. "I also want to let you know that Mr White has been escorted off the premises and has had his convention badge and access revoked. We have a strict no-tolerance policy for the kind of behavior he displayed earlier, and we take safety very seriously."

Min looked ready to collapse with relief, but she held it together. Hayden reached for her hand under the table, lacing their fingers together before he squeezed. When she turned to look at him, Hayden's eyes got lost in the raw emotion there, the anger and worry and beautiful tenderness.

He vaguely heard Brad say something else before the sound of the door clicked shut. He was alone. With Min.

She drew a shaky breath, still holding his hand. "I can't believe you did that."

"That I lost? Trust me, I tried not to."

A low laugh huffed out of her. "No, I mean… I can't believe you just revealed your identity. To everyone. This is your worst nightmare."

Hayden let his other hand touch her cheek, cupping it, pulling her a little closer as his fingertips grazed the softness of her hair.

"Min, it didn't take long for me to realize my worst nightmare was losing you."

Her pulse raced under his palm, and he watched closely as she licked those candy pink lips he couldn't stop thinking about. He could see a thousand questions fighting to be asked.

Finally, she blurted out, "We just met like a month ago."

Hayden shook his head, ready for this argument. It was one he had tried to make to himself all morning. And while logically he knew it was a good one, his heart felt otherwise. And he suspected Min's did as well.

"We've known each other for years, Min," he said. "We've played games and talked and gotten to know each other and pissed each other off for years. Maybe we didn't meet in person until a month ago, but you've been one of my favorite people since our first stream together."

She was blinking a lot, her eyes watering, and Hayden

tried not to panic. He had to do this right. He had to make her understand.

"Min, I know I was a huge jerk that first day in the elevator. I was reacting from anger and anxiety and fear. But since then, I've become addicted. I don't want to go back to only seeing you on stream. I want you in my life. Hell, I need you there. And at the risk of sounding crazy—"

"I love you," she rushed out, cutting him off. "If you're crazy, then so am I."

He felt it then. The relief that she felt the same way. His chest filled with a swirling feeling of affection and obsession and caring. The entire world shifted around him, like the last piece of himself had fallen into place and he was finally a whole person because of this woman.

He kissed her, giving her every thought and dream he had ever had about her, wanting her to feel his truth. When he pulled away, they were both breathless.

"I love you, too, Min. So much."

"No pressure, but I have a hotel room nearby," she whispered. And Hayden knew without a doubt he would follow Min anywhere.

"Let's hurry. I'm suddenly dying to ride the trolley with you again."

Min rolled her eyes, which delighted him. He kissed her again before standing, pulling her after him.

It wasn't the quick getaway Hayden had been hoping for. Min was stopped by Brittany and Randall, who had been waiting to congratulate her. Both gave him slightly skeptical looks, and Hayden could tell Brittany was whispering something in Min's ear, but Min just blushed and pulled away. Randall left with a wave and a "Tell everyone where you got that shirt." But Brittany crossed her arms in front of Hayden as if examining him under a microscope. Today she was wearing a military-style bomber jacket, lace-up boots, and a plain tank top, and she looked ready to rip off his head and spit down his neck. Hayden forced himself to endure the silent scrutiny. It was Min who finally groaned.

"Brittany, is this necessary?"

Brittany ignored her. "Min is my friend, DeathsHead."

Hayden didn't know how to respond to that, so he just nodded.

"She deserves to be treated a lot better than she has in the past. A lot better."

"She does. Min deserves everything. I plan on doing my damnedest to give her that." He was honest and could only hope the judgmental Brittany could see that. She was silent for another moment before she nodded.

"Fine. Please know that I'm a fan of true crime podcasts and that I know at least six ways to hide your body." Hayden's eyes widened, but she had already turned to hug Min again, whispering something in her ear. Finally, with a quick wave at Hayden, she was gone.

Hayden was already taking Min's hand in his. "What was that about?"

Min couldn't look him in the eye. "She, ah, wants details."

"About what?"

"About your… um… penis."

A laugh jumped out of Hayden as Min turned her eyes to the ceiling. Not able to resist, he pulled her into him, winding his arms around her and pulling her so tight he could feel the press of her corset against his chest.

"FlameThrower, my penis is crazy about you."

"Glad to hear it, DeathsHead, because otherwise this would be really awkward."

He laughed, letting her go, and followed her to her dressing room where she still had to change out of her persona. This time, Hayden got to watch. Seeing her strip away every piece of the person she presented to her fans, knowing that the woman underneath was just as incredible, if not more, humbled him in a way that made his heart ache. This felt like his future, his everything, and he could not wait to get started on showing her just how much he loved her.

With her wig finally carefully packed with the rest of her outfit, Min turned to Hayden, full of confidence and love.

"Let's get out of here. We got a trolley to catch."

Her eye twinkled as he pulled her in for a kiss. And he felt how perfect it was, how perfect she was, and he sent a thought of gratitude to the universe.

His future was here, and he was ready to embrace it.

EPILOGUE
MIN

Min surveyed the space, looking for any detail she may have missed. Theo's restaurant had been converted into a large spaceship, the design taken directly from Death Everlasting, Hayden's video game that he was finally launching. After Min won the tournament and began her year of sponsorship, Hayden was approached by several companies interested in partnering with him on the product. Although he had been leery of joining with a corporation—especially so soon after Bleeding Sword had tried to screw him over—his desire to put the game out into the world faster was what won him over.

It had been a year since the Bleeding Sword tournament. A year since Min's life had changed, since her real identity had been out for public consumption. It had been a bit of a roller coaster, one that was as exhilarating as it was nerve-racking. But Min knew in her heart that if she had to go back to do it all again, she would.

After the tournament, Brad had approached the board members about Dylan's behavior. Dylan was quickly fired from the company and blacklisted from working in games. Brad had then set his sights on restoring the reputation of the company. Though few outside of the streaming world were aware of Dylan's actions, it was enough to cause a ripple in the community that Bleeding Sword did its best to repair.

And then, when he felt like he had done everything he could for Bleeding Sword, Brad had surprised everyone and left to establish his own video game publishing company. He confessed to Hayden that he had always wanted to be on the creative side, working to develop new product and new creators. And while the situation with Bleeding Sword had been a setback, he was excited to move forward and finally live his dream.

When Brad had originally reached out to Hayden and Min a month after the tournament, it was only to again apologize and tell them he would testify in whatever court proceedings they wanted to bring against the company.

Min and Hayden had talked it over extensively after they had arrived back in LA. And though they had both been pissed, they also didn't want to drag out a lawsuit or anything, so they agreed on a settlement.

After returning to Los Angeles, Min had practically moved into Hayden's apartment, and he couldn't seem happier as he picked up her dirty towels or listened to her talk with her chat while on stream. If anything, the chemistry and connection they had found in Kimball had only grown brighter and stronger.

It had been a year, a year of both of them growing their brand and settling into their new lives together. And now here they were, back for the Kimball International Convention of Fans, only this time Hayden was launching a game and Min was about to announce a new year-long sponsorship with Bleeding Sword's new game.

"What are you thinking about?"

Min felt a warm hand slide into hers and she looked up, already smiling at Hayden. His eyes swept her body with approval. Min knew she looked good. Her hair was down, and she had let her sister do her makeup. She still wore her wig and outfits on her stream, feeling like she needed the separation between her and her streaming persona, and also knowing part of her audience simply loved the look. But Hayden loved her best when she was just herself. She did her own survey of him, enjoying seeing him in a suit. Her mind filled with memories of the morning, when she had put on that very same suit jacket and nothing else, determined to help him work through his nerves with the launch. The heat in his gaze told her he was thinking of the same thing, his eyes sliding down to take in her legs in the short skirt and heels, before coming back to stare at her mouth.

"You better check that look, Mr. Phillips. Your guests are about to arrive."

He pulled her into him, kissing her cheek before sliding his mouth to her ear. "Just wondering if you're wearing any underwear under that skirt." The hand at her back drifted down until it rested just above her ass, stroking the curve there.

She laughed. "That's something for you to find out later when we're done here."

"Min, this party is scheduled until two a.m., you can't seriously make me wait that long."

She patted his cheek, loving his torture. "Gonna have to keep it together, DeathsHead. Play the long game."

Hayden took a deep breath, and Min could see the nerves

still settled under his skin. In the year since he showed his real face to his fans, he had been lucky to receive mostly support. He rarely streamed anymore, but when he did he still kept his stream dark and off his face. The anxiety that lived with him almost every day before had faded into the background. They were private, as much as they could be, but Min always worried about him.

A hand clapped Hayden's shoulder, interrupting them. Min smiled at Theo with affection. The chef was walking chaos, something that she knew Hayden both loved and drove him crazy. Currently, Theo was frowning at the sight of his dining room.

"My god, look at this monstrosity. What have you done?"

Hayden rolled his eyes. "You agreed to it, asshat. It was your idea."

Theo shook his head. "That can't be true. I don't love you enough to let you do this to my baby."

"Too late now, Theo," Min told him, pulling Hayden closer. Over the year, she had gotten used to handling Theo's ever-changing moods. As much as he was despairing over his redecorated dining room, she knew he was proud of Hayden and what he was about to do.

Min threw the restaurant another glance. In the corner, her mother was standing with her sister, admiring the flower displays they had helped arrange. They had been wary of Hayden at first, knowing only that Min and he had been rivals for years and that she had been stuck with him for the tournament. But Hayden made it a mission to make them feel comfortable around him, and they quickly came around. Min had been surprised when they had agreed to come to Kimball for the launch, but she was happy they were here. And she had a suspicion that Hayden had specifically made sure they would be.

Hayden glanced at her then, and she must have let something show through her grin because he groaned.

"You already know, don't you?"

Min shrugged. "Mom's bad with secrets. She's been acting weird since she got here. Tried to blame it on gas. Don't be mad."

He shook his head, a sparkle in his eyes as he gazed down at her.

"I'm not mad. I just wanted it to be special."

"Whatever happens, tonight is going to be amazing, Hayden. You have to believe that."

She squeezed him for good measure, hoping to transfer some of her love and confidence to him.

"How good are you at acting surprised?"

"Really, really terrible." She kissed him then, sweet and quick. "But I swear, I'll try."

"Baby, as long as you give me the answer I want, I don't care about the rest."

She kissed him again, this time taking it deeper, pulling Hayden in with everything she had. They both ignored Theo's muttered, "Gross," as he walked away, once again sick of their PDA. After a long moment, Min put her forehead on his, leaning into him.

"My answer is always yes, Hayden. To anything you want."

She felt full, her love for him coming hard and fast yet again in a familiar jolt at the idea that they were actually here, watching his game launch, a team in a way that they always knew they could be. She couldn't stop herself from smiling.

Hayden's hand went down to her ass, caressing. "Even

when I ask if you skipped wearing underwear?" His fingers flexed as if he was trying to guess.

She grinned. "You'll have to wait and see."

He squeezed her. "You and me against the world, Flame."

She kissed him again. "Always, Death."

And then she walked away, going to help her mother set up another table with decorations. Out of the corner of her eye, she saw Hayden fiddle with the small box in his pocket and wondered if he'd actually make it to midnight and the fireworks before he popped the question.

Probably not. But she didn't mind. And she suspected he wouldn't either.

ACKNOWLEDGMENTS

I stumbled into writing this book much like a toddler stumbles toward an electric socket while holding a fork - with excitement and very little forethought. But I was lucky to find support from so many friends, old and new, who were able to ground me and willing to assist however they could.

So thank you to Daphne, for assuring me words were real after I obsessively stared at them too long.

Thank you to Nancy and Angela for giving much-needed opinions and suggestions about whatever I was currently having a meltdown about.

Thank you to Kristine and Ashley, my very first readers who were kind and also adamant about what this story needed.

Thank you to Coralie, for your guidance and wisdom.

Thank you to Ellie at My Brother's Editor for your support and exceptional eye.

Thank you to Sarah at Okay Creations for this cover I love.

Thank you, Ruby Dixon - you don't know me, but your books inspired and comforted me through a pandemic and led me down this path to self-publishing.

Thank you to gamer girls, for being there for each other.

Thank you, Mom, for the love of reading.

Thank you, Ryan, for the love of video games, even though I always had to be Luigi.

And thanks to all of you for reading Min and Hayden's story. It means the absolute world to me.

ABOUT THE AUTHOR

Ayla Chandler is the pen name for a writer turned author who loves romance novels and finally decided to try writing them. She lives in California where she is often in pajamas with two cats, drinking too much coffee, and staring at an ever-growing TBR pile.